Sometimes Satan comes as a Man of Peace
—BOB DYLAN

Whenever death may surprise us, it will be welcome, provided that this, our battle cry, reach some receptive ear, that another hand be extended to take up our weapons and that other men come forward to intone our funeral dirge with the staccato of machine guns and new cries of battle and victory
—CHE GUEVARA

ONCE AGO

2000. *Time is a hustler in black leather. Time is that which ends.*

Once upon a time, long long ago, long long before your time, there were two lads and one of them was me. He—the other—was wild when wildness counted. That's another story. Now it's six in the morning, after the dawning. Four years since I've been awake to greet the dawn, and that was due to illness. The time before that was due to sex best forgotten and the time before that was maybe fifteen years ago and due to me being still young and strong.

1986. *My firm sullen chin against a moonlit sky. Then. Someone touched a fiddle bow on a Kerry beach of a night. Then. Then... talking all the day and night with true friends who tried to make me stay. Sleeping. Dreaming in the night. Waking for the dawn. We stood by the Atlantic Ocean and we sang a song for Ireland. Made believe on a tin whistle. Our ancient glory. Our storied hills.*

I caught a flight from Shannon to San Francisco the next day. The sun was burning in the Pacific sky when I taxied into the new world, my pregnant wife alongside me, life before me and my family.

2000. *I can't sleep from bad trouble and that, as we used to say back in the epoch of analogue sound, is a wretched hungry feeling. The Corrs on* the TV boasting we are so young now, we are so young now.

"Now it's the winter time," said Johnny Whelan the Sunday after Horslips when we were tucking into a feed of his mother's bacon, potatoes, and cabbage. "Time for winter food."

Now it is the winter time again and time for winter food.

All is darkness, pain, and fear. We go groping on our knees for a sun that's disappeared.

Now it's time to leave the capsule if I dare.

PART 1

THE **SINGING FLAME**

THE BITTER IRISH WIND

"Mr Crowe?"

"Yes."

"Mr Liam Crowe?"

"Yes."

"The author of *Punk Rock Girls*?"

"I wrote it, sure." I'm getting a little tetchy. It's 3am and I'm listening to music, relaxing after a long evening with the computer. "Who am I speaking to?"

"Ah, you wouldn't remember me now Liam. I used to know you years ago here in Dublin."

"That must have been a long time ago. I've been gone from Ireland nearly fifteen years." I pretend jocularity: "But I've a pretty good memory. I remember most people."

"Ah, well…" he pauses indifferently; "I hear you're doing a book on Dan Breen, Liam."

"Yeah. Rewriting my very first book."

"Liam, you wrote an auld book about whores there, *Punk Rock Girls*."

The asshole is talking about my best known book, still doing well in paperback, about groupies in the Seventies.

"Yeah," I say neutrally, for this is all getting tedious. My caller speaks in an educated, middle class accent. Assured, amused, and arrogant. Not drunk. Maybe coked up. I'm out of Ireland so long I can't tell if he's a Dubliner or a provincial. They all sound the same to me now. I think he comes from the country but has lived in Dublin a long time.

"Well, that book you wrote on women is full of shit, let me tell you."

"What?" I laugh. This is the old Ireland of resentment and begrudgery I escaped from so many years ago.

"I said that book you wrote on women is a pile of shite."

With which my anonymous, belligerent stranger in the night hangs up, leaving me to the sound of rock music on the CD player and the bitter Irish wind howling outside.

IRA INTELLECTUAL

A lot of people have trouble digesting the truth.

I should know. I'm a biographer. I write up the lives of the selected famous dead. Eight books out, I'm in this thing in a serious way, I get nice advances for my books and I go on the talk show circuit to promote them.

I was a journalist—ultimately a music journalist—in Ireland. Now I write books about dead musicians and old whores. I think I'm still alive inside.

I'm back in Ireland rewriting my first book, *Against Tyrant's Might,* a biography of the IRA founder Dan Breen. It got published in 1981 when I'd just finished at UCD. To rewrite the Breen book—this time it'll be called *On The Run*—I'm taking time off from a lucrative three year project, *Mannish Boy*, a life of Rolling Stone Brian Jones which will 'get to the bottom of his mysterious death'. But Dan's anniversary is coming up, so a slick new Irish publisher asked me to do a new edition. It's a labour of love. For Dan Breen and for Rory.

There was nothing mysterious about Dan's death. He died an old man in the Sixties from old English bullet fragments embedded in his revolutionary body since the Twenties. There was nothing mysterious about his life either, a typically Irish mixture of romantic gesture, rock-hard action, and squandered, unwanted opportunity. So why am I rewriting my little book about him? I don't know. I must be mad. I understand why I wrote it in the first place and that seems to be enough.

I've got the biographer's disease, doing more work than is absolutely necessary. All that's required of me is 40,000 words, most of them platitudes. That's what I gave Benbulben the first time around, reckless, cynical, and free. Now some bizarre remnant of that long-ago megalomaniac of a young freelancer wants to do a *serious* book on Dan Breen, and the bright folks at trendy new Sub Urb have agreed to let me have a proper crack at it. So I've been cruising through books and papers that've come on stream since I did *Against Tyrant's Might* to find out more about Breen and his Third Tipperary Brigade of the IRA, a lethal panther-like group who were never really trusted by Michael Collins and the Dublin Republican intelligentsia.

A Dutch professor has written a boring-but-worthy book on the War of Independence, AKA the Tan War, in South Tipperary. Dutch is solid and sullen in his research. With his tweedy no-nonsense attitude, he obviously thinks Breen was a buffoon and a braggart. There is a sophisticated sneer in his read on Breen, like Dan was a mountainy man, a primitive loose cannon. If Dutch had been around in the Tan War he'd have been drinking coffee and plotting revolution from the safety of a 1919 Dublin redbrick, while Breen and the boys led shitty revolutionary lives.

What can some self-contented fuck sitting in front of a computer in a central-heated continental sinecure know about being stranded on a Tipperary mountain in the depths of winter, suffering from gangrene and starvation and frostbite and fear? What do I know about it?

I've plagiarised the Dutch. I've checked all his footnotes, but I'm not reaching his conclusions. He has enough attitude to light a cigarette.

I'm drawn to another IRA leader, a pal of Breen's: the intellectual fanatic Ernie O'Malley, known as The IRA Intellectual. Rich youthful revolutionary, collector of contemporary European art, Trotsky-like conscience of the IRA in the civil war they lost, author of the two best books on what they call the Old IRA.

Should I do a book on O'Malley when I'm done with Breen? It'd be a great life to write but I'm already way behind on *Mannish Boy*. I've spent the first half of the Brian Jones advance, and won't get the rest until I deliver a final text. It looks like *On The Run* is labour of love enough for one year.

THE BEST AND OLDEST FURNITURE

Johnny Whelan's mother had to write three different letters to St Fursey's to get me and Rory out for the weekend.

Johnny's mother said in her third letter that a Saturday and Sunday of home cooking plus a bit of mother's care would be good for us boarding school inmates. But there was never a mother in all the land less motherly than Mrs Josie Whelan.

Oh, she did her fair share of cooking and providing while we crashed in Johnny's place. Johnny'd hassled her into inviting us to stay because Horslips were playing that very weekend at The Star of The Sea ballroom in Youghal, a seaside town some miles from Johnny's farm. Every lad in Ireland wanted to see Horslips that winter.

The poignant thrilling Horslips rock'n'roll band reinvented Irish culture and teenage social life all in one swell 1970s swoop by wedding the glam rock guitar attack us kids loved to the naff fiddles and tin whistles we so very much despised. The explosion of that synthesis reverberated through every Irish kid's life. Sent the three provincial youths who travelled to Johnny Whelan's West Waterford home that weekend off on irregular trajectories. The consequences of our earliest musical passions remain unresolved, certainly for Johnny and for me.

Johnny's mother drove us to The Star of The Sea, doing a methodical forty miles an hour on difficult country backroads, in a sturdy old black Ford Zephyr. Johnny sitting in the front passenger seat where he could clearly hear Ken's Club on Radio Éireann. Me and Rory in the back, our ears angled forward like frightened rabbits, so we could just about hear Thin Lizzy doing their first radio session since the original line-up had broken up. Me just gone sixteen, Rory and Johnny a few months younger.

"Horslips have sold out now!" Johnny turned and shouted back to us. "The new stuff is not a patch on Happy To Meet."

Happy to Meet, Sorry to Part, the first Horslips album, sold so

5

fast that, when Ma bought it for me the winter of '73, shops were retailing vinyl copies without the elaborate hexagonal cover that accompanied it. They'd given out receipts with which you could claim your cover when they reprinted in mid-January.

A sort of shouting match then erupted between the three of us; Johnny backing Thin Lizzy, me supporting Horslips, Rory seeing merits in both bands. But he was prejudiced in favour of Lizzy because they had a black singer.

Johnny's mother, who wasn't up to speed with the concept of having 'sold out', stared at her Johnny like he'd just gone barking mad. Which, in retrospect, he had. Horslips and Thin Lizzy drove Johnny mad.

"Did you ever see that movie Moby Dick, Rory?" Mrs Whelan asked as we reached Youghal's outer limits. She generally ignored me, didn't trust me, something to do with my divorced background, while Rory was above board, from decent people.

"No, Mrs Whelan, I never saw it...yet," Rory replied meekly.

He was a tall, bony greyhound not fully grown then. As far as he was concerned, cinema was high art. He called it Kino, a word he'd picked up from his first cousin who was at UCD. Johnny's mam had his complete attention.

"Oh, John Huston made that fillum," she said as we pulled up in front of The Star of The Sea. "A gentleman. He hunted on our land several times—didn't he John?—during the making of Moby Dick. Which also starred the great Orson Welles."

"Orson Welles!" Rory exclaimed, impressed that the star of Citizen Kane had walked the streets of Youghal.

"Orson Welles, no less! We'll never forget him!" said Mrs Whelan with enormous pleasure, for she had dragged our talk away from the nasty rock'n'roll culture of our era to the polite movie culture of her own generation, and she had used the strongest amongst us to achieve her triumph.

Inside the ballroom—a damp seaside barn unusually stuffed and unusually warm—we mingled with a thousand other nascent rock'n'roll fans. An hour after we paid our admission the band hit the stage and a spiked mayhem kicked right in. Me and Johnny and Rory located ourselves in the third row of tight-pressed teenagers encircling a low stage bathed in white light and lime green light, me in front of Horslips' laconic guitarist, a feral and juvenile messiah. I'd seen Horslips three times previously. I'd never heard live electric guitar at anything other than Horslips gigs. Invocation, abstract penetration, rapture.

PARNELL SQUARE

June '99 an English sex shop chain opens across the road from the GPO where the 1916 Rising started. The English have played a long con, and their capitalism is swamping Dublin. Rumours of homosexuality swirl around Boyzone, as well they might.

I'm staying off Summerhill Parade, a rough inner-city ghetto within walking distance of the city centre. I have a whole Georgian house full of hand carved furniture and books and CDs to myself. I've rented it from an old pal who's in America for three months playing bass for Sinéad O'Connor. I'm pretty low profile here, otherwise the local vigilantes might mistake me for a drug dealer or a paedophile. The pebble-dashed Sixties-built tenement blocks overlooking my street groan under the burden of Dublin's white trash.

Hanging from the side of one building is a huge hand-painted banner demanding:

NO SPECIAL COURTS FOR ANTI-DRUG VIGILANTES. Another building insists:

CHILD MOLESTERS—HANDS OFF OUR CHILDREN OR DIE.

The house is big and gracious with barred windows and reinforced doors to keep out the neighbourhood. I've got my computer, my clothes, and some books I need for my research. The house has a professional musician's rack system complete with a DAT player and a MiniDisc machine. I'm buying CDs as I go. When I quit town I'll sell off the CDs.

I'm not far from the murky environs of Parnell Square where in 1920 Rory's grandfather Pádraic, then a very junior IRA officer, met with a delegation of senior officers returned in triumph that very day from Soviet Russia with the Russian Crown Jewels, donated by the cash-strapped Communists for the battle against British imperialism.

According to Pádraic, Trotsky met with the IRA delegation and told them:

"Comrades, we have no capital with which to aid you. We are a poor people raped by our rulers. These decadent baubles were the property of a gang of criminals who have robbed our people for a thousand years. The jewels carry blessings and curses with them. Sell them immediately so that the curses go with them. Put the money to work."

The War of Independence ended in compromise and civil war; a compromise rejected by Pádraic and Dan Breen and Ernie O'Malley. The jewels fell into the hands of the Republican politician de Valera who allegedly used the monies gained from their sale to fund and found his besuited constitutional party, Fianna Fáil. For sixty years Fianna Fáil pursued Irish reunification by 'peaceful means'. The Russian curse lingered over Irish history, sometimes an insignificant subtext, sometimes a monstrous malevolent shadow.

Revisiting Dan Breen has brought me face to face with my own past. As I walk through Dublin in the 1999 wind and rain, I can't help recalling the last time I went to write about Breen, with Rory looking over my shoulder, nudging me, shouting at me, laughing at me, speaking authoritatively of things I merely had romantic notions about.

I'm kind of addicted to CNN in my own glazed-over contented way. Gerry Adams—talking for Sinn Féin—appears with Martin McGuinness (allegedly the contemporary IRA big boss) standing to his left and Tina (the short tough woman I met twenty-five years ago in covert circumstances) standing to his right. Adams never appears on TV, substantially, without Tina being somewhere in the frame, a powerful shadow. But is Adams the true shadow while Tina holds the power? Has Tina moved over from the military wing to the political wing? Or is it all confused and have the lines gotten blurred as these ageing "revolutionaries" want to look honorable, presentable, decent...peaceful, safe? How does what I see on the global news network connect to the boy I was in the Seventies and the man I am today?

GET YOUR YA-YAS OUT

It was the Golden Age of Rock'n'Roll.

I was political in 1972, a somewhat creepy longhaired political adolescent, reading all the important books. The two Woodward/Bernstein books on Nixon, *The Diary of Che Guevara*, *Bury My Heart At Wounded Knee*, Dee Brown's history of atrocities against American Indians. Pregnant squaws having their bellies slit open by American soldiers. Deep Throat the disgusted Washington insider. Fidel forcing Che to smoke Cuban cigars to ward off mosquitoes in the jungle. Rory made me read those books, made me political. I can remember the Fall Of Saigon like it was yesterday. Me and Rory drinking vodka in Johnny Whelan's house, watching the reportage with the sound turned down, listening to Get Your Ya-Yas Out by The Rolling Stones and Too Much Too Soon by The New York Dolls on the Hi Fi.

I first met Rory in 1972 when he showed up like a surprise party just after the Christmas break at my lonely rich kids boarding school—St Fursey's College in Waterford, a dreary-but-exciting port town on the South coast of Ireland. I was fourteen when we met and he was maybe six months younger. He was big for his age, already kind of hirsute, with facial hair and some hair on his chest. He had a ruddy complexion, sensitive brown eyes, and jet black hair. He despised sports but worked out in the school gym every evening—when all the Gaelic games morons were elsewhere—before two hundred and fifty of us went into the refectory for dinner.

We met in the library five days after term commenced. St Fursey's had an excellent library; good collections of books on the Anglo-Irish Literary Revival and Irish history. I didn't look the library type in my rust coloured denim bell-bottoms, shiny black wet-look slip-ons, Rolling Stones Knebworth teeshirt, dirty blond hair hanging down my back. He looked a bit more reliable but there was already a python-like aspect to his demeanour. We got to talking. Talking kept going for three days.

At that boarding school, during those years, us guys who were interested in rock music had dinky little radios and headphones with which we listened to Radio Luxembourg under the blankets late at night. One time Riders On The Storm by The Doors was the Powerplay, which meant that they played it every hour, one minute after the hour, after the news headlines. Another time the Powerplay was Whiskey In The Jar by Thin Lizzy. The fact that we could hear an Irish folk song—played by a young Irish band led by a striking, lippy, black dude—on international radio filled us with pride, made us proud to be Irish. Now Thin Lizzy are just a memory and their singer, our black boyhood hero, is buried in Howth graveyard, which looks out over Dublin Bay.

"You're a big fucking eejit," Rory said to me in 1972. "You have brains to burn and you waste them talking shite about Frank Sinatra!"

"Yeah, well…" I responded, "you have brains to burn too and the only people who support the IRA are a load of old mountain hillbillies in Kerry."

"Sure. Sure those mountain hillbillies exist. But that doesn't mean I'm one of them." Rory paused as his scowl turned into a grin. "But you're still a big fucking eejit for liking Frank Sinatra."

He told me all the shit I could cram into my adolescent brain. We went to see this crap movie, Little Big Man, a harmless enough Western comedy about a little white kid captured by the Injuns and raised as one of their own. On the way to the cinema he had great expectations born out of the media hype; there were hundreds of pseudo-radical movies about the Indians—Soldier Blue and A Man Called Horse—doing the rounds right then.

"I want to go to America," he said all mock-heroic and cavalier. "I want to go to Wounded Knee and I want to fucking scalp every flabby, racist, degenerate, little American I come across. Slit open their pregnant women's bellies and see how they like it for a change."

"I think Charlie Manson has already made a start in that department."

"Well, ha! Maybe he has," Rory laughed. "A very small start from a very small man."

The cinema was full. Kids, mainly boys about our own age, dominated the audience. I was sixteen and Rory was fifteen. In 1974 there were lots of fur-lined parkas in the cinema not to mention tight blue Levi's jeans betraying horny adolescent male sexuality.

It was a shit movie which came as a surprise to Rory—always the hopeless optimist—though my teenage heartthrob Faye Dunaway did me proud, sexy as ever as a preacher's wife-turned-whore. As we left the auditorium, blinking in the brightness of the foyer, Rory was grim-faced and silent. He walked away from me to the cinema shop where he picked up twenty fags. I went outside, he eventually followed me, and we walked down the street towards Waterford's main square.

"What'd you think of it?" he asked in a pissed-off tone that told me this was a trick question.

"Ah, it was pretty good...I thought," I said nervously. He intimidated me then, and for a long time afterwards.

"Pretty good! Pretty good!" he shouted. Old women stared at

us, petrified. "You can't mean it! That shit Dustin Hoffman. I fucking hate him. I don't trust him."

"Rory, you don't know Dustin Hoffman so you can't trust him or not trust him. He's just an actor. I mean...did you 'trust' him in Mrs. Robinson?"

"The Graduate, you stupid cunt."

"Alright, The Graduate. Did you trust him in The Graduate?"

"Ah, would you ever shut up." But he was beginning to calm down. "You would like The Graduate, charming tale of middle class American Jews."

"Now you're being anti-Semitic as well, man. I think Hoffman was the only Jew there. I don't think Anne Bancroft is a Jew."

"Anne Bancroft? Anne Bancroft? Well, ya don't fucking know Anne Bancroft so how can you tell if she's a fucking Jew or not!" He paused triumphantly. "And how dare you call me anti-Semitic...that movie was based on the premise that any white boy can become an Indian."

"Even a Jewish white boy?"

"Yeah." He smiled, there was a crack in the clouds. "Even a Jewish white boy. You know, him and Jane Fonda and Donald Sutherland and all those so-called liberal Democrats, they're not wrecking the system. They're just holding it up by letting off a little steam, relieving the pressure."

"Rory, why're you trying to look like Che?" I goaded him. He didn't like being poked at but he had to put up with me—he didn't have that many pals. He *was* trying to look like Che with shoulder-length black hair, his expensive black leather bike jacket, the makings of facial hair, and a black beret sporting an enamel red star badge.

"The reason I'm trying to look like Che, asshole," Rory replied, never partial to ducking an issue, even when it made him look bad, "is because I admire what he did and therefore I want to be like him in every way."

"Oh really? So you want to be Minister for Finance, do ya?"

"Of course not—neither did Che. He quit the Castro cabinet to pursue his revolutionary ideals in swamps and jungles—not because he thought he would win but because he understood that his ideal was just that: a fucking ideal, more dangerous than anything he could have achieved in Cuba. Useless idealism is at the root of politics here. What was it that Pearse wrote...

'O wise men, riddle me this,
what if the dream come true?
What if the dream come true?
and if millions unborn shall dwell
In the house that I shaped in my heart,
the noble house of my thought?'"

It was just like Rory to pretend vagueness about the poem by Pearse, that strange lonely revolutionary whose 1916 Rising was hopeless, but whose actions sowed the seeds of our modern Irish aspirations. Patriotic piety was not his bag so, schoolboy recitation over, his face flushed with embarrassment, Rory immediately put distance between himself and simplistic platitudes:

"What is it with all these Irish revolutionaries anyway? Why are so many of our heroes queers? Pearse... Casement...Brendan Behan...Michael Collins. Did you ever read that stuff about how fond Collins was of wrestling? Apparently after meetings of the Army Council he insisted on wrestling with the other commanders, some of whom were right bogtrotters and gobshites...fucking horrified by The Big Fellow, as Collins was so aptly known."

"Maybe they liked dressing up in uniforms," I laughed. "Country boys in sexy green tight fitting uniforms, consumed with a love of Auld Ireland. And The Big Fellow."

LUCIFER WAS A GOOD REBEL

The UN says Ireland has the second highest level of poverty in the industrialised world. An IRA gun smuggling plot is discovered in Florida. The big question is: do these guns belong to the Real IRA or the Provos? The radio full of bullshit about whether a big metallic spike on O'Connell Street is an appropriate way to commemorate the Millennium.

In the National Library I find a photocopy of an interview with Dan Breen in old age. In it Breen says if he'd known what sort of a fiasco the independent Ireland would turn out to be, he'd never have lifted a gun to seek our freedom. "The revolution didn't work out. To get the government they have now, I wouldn't have lost a night's sleep." I also locate an interview Ernie O'Malley gave to *The Irish Press* in 1948:

In Ireland it is so unusual for a man to have a sense of duty that when we do see a man doing his duty, we all burst into applause. The right thing to do, of course, is to carry on a man's work if you approve of him that much. It's all well and good to be singing rebel songs, but I have no respect for people who sing these songs but do nothing about the cause those songs celebrate. Rebel songs are despicable when they come from the mouths of hypocrites and charlatans.

Sitting off Summerhill Parade in Georgian splendour, I tend to agree with Breen. What kind of bizarre beast has Dublin become? How did the guns and bullets of the Tan War give way to the Soviet-style corruption and state hypocrisy which prospered for sixty years before descending into British Intelligence-orchestrated moral chaos?

I call into the Sinn Féin bookshop on Parnell Square looking for stuff on Breen. Although the ceasefire holds firm, the building is heavily protected by metal doors, security cameras, a buzzer entryphone. Two paranoid Volunteer stalwarts—huge guys in regulation black leather jackets, blue denims and black shoes—linger in the hallway.

A woman is inquiring can the IRA do nothing about the traffic congestion on O'Connell St.

"It took me an hour to drive from Westmoreland Street to Parnell Square," she moans. "James Connolly would be disgusted."

I pick up *My Fight for Irish Freedom* by Dan Breen. A dubious war memoir written for propagandistic reasons. Ma's father, who opposed Breen in the Civil War, said it was the book in which the word 'I' was mentioned the most often in the English language. Certainly it is vainglorious and somewhat vulgar with little by way of intellectual input. But then Breen left school at fifteen, the book is ghost-written, and anyway today I found a letter in the National Library in which Breen says:

When *My Fight for Irish Freedom* was put together, I thought I was about to die from my wounds in the Tan War. The IRA'd just lost the Civil War and the cause of a free Ireland seemed lost forever. Our movement was destroyed. Some of the men approached me and told me that a book by me would act as a source of inspiration for the people in the countryside. So I let a young lad get on with writing it. I did seven interviews with him and my wife guided him through the rest. At the time I was happy enough about it; I didn't expect to live to see it in circulation for nearly forty years. But that's life.

I flick through Ernie O'Malley's autobiography, *On Another Man's Wound*, which is in a whole other league and on a whole other level. I don't know if Rory consciously wanted to be in the O'Malley mould but, certainly when he was younger, he wanted to combine his fanatic gunplay with being a thinking man.

I go to the Benbulben offices to look at their *Against Tyrant's Might* archive. A smart Dublin lesbian in her late twenties—a former journalist—runs the Dublin end of the business from elegant rooms in Temple Bar. Five men in their mid-twenties work on computers, administrating the book distribution business which has supplanted publishing as Benbulben's main activity. Formidable computer fire-power. Liston died eight years ago, the lesbian tells me, and his three sons own the business. They do about four new books a year now—in Liston's Sixties heyday it was more like a hundred—mainly folkloric and historical titles. The backlist of nationally-related titles (ie gung-ho rebel writing and legitimate historical studies) is kept permanently in print, and sells vigorously.

The archive is in a well lit back room along with a library containing every book Benbulben ever published. The lesbian says she'll get me some coffee, goes to an old mahogany sideboard and lifts up a green document file which she silently hands me. She leaves me to my memories, never returning with the promised coffee.

I take out the contents of the file, about seventy pages of A4 paper from the epoch of typewriters and carbon copies. Most of it is stuff I have in my own files but there are notes in my own handwriting that I'd completely forgotten about.

One page is headed *Autobiographical Fragment By Breen*:

It was common in the hot summer and early autumn to see the men of a flying column bathing in a river or in the pool of a mountain stream. The usual procedure was to get up a good soap lather and swim about for a while. If no towel were available, the men would roll in the grass when they came out of the water naked. Shirts were washed by being immersed and rubbed in the water. When they had been wrung out they were hung on bushes to dry. The men dressed minus the shirts and by the time the column was ready to parade the shirts would be dry and well aired.

Another page is headed *Quotes From Countess Markievicz*. I know she was pally with Breen but I don't know why I took down her quotes.

"Lucifer was a good rebel," she once wrote to her sister. On her deathbed she said to a pal, "How could I face Paddy Pearse or Jim Connolly in the hereafter if I ever took an oath to a British king?" After working in the Dublin slums she commented:

I've never seen worse slums or met nicer people. If only I could get the people to understand that politics ought to be nothing more or less than the organisation of food, clothes, housing and transport to every other unit of the nation, I'd get a lot further.

I find a copy of Dan Breen's last interview stapled to a photocopy of a letter he sent to an old comrade. In the letter he says,

Dublin is still Dublin and it is still pro-English. The Anglo blood is hard to change. You may change one or two of them but the great majority will always be anti-Irish. They tasted the ways of empire and served it for a way of life—so they can never change.

Poor old Dan was right there—they can never change. Dublin is wall-to-wall shitheads.

Down at the very bottom I place my hands on three sheets of ruled paper written in Rory's strong emphatic hand. I gasp and my heart misses a beat. A ghost has crawled out of the ether to grab me by the balls. I don't know how it ever got here, how or why I passed it on to Benbulben. I remember Rory presenting me with his assessment of Breen when I started on the book.

Daniel Breen (b.1894, d.1969)
Born into peasant stock on the Tipperary/Limerick border when Ireland was a part of the empire. Lucky to have an indulgent, liberal landlord. Inspired by a nationalist schoolteacher, Breen helped to organise the earliest manifestations of the modern IRA in 1915 in Tipperary.

The day that the rebel Irish parliament met in Dublin in 1919— an exercise in constitutional but revolutionary nationalism—Breen lanced the boil by gunning down some Brit police in Tipperary. Breen began the War of Independence. Took no part in the Civil War. Too good a heart to involve himself in brother against brother. Ostracised by the anti-Republican winners of the Civil War, Breen ended up living like a dog in a hut in the forests before emigrating to Chicago. Later, when Al Capone asked him to leave town, Breen moved on to New York where he opened a shebeen during Prohibition. Saw other old IRA pals—frozen out of the new Free

State—become New Yorkers. His first cousin, John Phelan, heroic leader of a Mid Tipperary Brigade of the IRA, gunned down by gangsters raiding the warehouse where he worked as a security guard. Hung out with IRA boss Mike Flannery who, in our time, is the head of NORAID, the main American fund-raisers for the Provos.

My mobile phone rings. Somebody has given my number to the current editor of *Anna Livia*, which has changed hands three times since my time, and also changed with the times. Now it's all buxom babes on the cover and soft interviews with Will Smith inside. In my time the cover babes were Natassja Kinski or Patti Smith and the interviews were with Daniel Ortega or Joseph Beuys. Anyway, *Anna Livia* want me to interview George Michael. I decline politely and tell the editor she should approach me through my agent and where'd she get my mobile number? I don't bother telling her I don't want to interview that self-important piece of shit, that I'm way out of her price league, that there's no such thing as for old time's sake—especially in Dublin. So will I review the new Marianne Faithfull album for them? No. Will I agree to be interviewed for an article on Dublin in the Seventies "when Neil Jordan and Bono and Bob Geldof walked the streets like mere mortals," she quips.

"Sorry," I tell her, "I think nostalgia is a nervous disease."

So will I agree to do their celebrity questionnaire box thing? She is nothing if not persistent so I say "Oh, alright, that can't hurt. So long as we do it right here right now."

She is on for this and it takes her about ten seconds to get the list of questions up on her screen.

What was my earliest ambition? *To live forever.* What would be my dying words? *Why me Lord?* What is my most treasured possession? *An original copy of Brian Jones Presents The Pipes of Pan at Joujouka. Worth about $200, but priceless to me.* (A lie. My most treasured possession is Pádraic's old Smith & Wesson that Rory eventually gave me, which is carefully buried under a pile of ancient NMEs in Kilkenny). My favourite album? *Ramones Leave Home, or Animal Boy by The Ramones.* My favourite book? *The Pat Hobby Stories by F Scott Fitzgerald.* My favourite Irish book? *The Singing Flame by Ernie O'Malley.* If there was one thing I could change about my appearance, what would it be? *The colour of my skin.*

Three questions later we're finished and I still don't know how she got my number. I get her off the phone quick enough because I want to get back to Rory.

Back in Ireland Breen joined Fianna Fáil, constitutional nationalist party, and got a seat in the Dáil where he spent the rest of his days polishing his stories and fulminating against the mediocre nature of what he'd achieved. When he was an old man living in a fancy old people's home outside Dublin in the Sixties, I got to meet him. My Grandad Pádraic and I were brought there on Sunday afternoons by Dad, a Fianna Fáil safe pair of hands. Breen and Pádraic had fought together. My father was a bit of an amateur historian and felt that, with Breen bedridden, it would be safe enough to visit him. Dan was sick a lot of the time. He still had Brit bullets in his body. I don't think he liked my old man, but Dad took him out for drives around the Dublin Mountains and that was something.

When I got a bit older I'd take the bus out to the home, the St John of God's in Kilcroney, and read books to Dan. He gave me a present, a little silver cross made out of the medals he got for his IRA activities. He'd had them melted down and turned into a series of small silver crosses. Most of his life he'd been violently anti-clerical but he embraced Catholicism again in his last years. Who can blame him? Who amongst us doesn't cower in the face of Death's tyranny? Religion is no answer to our problems. It falls to people like you and me to be precise in our revolutionary analysis of the world we live in.

Like many a man of his ilk, Dan Breen would have been better off if he'd died when he was thirty. He'd done all his important work by 1922.

I pick up Rory's slick testament and inhale. I think I can still smell him off of it. I slip the yellowed document into my briefcase. It was mine anyway. The only other thing of interest in the file is a carbon copy of a letter from Liston to me, cancelling publication of my book on Seán McBride.

GUERILLA DAYS IN IRELAND

Rory told me that he had been dumped in St Fursey's because his parents were sick of him. Why were they sick of him?

"Last summer holidays," he explained to me the third day I knew him, "I thought the folks had gone to the country to visit some culchie cousins. In fact they were visiting some new shopping centre that'd just opened down the road. See if they could find some interesting frozen beans or yet another plastic deckchair for the back garden. The biggest Dunne's Stores in the fucking world or something. I had these bomb making plans my cousin gave me so I decided to have a go with them. They worked real well! Just as Dad drove into the driveway the biggest mushroom cloud they'd ever seen in Cork erupted behind the house. When everybody'd calmed down a raid on my bedroom revealed my copies of *The Anarchist Cookbook*, Mao's *Little Red Book*, and *My Fight for Irish Freedom* by Dan Breen. The Breen book—an autographed copy I got from Grandad—gave the worst offence—too close to home for Dad. So I says to him, 'You stupid moron, your own fucking father gave that to me! You should be ashamed of yourself. I'm sure Grandad can't stand the sight of you!' And that shut the fucker up for at least half an hour before it started all over again."

Rory's parents were worried about the bad influence he was having on his young brother Tony. When the Guards visited his home for an 'auld chat' with his parents and told them Rory had been seen hanging around with Sinn Féin Provo types, this proved one embarrassment too many for his civil servant father, a pillar of Catholic society in the provincial southern city of Cork.

Ireland was sufficiently a valley of the squinting windows for domestic visits from men in uniform to wreak devastating social havoc. The father got promoted to a big job in Dublin and he decided, prior to the move, to solve the Rory problem once and for all. Through Department of Education connections, a good middle class school—my school—was found for the proto-urban terrorist.

There was no lack of love in my life but I got dumped in boarding school because my folks had just split up. I lived in Kilkenny with my mother. Ma had money; she owned an antique shop, a share in her family's bottling plant, and a couple of houses in flats. She felt, correctly, that I would have a stable bunch of school friends if I was educated in a stable environment.

My old man was a farmer who lived near the village of Urlingford where he owned a newsagents, a pub, and grocery store. I went to stay with him one weekend a month during the summer holidays. I think I loved them both, but I have everything in common with my mother. My father remains a distant man consumed with his own affairs.

My mother was a tall, thin, bony woman with bright red hair and a taste for expensive sunglasses, who drove an old cherry-red MG sportster that was her pride and joy. Her skin was unusually pale and translucent, relieved only by two bright red cheeks. I don't know what she ever saw in my father, who can best be described as looking like the smalltown entrepreneur that he is.

Me and Rory were on different wavelengths, that's why we became good friends. He was difficult and severe in his dealings with the outside world but internally tender. I was a more successful operator, very smooth and pleasant on the surface but tough as old leather deep down inside. He had a family. I just had a mother, really. I didn't (and don't) give a fuck about anybody else. He cared way too much. He seemed to be the extremist and I seemed to be the moderate, but life is a long song. I reckon I've grown to be a typical Twenty First Century man, cold, self-obsessed, unimpressed by ideas/ideals and their ramifications. He was a Nineteenth Century man caught in the crossfire of swiftly changing times.

At St Fursey's he listened to black sounds like reggae and Stax. Hard to believe it now, but very few pseudo-cool white boys listened to actual black music in '72 and '73. Most of us absorbed it second-hand from the Stones or Dylan. At the time I reckoned Rory was listening to unadulterated champagne music and that the only valid form was guitar-based rock'n'roll wrapped up in twisted kicks. Which is not to say that Rory was twenty years ahead of his time, or that he had some faultless ability to spot needles in haystacks, just that he was right about some black records. He also listened to a lot of bad soul music, and would occasionally produce worthy-but-dreary tapes of American Indian music.

"Turn that shit off, Rory. You play any more of that stuff and I'll begin to side with the fucking Cavalry against Geronimo," I said one time. "If you want to sing a song, sing a love song."

"I don't know any love songs."

"We all know love songs. You just don't know about love."

"Love is not worth the bother." He'd get uncharacteristically tongue tied when the talk came around to sex.

"Sure. Love is not worth the bother but the ride is. Did you ever get the ride, Rory?" I taunted him.

"No." He was nervous but honest. "I'm terrified of the lead up...you know what I mean. How do you ask her? Where do you go? How do the two of you get to take your clothes off?"

I laughed at him then but now I know that these are universal questions that never quite got away.

Six foot and handsome in a broody way, dressed in denim, thin and muscular, he let his hair grow long after I insisted on it. Rory could be competitive in his own contradictory way. When I read about skinheads in the Sunday Times colour supplement I went straight out and got a skinhead. The cult of skinhead was then the sexual vogue, at least partly due to the rape and pillage skinhead novels all at St Fursey's read. Rory was pleased with my haircut but, on the other hand, pissed off that he hadn't thought of it first. He was somewhat manly but still a boy. Father Joseph, the St Fursey's President nicknamed Joe Spunk, denounced me on front of the whole school as a 'stupid fucker'. Rory later made a long speech on this great incident.

"To get that pompous queer fascist," he maintained, "to use the word 'fucker' in front of the whole school was excellent. To annoy Joe so that the reactionary moron was speechless, to show him something, even just a fashion thing, that he had never seen before, was like taking out your knob and asking him to suck on it."

Rory was the first in a long line of New Friends that Old Friends warned me against:

—Keep away from him…

—The Guards are watching him…

—He'll get you into trouble.

—He's IRA!

—The Provos are only killing their own…

—You can't bomb them into a united Ireland…

These were the things that my friends said to me as we ate shepherd's pie, which we called shepherd's shit, followed abruptly by hot apple tart and cold custard, in St Fursey's cavernous refectory.

I got a very hard time of it; it was as if I suddenly turned into a gothic Neanderthal bent on mayhem and destruction. My previous reputation as a harmless hippy, eccentrically dressed in a dirty peace-symbol teeshirt, took a terrible battering and didn't fully recover for at least six months.

Rory and I enjoyed taking Irish language classes together. Our teacher was a gentle soul in his late fifties who'd been a priest all his life. Left the priesthood to marry, enjoyed the private miracle of having a child, was now starting life again in society, before our very eyes. He was particularly good on modern literature in Irish. We were impressed by his enthusiasm though neither of us understood very much Irish.

The Jesuits were none too happy with Rory, for those were tense days. The Northern Troubles had swung into action, and nationalist feelings were running high in the South where minor aspects of society were crumbling under the weight of the Northern upheavals.

When I first went to the school, it was a mark of pride with Father Joe that the son of the local Fianna Fáil minister was a Fursey's pupil, a timid lad whose main interest in life was Gaelic Football. Then, as all hell broke loose in Irish politics, the minister resigned from the government, his Mercedes and Fianna Fáil to join a fringe Republican party, Aontacht Eireann (Free Ireland), thus bringing shame and odium onto our school. This fall from grace was bad enough, a complete marketing disaster. The last thing Joe wanted—adding insult to injury—was a recruiting officer for the Provos in our midst, turning our tender minds towards anarchy or insurrection.

Then on January 30th, the British Army fired into a crowd of unarmed Civil Rights marchers in Derry, killing thirteen. Bloody Sunday. Joe Spunk closed the school for a day of mourning and we were all instructed to attend a memorial service for the slaughtered in the town centre. We were addressed by the Bishop, local Fianna Fáil worthies, and a severe character from the IRA. Six hooded youths wearing blue jeans and army jackets stepped forward from the crowd to leave off a volley to loud cheers.

An enthusiastic student of Irish history, I was agog. I'd never seen anything like this, never set eyes on the IRA in the flesh. Neither had Rory, and the sight of the Volunteers—proud, virile, free—had a profound influence on the two of us. Church, State, and Republicans would subsequently splinter into a hundred factions. The meeting, and meetings like it all over Ireland that day, were supposed to calm things down. They merely fanned the flames. The IRA, moribund since the Thirties, was back in action. In the years since then Ireland reaped the whirlwind.

Rory and me gathered around ourselves a forlorn gang of dispossessed middle-class bell-bottomed Irish boys hung up on Led Zeppelin or Marlon Brando or Jane Fonda...talking bullshit about Bob Dylan's comeback...one guy insisting that Dylan was only copying Rod Stewart...Paul McCartney recorded Band on the Run in Nigeria and he played all the instruments himself...Horslips were researching ancient Irish melodies in the National Library...

Stranded in a port town full of hustlers and sailors and whores and queers, we were glam rock revolutionaries committed to the destruction of society. Society is a nasty brute to tangle with; it has a way of taking its revenge.

BOOK OF INVASIONS

Anna Livia is banned, temporarily, by the censorship board. At the end of August 80,000 people catch Robbie Williams at Slane. Where I, in my epoch, saw the Stones and Dylan. But there are worse things in Ireland than Robbie Williams. Such as Westlife, a

Boyzone satellite who, no doubt, were put through their paces before superstardom beckoned.

Staying with Ma in Kilkenny for the weekend, we go to Waterford on Saturday. She is ageing now, grey haired and brittle, but she still has her fantastically rosy cheeks and her saintly cheery disposition.

She buys me lunch in the Tower Hotel where all the local worthies tuck into roast beef smothered in gravy or roast chicken smothered in the same gravy. Garth Brooks is singing through the tannoy.

"Liam, you should come back to Ireland," she says smoking a Benson & Hedges while I grimace at the damage she is doing to herself with cigarettes. "While you're still young enough. While you still have the time to find a nice Irish girl and marry her."

She is too old and close to the end for me to argue with her or tell her home truths. Like that I have a home I own in America and I won't be coming back. Like that I was once married to "a nice Irish girl", that it was a complete disaster, that we have a daughter who is her grandchild.

The real thing I cannot tell my mother, cannot tell anybody in this godforsaken country, is that Ireland means nothing to me now. I sailed away a long time ago and I never returned. They don't owe me anything, I'm not interested in them. I still say the English should be kicked out of my country but I'm no longer qualified to comment. Anyway, that whole aspiration is now out the window for the time being. And I ran away from the local mess so, in terms of the Irish, my opinion doesn't count. I'm partial to Chryslers. The Chrysler is a good travelling car.

After lunch Ma goes shopping for a few hours and I head for St Fursey's. The boarding school has long closed down. The dormitories and refectories where we lived and ate have now been converted into a weekend conference centre; the elaborate gardens and grounds where I marched, a strong young colt, were destroyed to make way for a sprawling modern urban secondary school complex. Still run by the Jesuits, still a happening place in a restive world, it touches me with a certain energy.

I walk across the three football pitches leading to the banks of the Suir where we used to go to smoke and bullshit. I stare across the river at the now closed meat factory. I can just about make out the rust and decay tearing the old steel/aluminum building apart. A mushroom cloud of crows rise up from the factory, scattered by some unaccountable disturbance.

I'm caught up in reverie when I hear some life to my left. A boy about fifteen is standing staring at me. For a moment I think that he is a pupil from St Fursey's but then it dawns on me that he is cruising me. I say hello and leave quickly.

Later I walk down the quays and stand outside the post office, looking at the selfsame phone booth from which Rory called me in Dublin twenty-three years ago. I shiver.

Me and ma stop off in Tramore where we walk the prom, the good salty wind blowing in from the sea.

"There is rain on the wind," she says to me, nestling up close to my man's shoulders.

To the best of my knowledge there were no men in her life after my father.

I drive Ma back to Kilkenny. She got rid of the MG decades ago; she has an Isuzu four wheel drive back home, plus this more modest Volkswagen Polo I'm using for the weekend. The talk comes around to *On The Run*. I explain that this time around I'll get to do the book I always wanted to do.

"My school pal Rory always said I shouldn't be afraid to criticise aspects of what the IRA did. He said a hagiographer is not a good friend, that the truth is a weapon in the hands of a true revolutionary."

"And are you a true revolutionary?" Ma asks waspishly.

"No. Of course not. I just write about musicians. Some of them are revolutionaries, and I'm glad to write about them. *Mannish Boy* and *On The Run* are both going to be good. I never became a revolutionary...but Rory was a revolutionary."

"Yes he was," she says, rather nastily in the context. She never approved of that friendship, no more than anybody else. Ma hates Republicanism in every form.

There is silence for a moment.

I take my eyes off the road for just a second to take a good look at her. She is old now and more worried about keeping warm than about looking stylish. But she still looks fancy to me. I bought her an old Deco brooch in San Francisco before I came over. She has it on the lapel of her black silk jacket, the work of some trendy Irish clothes designer taking the world by storm. Her cheeks still have that miraculously rosy glow. She is as smart as she ever was, richer than I remember. She inherited everything from Uncle Alan. One day, we both know but it is something we could never talk about, she will be gone and all she owns will belong to me.

"What do you think Dan Breen would make of the Peace Agreement?" she asks whimsically.

"I think he'd hate it but who knows? That was another place and another time."

"And Rory? What would he think of your Mr Adams?"

"He's not *my* Mr Adams, I can assure you. Rory..."

I stare ahead at the tail lights of the cars in front of me: at this godforsaken moment in time the whole fucking world has decided to drive from Waterford to Kilkenny.

"I think Rory would personally assassinate Adams. But of course…who really knows? That was another time and another place too."

My old Sony turntable, connected to my old Phillips amp and my handmade speakers, stands proud as a Seventies cock rocker in my bedroom. Thanks to Ma's curatorial skills, all I have to do is plug it in, press the On button, and I have access to my original, pre-CD record collection. If only life was that easy. Life's a river flowing to the sea.

I listen to The Book Of Invasions by Horslips. Their comeback album, a return to the Celtic mythological cycles of The Táin. The same blending of Irish and rockist musical themes. But not, I think, as good as The Táin. What went down in the flood.

I arrange with my mother to have all my LPs freighted to the States. This dismays her a little although she knows I won't be returning to Ireland—not during her lifetime.

REMAKE/REMODEL
One fine summer, the summer of '74, the Seventies were in full kitsch swing. It was plotted between Rory and me, later agreed upon by our parents, that I'd go stay with Rory's family in Dublin for two weeks. The arrangements were made in May, before we

broke up for the summer. British Intelligence let off car bombs all over Dublin, killed 23 people. There was talk of blood flowing down the pavements of Dublin. Patty Hearst was in the jaws of the Symbonese Liberation Army, and Shaft in Africa was playing in the Regent Cinema in Waterford.

We looked like Robert Plant and Jimmy Page from Led Zeppelin—or at least we thought we did, which was the same thing. So Plant (me) and Page (Rory) sat down on the banks of the Suir smoking and staring at the Clover Meats Factory across the river. We were good friends by then, we'd known each other two years, so our talk could occasionally be frank. I guess by saying we were like the Zeppelin boys I'm saying that I was the better looking of the two, though only by a short head, and neither of us was particularly handsome. We were both tall, but Rory was filling out more than me, deliberately, and his dress sense was significantly duller than mine, being a copy of mine. We had a good deal going. I was copying his mind and he was copying my body.

"You could come and stay with me in Kilkenny only Ma is not that hot on having visitors to stay. She avoids hassle as much as she possibly can. Anyway..."

"Anyway you fancy a trip to the big smoke where you can be all cool at my expense."

"At your expense?"

"Well, you get to have a good snigger at my fascist father and my lunatic mother."

"And to see your Confirmation photographs. I'm really looking forward to that."

I guess his folks were pleased that he was making friends with nice respectable kids like me but, Rory told me, they were

33

distressed by the fact that I came from a broken home. They had Rory down as a loner and presumably they thought that I was a flawed companion but a better friend than no friend at all.

Who knows what they made of me when they got to know me? Neither of them had ever set eyes on me prior to my trip to Dublin. I was resolutely dedicated to my lifestyle of long hair and the clothes and opinions that went with it. At sixteen, I had already developed many of the anti-social habits that still govern my life—I liked to dress casual, talk too smart, and do very little.

Ma drove through the Kilkenny afternoon traffic jam to the railway station. Before we left the house she gave me money, told me not to spend it all, that it was just in case I needed something in an emergency. She packed into my knapsack her gift, a jar of homemade blackcurrant jam, for Rory's mother. The train, arriving from Waterford, pulled onto the platform. I leaped aboard delightedly, in a rush to begin my first adventure alone in the big city, and found an empty seat with a good view. Two hours later I got into dreary old Heuston Station in Dublin, where Rory was waiting anxiously for me at the end of the platform.

"Uh, hiya, Liam," he said a little stiffly. "My dad's outside in the car."

I followed him out to the car park where his father waited patiently at the wheel of a new-smelling Volvo hatchback.

"Hello there Liam, I'm Séamus. Call me Séamus," said the father.

He smiled disapprovingly, held out his big country hand for shaking, so I shook it. I never ever, in all the years since then, called him anything other than 'Mr Murray'. He was approximately fifty, wore brown-rimmed glasses, had Tony

Curtis-style greying brown hair, was in good condition for his age, about five ten and stockily built, wearing his weekend casuals, synthetic navy blue slacks, expensive brown brogues, and a Clancy Brothers jumper.

Séamus had an especially strong Munster accent. It went with the job. Most people who spoke Irish on a regular basis talked a heavily accented version of the English language. Commitment to Irish was de rigueur with educators, ambitious civil servants, Republicans, and supporters of Fianna Fáil. Old Séamus came under all of these headings except Republican.

Fianna Fáil in those days were like the Eastern Bloc Communist Parties (in those days). Always in power, their commitment to The Language (as they called it) was like the Soviet commitment to global revolution. As well as being fluent in Irish, civil servants and school teachers had to pay lip service to the notions of Eamon de Valera, the Spanish-American freedom fighter and founder of Fianna Fáil who dominated Irish politics between 1930 and 1960. The central elements of Dev's creed were that:

—Ireland would one day be reunited by peaceful means.

—The Irish language would eventually be spoken by the people of Ireland.

—The youth of Ireland would be strong lads and comely maidens, busy dancing jigs and reels at country crossroads.

—We've never had it so good.

Genuine IRA Republicans were to Fianna Fáil what Trotskyists were to the Soviets; potent dangerous distant brothers and sisters who'd strayed off a sensible and lucrative path, who took things literally enough to actually believe the approved party line rhetoric bullshit.

Séamus was a typical Fianna Fáil man of his time. His father Pádraic had fought in the Tan War. Pádraic's IRA generation founded Fianna Fáil out of the ashes of defeat in a bloody civil war. They were good men, really. Pious, responsible, conservative; perhaps they meant well. Séamus was one of the privileged next generation who got to live a confident, affluent Kennedy-era lifestyle. The men who inherited control of Ireland in the Sixties thought they were having their optimistic day in the sun. Too much sun gives you cancer.

By the end of the Sixties their swish lifestyle gave rise to its own malignant contradictions, and by the time Rory and me were on our way to Séamus's comfortable Howth homestead, Fianna Fáil had undergone all manner of turbulences. The most traumatic of these was the second coming of the IRA who—calling themselves the Provos—waged a full blown war against the British presence in the North.

On the home front, the Seventies and the drug counterculture it brought with it took a traumatic toll on family life. Ireland was a lower middle class redneck mausoleum full of petrol pump attendants, nurses, bank clerks, and office workers who liked bad country music. Now the smart cosmopolitan children of Fianna Fáil were growing up to be dope smokers or Scientologists or guitarists or lesbians or pro-Castro. The plan went badly wrong.

Assailed by a hostile media who unearthed endless financial, sexual, and ethical scandals, Fianna Fáil survived, a mere shadow of the monolith it once was. The thing you always hear them saying about Fianna Fáil in Ireland is: 'They're finished now'. Fianna Fáil rules Ireland today. And probably always will.

I remember Séamus's big powerful Volvo gliding serenely out onto the busy dual carriageway; our smooth progression through

Dublin's sleepy city centre.

Why is it that assholes always make such good drivers, I thought to myself as Mr Murray effortlessly negotiated with the bleak streets of the city. I stared out the window like a dim nine year old. Eventually we hit the coast road which took us out to Howth, the fishing village jewel on the northern lip of Dublin Bay.

In those days a lot of Protestants still lived in Howth, benign remnants of an imperial past. There were also a few working class Dublin types, happy slaves who travelled by slow bus into the city centre every morning for work. But the dominant element in Howth was the rising Irish bourgeoisie, aspirant Eurocrats and contented Catholic bureaucrats like Séamus Murray, people whose children—my generation—would grow up to destroy the sureties of the calm, cool, swinging Ireland of those days.

A Catholic nationalist bureaucrat by profession, in his spare time Séamus was a grey eminence in the Irish language revival movement and a gung-ho amateur historian; too intelligent to be dismissible, too conventional to ever understand Rory. I guess he really believed in the reunification of Ireland by the 'peaceful means' of Fianna Fáil. He was an archetypal Seventies man: confused and busy, fond of gravy on his steak, and sugary whipped cream on his sugar-infested apple tart. Probably nice enough in his own self-consumed way but that meant nothing to his son or to me, two boys who saw themselves as heavy hitters in the cerebral stakes.

Eldest sons and fathers often don't get along and the usual reason given for this is that they're much too alike to ever be pals. But I could never see any similarity between Rory and

Séamus other than a quick and steady intelligence.

On the drive to Howth, Rory sat in the passenger seat with me in the back. Séamus spoke at me throughout the journey. Every once in a while Rory would turn around in his seat, smile, and raise his eyes up to heaven. Séamus spoke of Parnell, the fallen Nineteenth Century parliamentary hero whose home is now owned by the State. He was on some committee to do with restoring the house to its Parnell-era glory.

"Ah, yes, well," he said matter-of-factly, 'if we had more men like Parnell in Ireland today we'd all be a lot better off, and people would be much happier."

As it happened I knew a lot about Parnell, having read the standard tome-like biography. Therefore I ended up yapping about him with Séamus. It was all platitudes on both sides but Séamus looked briefly disturbed when I quoted Yeats on Parnell:

"When the strong silent man was at hand he organised their people, and they looked like a heroic people."

According to Fianna Fáil the Irish didn't look heroic, they *were* heroic, but that heroism—valid during the revolutionary period—was no longer called for.

The fact that I fraternised with Séamus disappointed Rory. That part of me that will talk to the father, pretend to be the regular guy, has always hurt and disappointed my friends. I'll always be the snake in the grass who will see the other guy's point of view. I'm quick and sharp, given to a snappy venal cynicism. Later I knew that Rory was a mixture of his father's educated classicism, his mother's neurotic unhappiness, and his own genuinely leftist world vision.

Frank Sinatra singing It Was A Very Good Year on the radio as we pulled into the long pebbled driveway of the house in Howth.

"I'll go in ahead to alert Maeve!" said Séamus humorously, grabbing his keys and rushing into the house.

I guess he felt he'd better warn her that I looked like a youthful refugee from Woodstock. Ma'd cleaned me up a fair bit before the journey but I refused to get my hair cut or to abandon assorted rather zany medallions and bangles which swung around my neck, jingling and jangling anarchically. I was wearing a Rick Griffin psychedelic teeshirt, purchased via a mail order firm in Wales, featuring a huge fat joint. All the photographic evidence suggests that until about the age of seventeen I was a total provincial jerk.

We gave Séamus five minutes and then we entered the house together, using the back door which, Rory warned me, led straight to a kitchen where his mother invariably lurked and ruled her empire, where she would be waiting to greet us and sniff me out.

It was like I'd known Séamus and Maeve all my life. Rory'd told me all about them during the cold winter evenings when we'd walked around the extensive wooded grounds of our school in Waterford.

"My dear mother is totally fucking crazy, the poor woman. I hate her. I'd happily shoot my father. He has done so well out of this country, and he just wants more and more and more," he said one wet Sunday as we shared a joint down by the banks of the great River Suir, full of the vile smell of blood from the meat factory.

They lived in a large Thirties house, a redbrick detached place with vast well-maintained grounds. The house had been updated along the way and the internal decor was very chic in a prosperous Sixties mode. The kitchen we entered was very much the family room, where Maeve and her sons communed with one another. Séamus lived in a salubrious wood-paneled lounge where, master of all he surveyed, he listened to Bach, The Clancy Brothers, and Herb Alpert's Tijuana Brass on a state-of-the-art Hi Fi, complete with an enormous Tandenberg reel-to-reel tape recorder. Maeve, who seemed formidable enough and intelligent if batty, was in her early forties then. Kind of good looking, or at least still thin. She seemed pleased to get Ma's blackcurrant jam and offered me food. I just wanted a glass of Coke so I said that to her.

"It'll be waiting for you in five minutes," she said kindly, "but first go and leave your bag up in your room. Rory'll show you."

I was to share Rory's room with him, she explained. I would sleep in his bed and he would sleep on a spare mattress on the floor.

His room on the second floor was smallish but jaunty enough, his books neatly arranged on built-in mahogany bookshelves; his library typical of the formidable intellectual battery at the disposal of the prosperous Seventies adolescent; Mailer, Hesse, De Beauvoir, books of his I'd previously seen in St Fursey's covering Cuba, American Indians, and Irish history. When I first met Rory his interests had been largely internationalist. He was particularly interested in the history of the Indians and in the never-ending Arab/Israeli crisis. As the situation in the North got out of hand—after Bloody Sunday—he turned his focused attention towards his own country's problems. He had always been Republican and engaged. After Bloody Sunday it seemed to him that the removal of the English from Ireland was the most important of all his personal priorities.

Séamus and Maeve had the biggest bedroom. Rory,

sniggering, showed me their lavish quarters complete with huge double bed, bay windows, and wall-to-wall carpets.

"Sorry about the Ku Klux furniture," Rory said. "Interior decor isn't their strong point."

He had two brothers—a four year old whose name I can't remember and Tony, a mischievous nine year old close to Rory. The three boys had a bedroom each.

"Their rooms are a mess, no point in going in there," he said, respecting their privacy as he certainly didn't respect his parents's. Rory was very fond of his brothers. I didn't see much of them on that visit, I think they were kept away from me, but I subsequently met Tony from time to time with Rory.

I spent an hour being civilised in the kitchen, sipping my Coke and chatting amiably like a good boy while ducking and diving to avoid leading questions.

Maeve was undoubtedly mad, but could hold her own in conversation and was reasonably well read—a big fan of the novels of Edna O'Brien and the music of The Dubliners folk group.

"Is this your first trip to Dublin, Liam?"

I told her it was. She launched into a speech about the joys of travel, while she poured out the promised glasses of Coke and presented them to us along with a plate of biscuits.

"We go to France every summer for our holidays. We always get the car ferry from Cork. Driving really is the best way to see France. I love Paris because that is where Séamus and I went on our honeymoon. My only regret is that I've never been to America because I'm afraid of flying."

"Come on, Liam," Rory said eventually, "you have to come and meet Pádraic, he's expecting you."

Rory's grandfather—Séamus's old man—was the only adult

in the family that he got along with, and the only member of the family I was looking forward to meeting.

A retired schoolteacher from rural Munster, Pádraic was in his late seventies when I got to meet him. A delicate trim man who always wore a good jacket of Donegal tweed, he lived in a granny flat—a converted outhouse at the bottom of the garden—where he passed his days reading and listening to the radio. He was a witty, sophisticated, old character of Victorian demeanour, with a big collection of books on Irish history and a lot of books in the Irish language. The furniture in his place contrasted sharply with the style in his son's house; solid old-fashioned mahogany items brought up eons back from the family farm in Munster.

Pádraic's was a romantic but dwindling world. He talked of Raftery, the famous blind harpist/poet from before the Irish Diaspora. In his muscular drawl he could recite, in Irish, long passages from the poetry of Raftery:

Mise Raifteirí, an file, lán dóchais is grá
le súile gan solas, le ciúineas gan crá,
ag dul síos ar m'aistear le solas mo chroí,
fann agus tuírseach go deireadh mo shlí;
tá me anois lem aghaidh at Bhall,
as seinm cheóil do phócaí falamh.

I'm Raftery the Poet, full of hope and zeal.
My eyes see no light, see no misery.
The end of my story is surely to be
Worn shoes, old rags and banter to hear,
So I'll play no perfect melody,
For empty pockets who care nothing for me.

42

Pádraic talked of the Irish mythological cycles which I knew little about. Raw unpasteurised Irish culture was an outmoded style in the mid-Seventies, and the old man's interests seemed noble and very pure to me.

Rory and I went to see him every night during that visit. He'd be watching TV, the evening meal prepared by Maeve cast to one side half-eaten. When we'd arrive he'd stand erect, walk to the television, and turn it off like it was unworthy of him, like we'd caught him looking at a porn mag. Oddly enough, Pádraic favoured the BBC, which he said showed the best films and documentaries.

Cute enough in his honest way, he never said anything negative about either Séamus or Maeve. This old man had been around the tracks a few times and seen a thing or two—his own wife had died young from cancer and he'd reared both Séamus and Séamus's sister on his own. He didn't pretend that he'd been some hero in the Tan War. Quite the contrary. As he said to us one evening:

"I was a very ordinary young man but through my brief dalliance with the IRA I was privileged to witness some heroic men in action. To observe thrilling moments in history, such as you might read about in Joseph Conrad or Rudyard Kipling. But the problem with the Irish is that we're a peasant people. We don't have the heroic spirit in us. So you have endless revolts led by decent middle class lads—with no support from their middle class pals—who then get let down by working class lads who're not thinking Sinn Féin (Ourselves Alone) but Mé Féin (Myself Alone). Same thing happened with the Russians. Mr Lenin was an aristocrat, guided only by noble motives; Stalin was a dangerous, mischievous, ambitious cur who came from cottage people!"

I liked Pádraic a great deal. We talked books a lot. He was merely amused by rock music and by my long hair. Much of the talking had to do with Irish history, Rory and his grand-dad swapping tales of English infamy and Irish stupidity.

Pádraic left Rory all his books and a little money. Some of those books are in my San Francisco library today.

IF YOU WANT TO SING A SONG

October 6th Ireland signs up to the Partnership for Peace, a NATO umbrella organisation. The great achievement of the founding fathers—our neutrality—is casually forgotten.

I stand in front of a redbrick house on Raglan Road in Ballsbridge. Brendan Behan used to hang out on Raglan Road back in the Fifties, after he quit the IRA and before he became a writer/weirdo/chat show superstar. Now it is three in the 1999 afternoon and the rain is torrential. I stare at one of the terraced houses, Number 37. Inside that house in 1980 I signed my contract for *Tyrant's Might*.

My publisher, a Galway-based pirate called Dick Liston, was the owner of Benbulben Books, a legend in Irish publishing. By 1980 Liston was past his prime, reduced to putting out maybe fifty paperbacks a year, usually on political, historical, or rural themes. Benbulben covers were very bad indeed, and the quality of what went between the covers varied a whole lot.

In the early Sixties, when he was the most prominent Catholic publisher in Ireland spitting out morally uplifting Vatican-approved texts by the new time, Liston, a happily married family man, maintained a Ghanaian mistress in a seafront apartment in Salthill, a tacky seaside suburb of Galway. When his wife of thirty years, mother to his three sons, went down with cancer, he got her to keep a diary of her final days. This sad diary he published for the edification of the Faithful: 'The story of one Catholic woman facing death and her Maker with faith and trust in Jesus.' Six months after she died, Benbulben published Liston's own recollection of the trauma of seeing his wife die of cancer. Then, a year later, he published a memoir by the Ghanaian mistress on what it was like to be the mistress of a Catholic man (unnamed) whose wife is dying of cancer.

By the time I met Liston he was getting on for seventy, a professional gone-to-seed rogue who devoted all of Benbulben's considerable clout to supporting the Provos and Charlie Haughey, the scandal-rich Fianna Fáil bandit king. Academic sources had told him that my BA Mini-Thesis was on Dan Breen. As had luck would have it, he was doing a series of paperback biographies of the heroes of the Irish War of Independence: Ernie O'Malley, Seán McBride, Countess Markievicz.

A letter on Benbulben headed paper arrived, asking did I want to do the Dan Breen book. I'd just left university, and was thinking of doing a bit of writing. I rang Rory and he said "Go for it. Dan Breen knew how to deal with the Brits. You know, I knew him through Pádraic...I don't know, maybe he was a bit of a clown but...I think he was good. He did good."

I called into Benbulben's Dublin offices on Pearse Street where I met an ancient fusty librarian-type called Tom Flannery, who administered the firm's activities in the Big Smoke. A kindly alcoholic with a rosy red nose, glasses held together by sellotape and a smelly Harris Tweed jacket that'd seen better days, Flannery was all too glad to see me—I relieved his boredom.

The Pearse Street premises was mainly a book distribution warehouse with two tiny offices tagged on. Downstairs was a bleach factory where they took bleach concentrate, mixed it with water, and put it into plastic bottles for distribution to pound shops and cheapo supermarkets. I became familiar with the stink of bleach over the next year; if working for Liston hadn't driven Flannery to the drink, the bleach would have done the job. While I was sitting there that first day Flannery got on the phone to Liston in Galway to arrange an appointment for me. I was to make my way to Raglan Road the following Saturday afternoon at half past two.

"And don't be late!" Flannery advised me by way of a parting shot. "Himself will expect you to be on time."

Rory called around to see me the night before my meeting with Liston. He was more excited about my impending contract than I was.

"You'll never get a penny out of Benbulben," he said, "but you'll get your say. Liston has a mistress in every town in Ireland. This place you're meeting him in is probably the home of his Dublin whore."

But when I walked up the steps of the redbricked, terraced house I was greeted by a respectable Ballsbridge matron, the widow of the man who introduced peat briquettes—a phenomenally popular domestic heating fuel reclaimed from the otherwise useless ubiquitous Irish bogs—to Ireland. She explained in her refined Galway accent that Liston—she called him Richard—had been to UCG with her late husband, and the basement of their home had been his Dublin base for many years.

Her hallway was genteel and old fashioned, spotlessly clean and smelling of floor polish. An invisible grandfather clock tick-tocked from behind a closed door to my left. I could also hear opera on the radio somewhere.

I was led down to a basement where the walls reeked of tobacco smoke, the furniture was ancient and scruffy, and floral patterned wallpaper gave things a squalid aspect. This was a man's den, and only masculine needs were catered for. I subsequently called to see Liston several times in his basement, and there was more to those quarters than met the eye. This was the home of a schemer, a desperado, a player, a cowboy. The basement saw them come and saw them go. It saw me come and go.

"Come in Liam, come in," Liston roared like a lion as my feet touched the basement floor.

"I'll leave you now, Mr Crowe," said the lady of the house, withdrawing demurely. The thought struck me that there may well have been some truth in Rory's lewd innuendo. Maybe this old bird did have a thing for Liston.

He didn't get up to greet me. Huge and ancient, he sat in his creaky armchair to the left of a roaring fire. A bottle of whiskey, some glasses, and a jug of water lay on a new Formica coffee table. A cumbersome old Rediffusion wireless with stations like Hilversum and Luxembourg listed on its dial was blasting out The Waltons Show, presented by a theatrical old guy called Leo O'Grady. Waltons were an old Parnell Square outfit who sold musical instruments, sheet music, and records. The Waltons family had done their part in the War of Independence. They had their own record label.

Every week The Waltons Show ended with Leo O'Grady

advising: "If you want to sing a song, sing an Irish song."

He played records issued on the Waltons label like Come Down From The Mountains Katie Daly and

The Sea, Oh, The Sea, Grá Gheal Mo Chroí,
Long may it flow between England and me.
It's a sure guarantee that some day we'll be free.
Thank God we're surrounded by water.

"Help yourself, boy," Liston gestured in the direction of the whiskey bottle, growling in his smoky Galway brogue as The Stone Outside Dan Murphy's Door blared out of the radio.

"If Dan Breen was with us today he'd be very happy here by the fire, with a bottle of Powers, good company, and auld Leo there on the radio where he belongs playing the grand old music. Sure I knew Dan well, of course, I was always trying to get the fucker to write a book for me but he had…other ideas."

BLOOD ON THE TRACKS

March '75 Da Nang fell to the Viet Cong, pandemonium everywhere. The end of April Saigon fell, and me and Rory were staying at Johnny Whelan's farm whooping it up—watching unfolding events on a TV in the kitchen. Johnny's folks were gone to Dublin for the weekend, and his much-older sister (she was twenty) was supposed to be in charge. In fact she was a cool chick, not unlike Johnny in many ways, and spent the weekend in her bedroom with her boyfriend who was studying engineering in Trinity and who subsequently disappeared without trace in the mists of the decade that was in it.

While she was getting it on we admired sexy Cong guerrilla girls being welcomed on the streets of Saigon as frightened Yanks escaped on helicopters to the coast. I was preparing myself for going to university the following Autumn so it was a perfect time for the Commies to score a victory. It was going to be a great time to be a student. When all the news we could catch on one TV channel was over, we continued the celebrations with a bottle of vodka and Too Much Too Soon blasting out of Johnny's Dansette, which he'd dragged down from his bedroom for party purposes. The Dolls album belonged to Johnny, I'd never heard them before. I knew nothing of the psychotic Catholic/Jewish immorality they celebrated, that sweet and sour invincible spirit that went on to create punk rock music. Suddenly all the dippy singer-songwriterish bullshit I'd wallowed in through my early teens (Neil Young, Randy Newman, James Taylor) went out the window, deeply suspect and bourgeois. The suspicious connection between sex and music had been unclear to me until Johnny brought the Dolls into my life. The Dolls howled about trash, don't pick it up, promised I'd never be safe in Babylon. So I spent the rest of my life picking up that very trash in Babylon.

The summer after the fall of Saigon I was off to Dublin again to stay with Rory. I was growing addicted to the city, and the addiction just grew and grew until, eventually, I snapped right out of it.

Rory still had a year to go in St Fursey's but he had changed a whole lot. He was no longer exactly a boy—hair was sprouting everywhere—but he still maintained his interest in soul music and worldwide revolutionary politics.

In the months since my previous visit I'd started taking drugs a lot and I'd visited Dublin under my own steam, crashed on people's floors and had sex twice. At an allnight teenage party in Rathmines I smelled what a city was like, noxious and cynical, and the bad part of me liked that smell. It didn't work out like that for Rory. I think he was too intense for the casual moment.

The second time I stayed in Howth Ma didn't drive me to the station. In a way she was happy that I was growing up and spreading my wings. She was a big believer in standing on your own two feet, but once again she gave me loads of money and a gift—this time a rich fruit cake—for Maeve.

Maeve was frantically intense again but Séamus was still placid in his appallingly cold way, busy with his civil service career and his historical hobbies. He'd invested in Reader's Digest boxed sets since my last visit; every blessed thing Herb Alpert and his Tijuana Brass had ever recorded, plus a Glenn Miller six-album compilation.

A month or so before my visit, old Pádraic had died. One evening while watching the American comedian Jack Benny on TV, he had a laughing fit brought on by one of Benny's routines. The laughter turned into a heart attack and the following day, in a Dublin hospital, he died. Rory showed me the small obituary that had appeared in the *Irish Press* two days later, which he had cut out and kept:

Pádraic Maloney was an IRA student revolutionary in 1917. He played a minor role in the War of Independence, a bigger part in the Civil War on the Republican side, seeing active service with Ernie O'Malley in Tipperary and Kilkenny—the hotbeds of Republicanism—during the last, disillusioning days of the Civil War.

He returned to university after the IRA's traumatic defeat in 1923, and was a founding member of Fianna Fáil. He was a respected friend of Republican activists such as Dan Breen and Seán McBride.

I spent the first couple of days of my visit walking around Howth with Rory.

"Sometimes I feel like my head is going to just explode," he said, referring angrily to the behaviour of the Brits in the North. "I just want to do something about it. I can't go to fucking Palestine or help the Indians and in any case I'm Irish so my first duty is here."

I rang Davit, my old friend from St Fursey's who'd been in Dublin a year at this stage, studying linguistics and folklore at UCD. Everybody said Davit was destined for great things, he was always deemed 'brilliant'. We arranged to meet Saturday afternoon.

I got on well with Davit who was an eccentric boffin, an old head on young shoulders. When I'd met him at Fursey's he was a geeky precocious intellectual boy who had read Sartre, all of James Joyce, much of Beckett.

Davit came from a family of clever but poor scholars. His old man, a quiet civilised well read sort of man, held a low position in the provincial civil service—I think he gave out grants to farmers who wanted to buy modern farm machinery or build haysheds. Davit's great-granduncle, a priest and Professor at the Catholic University at Maynooth, had been involved in the biggest Irish academic controversy of the 1900s, concerning the mutually hot potatoes of Irish Ireland and the Catholic Church. Davit's eldest brother was in the Army Intelligence Corps. Another lectured in linguistics at Trinity College. A third was a too-brilliant translator whose eccentricities got the better of him and forced him off the rails, leaving him more or less grounded in the family home five miles outside Waterford.

Davit said it got serious during the Eurovision Song Contest, then a source of huge celebration and excitement in Ireland. As each song came up during the annual songfest Davit's mad brother would bark out a simultaneous translation of the lyrics, no matter what language the song was sung in. The translations, Davit said, never quite captured the romantic aspect of the ditties in question.

At school Davit had been politically radical but denunciatory of the IRA. A radical pacifist who felt, with real ardour and conviction, that violence polluted mankind, he had been one of the many who disapproved of my friendship with Rory, whose intellect he endorsed but whose politics he regarded as being both coarse and simplistic.

The first Horslips album featured the band posing in front of an ancient Celtic cross.

"A perfectly good photograph of an important cross ruined by these fools in their velvet trousers," said Davit.

Davit spent his first year at UCD's Belfield campus hanging around with Trotskyists, and their friendship had radicalised him in a new way. When I rang him to arrange our assignation, he made it clear even before we got down to 'How are you?' and 'What's happening?' that he now fully supported the armed struggle to drive the English out of Ireland in general, and that he approved of Rory in particular.

I asked Rory if he wanted to come into town with me to meet Davit but he said I'd probably enjoy myself more if I travelled alone, which was true. "Davit thinks his shit don't stink," was Rory's analysis of the situation.

"He says he approves of the Provos now," I defended my pal. "Maybe you should come along."

"Just because he approves of the lads don't mean that I have to approve of him."

We were talking in his bedroom as I changed my clothes before catching the bus to O'Connell Street. He had a fair point, common enough with him, but he also had other, more pressing business. He was going to meet up with an IRA woman who lived about ten minutes walk from his home.

Tina was on the Army Council of the Provos, which meant she was a big player in Provo ranks. She was Rory's liaison with the real world of bombs and sawn off shotguns. Tina came from Belfast but had been living in Dublin for six years. Her husband was doing twelve long years in the H Blocks of Long Kesh—a hero of the revolution. She lived in Howth with a ten year old daughter and a young Volunteer (the term used by the IRA for their own members) who fulfilled the dual functions of bodyguard and lover. She went to work every morning at the Sinn Féin headquarters in Parnell Square, holding the title of Youth Organiser or something like that. Though the only youths she organised were young Volunteers doing active service for the movement and, evidently, in her own bed from time to time.

My bus took an easy hour to get into town which was no big deal to me. I was by then a slightly weird kid who liked being stoned on a bus, staring down at people out of the top floor, hoping to learn something about what keeps mankind alive from in-depth distanced study. I'd arranged to meet Davit in Bewley's Café on Westmoreland Street at three and, in accordance with my plan, I got into town well before two. I spent my spare hour in record shops and bought two albums—Too Much Too Soon by

The New York Dolls and Aquashow by Elliot Murphy.

Dublin is always good on Saturdays. All the schoolgirls come into town on the buses and, if the sun comes out, the town is full of excellent things to see. All the boys walk around dressed up for each other. I associate Dublin Saturdays with Grafton Street, loud music blasting out of independent record shops and interesting bookshops full of radical pamphlets and small poetry magazines.

They said Elliot Murphy was the 'new Dylan' and that put an end to his prospects. He drew much inspiration from F Scott Fitzgerald. So did Dylan, so did I, so did the most of us. The more-or-less collected works of Fitzgerald were available in popular Penguin Classic paperbacks, with slick Art Deco-ish covers featuring attractive women showing a little mild cleavage and men in white suits and trilbys. It was a time for denim and tie-dye teeshirts but in some contradictory way the foppish vanity of Fitzgerald was also in vogue. Jagger was at his most dandy, my generation swooned to *The Great Gatsby* and *Tender Is The Night*. Scott Fitzgerald was a romantic writer and ours was a profoundly romantic time.

Elliot Murphy proved way too erudite for pop music and never really made it. Later he became a writer in the Scott Fitzgerald mode and wrote some OK stuff for Rolling Stone. Then he disappeared without trace. I bought Aquashow again on CD a while back and played it once or twice. I just can't work out what it was that attracted me all those years ago or what all the fuss was about. My last literate emotional I'm-bourgeois-just-like-you singer-songwriter, I think. The New York Dolls, by way of contrast, just became more and more influential and relevant as punk rock eclipsed all other forms of guitar rock.

Davit was sitting in Bewley's waiting for me when I got there. Bewley's Westmoreland Street was a huge Nineteenth Century Quaker coffee shop serving sticky buns baked by Bewley's own bakeries, dairy products from Bewley's own farms, and tea grown on Bewley's tea plantations in India. A very laid back and cool place for students to liaise, for up and coming rock groups to hang out in, justly notorious as one of the best places in Dublin to buy dope.

Davit dressed in conservative rural mode, totally out of step with the sartorial wisdom of the age, the regulation uniform of big hair, battered leather, and faded blue denim. Bushy brown hair erupted in every direction at once as he peered at me from behind the same sensible glasses he'd always had in Fursey's. He wore a sensible woollen jumper and grey slacks, while I sported old jeans, hippy sandals, and a Led Zeppelin teeshirt. He looked like a twat but, it must be said, I looked like a twat too. Talk was of mutual friends and what he was up to and what I was up to.

"So, Liam, what records have you got there?" he said, all professorial and sensible like an erudite old priest, after our initial conversation died off. With a twitchy nervous look he eyed my plastic record shop bag holding Elliot Murphy and The New York Dolls, like he was entitled to ask stiff questions, perhaps being in some way more serious, lofty, and therefore more worthy than me.

I proudly pulled Aquashow out of my bag and explained the Fitzgerald literary connection. Davit gave me a barbed look which implied that he very much doubted that such a character, in a pair of tight white satin trousers, could ever have read anyone published in Penguin Classics. He was aghast when I pulled out the New York Dolls effort.

"This is what Sinatra calls Fag Rock," I said smirking.

"Right," he said dubiously, looking around to make sure that nobody'd overheard me or seen the cover of Too Much Too Soon, which featured my new heroes dressed in spray-on shocking pink plastic, eyeliner, perms, and superstar lipstick. David Johansen, the puss'n'boots singer, the very first wannabe Mick Jagger to take a postmodern approach to his carbon copying. Guitarist Johnny Thunders, street urchin from the boulevard of broken dreams, the first postmodern Keith Richards. Johansen sprawled on the back cover in navy blue lurex trousers. Thunders on-stage clutching a girl doll on the front cover. A second guitarist wearing leopardskin boots with two inch risers.

A fraught silence for just a moment.

"I just don't see how someone as bright as you, Liam, can listen to music made by people like these fellows. What kind of people are they when you get right down to it? Prostitutes. Charlatans."

Davit pointed with genuine horror at the photograph of the New York Dolls—undoubtedly whorish chancers, demented, over-sexed, gone wrong, queered out escapees from the New York demi-monde—his bony index finger tapping the cover of Too Much Too Soon triumphantly, angrily. Davit was eighteen, knew his Flaubert and his Ezra Pound, was wrestling with linguistics, spoke the Irish language fluently, but he had missed out on rock'n'roll on the road towards commitment and/or enlightenment.

Years later Davit developed a chronic addiction to prescription drugs and also changed his views on rock'n'roll. The same people who turned him on to the Provos eventually turned him on to Bob Dylan. By his mid-twenties he'd conquered his drug problem, landed a job in the Linguistics Department at Belfield.

Then one day he took the train from Dublin to Belfast to give a lecture at Queens. He was reading a detective novel but the sun was shining into his weak eyes so he moved to an empty seat some way down the carriage where he could sit with his back to the sun. An hour later, as his train was coming into Belfast Station, the bomb under Davit's previous seat exploded, killing both those who'd been sitting behind him and the woman who'd been sitting right opposite him. The train ground to a halt, blood and guts everywhere. There was a deathly silence for a second before depraved primitive confusion erupted. Davit quietly got to his feet in shock, stumbled towards the nearest exit. The confusion was total so he made slow progress, getting stalled in a packed and demented corridor. Then he imagined he heard, under the seat alongside him and clear as a bell, the sound of a clock ticking—of a second bomb. He kept very calm and said nothing to anybody as the collective panic was already too much.

In a complete daze, Davit escaped off the train and out onto the safety of the tracks. Five minutes later the imagined second bomb, the one he'd heard ticking, went off killing two more people and maiming eight. He wandered around the train tracks in confusion until two railway employees found him.

That was the end of Davit's struggle against drugs—he succumbed to the prescriptions entirely after that. He lives in Canada, a successful published-in-footnoted-journals academic married with two children. I've seen him once in the last eight years, for maybe an hour. He was working on a biography of his priest great-granduncle and the controversy that priest fought.

Davit retained both the arrogance and the unsullied intellectual hunger of his youth.

I got back to Howth to find Rory in charge of the house, his folks out for the evening to attend the opening of a play; a new production of an old Seán O'Casey play at the Abbey Theatre, founded by Yeats, the repository of traditional State-approved and sponsored culture.

"Every two months they open a new production there," Rory spat out, "and every old homo in RTE comes all the way from Donnybrook to interview every Fianna Fáil politician in the country about O'Casey or Synge or Wilde. I don't think they're allowed to put on any plays in that place that were written after 1950. So, how'd it go with Davit?"

"It was shit seeing him, really," I whinged like a spoilt brat, "and he was really down on my records. I don't know if I want to see him again."

"Davit just thinks his shit don't stink, like I told you already," said Rory.

"Correct," I said laughing. "And how was the day for you?"

"I just hung around with Tina all afternoon, getting pissed and complaining about the Dublin leadership. They're all stupid old cunts living off of past glories and holding everybody else back. A pile of jokers, Holy Joes."

Rory was always annoyed when he spoke of the IRA's Southern leadership.

"So do I get to call around to see her?" I asked; he'd promised he'd try to organise something.

"Yeah. I said I'd arrange it, didn't I? I told her about you and she's interested in meeting you. I'm to ring her and arrange a time tomorrow she says."

As he spoke he was flinging one of Séamus's Carpenters albums off the Hi Fi, replacing it with Bryan Ferry. As Ferry reconstructed Hard Rain's Gonna Fall, changing it from a surreal protest song into a sleaze anthem, Rory shimmied over to the drinks cabinet, grabbed a bottle of vodka plus two glasses, joined me on the couch. Séamus was a member of this bizarre Catholic teetotaller organisation called the Pioneers (the Pioneers Total Abstinence Association) but—having to entertain fellow bureaucrats from time to time—he maintained a reasonably good drinks cabinet.

I rolled six pathetic, wizened, little joints that we, me mainly, proceeded to smoke. I'd picked up a rip-off five-spot from a worthless American scumbag dealer in Bewley's.

"The cunt never touches booze. Mister Mellow, Mister fucking Nice and Easy, Mister Go Slow, Mister Give and Take," Rory spat out half plastered. "Just leave enough in the bottom of the bottle so when we refill it with water, it'll still have the smell of vodka."

We did meet Tina that Sunday. We got up early with pounding juvenile hangovers. Breakfast was bright and early because we were supposed to be on our way to Mass but the atmosphere was far from bright.

Maeve was cruising on the edge of hysteria and, like most neurotics, tended to blurt out the exact questions you least wanted to answer. She wasn't at all happy about me now that she'd had a long hard look at me. The cause of her dislike was her fear that I was in the process of recruiting Rory into the Provos. She was scared shitless that her son would end up with a bullet through the head or doing ten years in Portlaoise Prison or Long Kesh—fears that were fair enough and rational enough. She just had the wrong end of the stick; Rory was recruiting me, not the other way round. But Maeve was a fine cook, as neurotics often are, so with breakfast looking good and smelling good, we told her that we wouldn't take Holy Communion. Taking Communion involved fasting for an hour before Mass, and the bacon and eggs looked more appetising than the Body of Christ.

Table talk concerned the O'Casey play from the night before.

"What'd you think of that production, Séamus?" Maeve asked loudly, drowning out Doris Day singing Que Sera Sera on the radio.

"The best thing we've seen there in recent years, certainly, Maeve," responded Séamus, leaning back on his kitchen chair, all relaxed like he'd just been given a satisfactory blow job.

"How do you think it compared with Siobhán McKenna in The Plough and The Stars?" asked Maeve, perhaps imagining that she was presenting a chat show on the radio.

"Ach, there will never be another Siobhán McKenna," said Séamus theatrically, his provincial brogue to the fore.

"She's a great woman, that's definite," Maeve chortled. "But…last night…I'm not sure."

"It was a real triumph for The Abbey," Séamus insisted.

"I don't know about that," Maeve said. "I didn't think that Shane Maloney was very good. He's been on the radio in The Kennedys of Castleross as a priest for donkey's years, and then all of a sudden he's meant to be a soldier?"

All this bland suburban culture chatter was designed to render Rory psychotic. To add insult to injury he really liked O'Casey and approved of his writings. He'd never seen the plays but he knew the O'Casey autobiographies and believed that, had the politics of O'Casey and James Connolly won out in Ireland, the likes of his parents would have been put up against a wall and shot. He may have been wrong about this—all revolutionary periods eventually produce bureaucrats, not to mention the unhappy families that such bureaucrats insist upon breeding.

The alleged arrangement was that we'd go to eleven thirty Mass. In fact we were going straight to Tina's place. The previous night Rory had brought me for a drunken stroll past St Peter and Paul's Church so I'd be able to describe its location and interesting features just in case I was later quizzed by nervous parents. Peter and Paul's was a snappy modern structure; no great shakes architecturally but it reflected, as places of worship are supposed to, the prosperity and respectability of the suburbanites who lived around it. We walked in around the back and took a piss.

Tina turned out to be a short woman with dyed black hair who slopped around in a cardigan and jeans. Not attractive in any modern or urban sense, but she did look healthy and robust. Her boyfriend was a sulky but likable handsome teenage lout from Derry who resented Rory and, to a lesser extent, me. His shoulder-length brown hair was victim to split ends, he wore tight black corduroys, and he had a nervous jumpy bug-eyed aspect to him. He was maybe a year or two older than me, but I got the feeling that he'd seen pretty hard action in his time. He said very little, sat in a corner reading a biography of Hemingway.

I'd never been in the home of a bona-fide guerrilla fighter before and Tina was an adult portion, a strong woman. Her Volunteer lover left his revolver on the sideboard in the living room, in between framed family photographs and African handicrafts. Tina's was a conventional, indifferently furnished suburban home, so long as you disregarded that one delicate feature—the gun resting on the shabby old inlaid sideboard. Tina knew Rory well and must have trusted him implicitly because all their talk had to do with a local Active Service Unit and their bank-robbing 'activities. Presumably Rory had vouched enthusiastically for me, for their chatter was wildly indiscreet, jeopardising security in a big way.

It was a hot day for Dublin, and hot enough for most other places. Rory wore a new pair of jeans and blood red wet-look boots. I sported an expensive pair of old Ray Ban sunglasses my father'd grown tired of. I had on my Led Zeppelin teeshirt but, having just discovered the Dolls, I felt seriously self conscious and hick. I made a vow to myself that, before going back to Kilkenny, I would waste some of my mother's money buying cool new clothes, more suited to the imaginary brave new epoch I foresaw myself stepping into.

With Blood On The Tracks playing on her stereo, Tina regaled us with explicit details of bombing runs that she'd participated in, defiant capers that went wrong, comrades who'd been shot or killed by the Brits. None of these war tales frightened me or horrified me but incidental references to Volunteers serving mercilessly long sentences in Portlaoise or Long Kesh filled me with a kind of pessimistic dread I've never liked in myself. I could imagine shooting it out with the enemy just like John Wayne or Che, or conspiring intelligently like The Third Man, but I knew that spending ten years masturbating in a grim prison cell could never be a part of my foreseen future.

A photograph of Tina's locked-up husband hung on the wall over the sink in the kitchen. He looked young and big, fanatical but humorous. It struck me that her marriage, one of those long ago revolutionary marriages, was finished with.

Rory told me on the way home that he'd become a member of

the Fianna, the youth wing of the Provos. Everything I'd seen and heard at Tina's place led me to believe that my friend was indeed putting theory into practice. He swore me to secrecy. My own more nebulous sense of revolution was grounded in Lou Reed albums, Marlon Brando movies, and books about the hippies of San Francisco. Now that I'd suddenly discovered The New York Dolls, my self-centred sense of personal revolution was operating on a whole other level. Rory was obviously swimming in more deeply troubled waters, spending his weekends up in the Dublin Mountains learning how to make proper bombs, how to fire killing guns, and about the serene distressful history of Ireland.

Every time I turn on the TV in Summerhill Parade, it seems, Tina is discreetly shadowing some Sinn Féin media superstar, negotiating with the Americans or the English, a grey eminence of undoubted importance. What exactly is she today? Is she the Provo Chief of Staff? I don't know. She is undoubtedly a middle aged woman, a past-it revolutionary guerrilla fighter. Her presence on my TV screen is now the only real link I have with Rory or my visits to his home.

CHAOS AND NIGHT

1975 was a time for philosophy and penetration. I was howling out my support for the Viet Cong while checking out Rock'n'Roll Animal by Lou Reed, a vulgar album by a man busy abandoning poetics in favour of populism. At least it familiarised us with old Velvets songs like Heroin. And I feel just like Jesus's son.

That summer, after my Leaving Certificate exams were over, I went on holiday with my mother who loved me, indulged me, did everything in her power to keep me happy. Now I understand that I behaved like a precocious shit towards her but that is an unhappy part of the biological process.

When she was little, Ma's parents used to rent a cottage every summer in the Victorian seaside resort of Ballybunion on the wild West Coast of Kerry. After the divorce, we always spent August there. Ma's unmarried brother, my Uncle Alan who worked in the Department of Foreign Affairs in Dublin, accompanied us that particular year. Alan had film star good looks, stood about six foot two with our family's blond hair and cold blue eyes. He never had any close relationships with women or other men—none that I knew of in any case. I went for long walks with him along the cliff front while my mother stayed at home listening to the radio and reading magazines. Alan and I provided each other with airtight alibis. I didn't want to know what he got up to when he went a-rambling alone and vice versa. It was a busy sex-in-the-sand-dunes period in my life. Weekend nights I loitered outside ballrooms listening to crummy showbands like Dickie Rock and The Miami Showband.

The Miami were later slaughtered in the North by Loyalist paramilitaries, on their way back to Dublin after a gig. By that time Dickie had left the band, bought houses of flats all over Rathmines, an extensive collection of wigs to cope with his receding hairline, and changed the spelling of his name to Dickie Roc in order to pursue an international career!

Ballybunion afternoons I escaped to my room to listen to Larry Gogan on RTE radio. Larry was a veteran of Sixties radio shows sponsored by jam, insurance or soup companies; the greatest of these being the TV Club Show, recorded in the Eamonn Andrews Studios located, as Larry used to say, 'in the

heart of Dublin over the TV Club, the home of With-It Dancing.'
In the Sixties Larry used to play the Stones and the Beach Boys;
by the time I was in Ballybunion with Ma it was The Doors, Joni
Mitchell and the first Irish rock bands: Grannies Intentions and
Thin Lizzy. He championed the rise of Horslips who, blending
guitar rock with Irish ethnic tones, wiped out the showbands.

The people of Kerry were, by general consensus, the best
educated people in Ireland. This powerful county of bad boggy
land populated Ireland with civil servants, cops, writers and
school teachers in the decades after independence. They say the
lost land of Atlantis exists beneath the waves, out in the Atlantic
off the turbulent coast of Kerry.

Our last Saturday in Kerry we went to Listowel so Ma could
visit an old school friend. Alan decided not to go with us; "I have
other fish to fry," he said enigmatically. Ma dropped me at the
town centre, giving me a twenty pound note. Listowel had a kind
of chic arty area down a back lane with two antique shops, a bad
art gallery, plus a secondhand bookshop.

One antique shop looked more promising than the other so I
hopped in to check it out. The old dear who ran it gave the
impression that the shop was just her little hobby, that her
husband had been a well-to-do professional gent who'd left her
generously provided for. Her shop smelled of floor polish,
piquant perfume, and cigarette smoke.

She had a glass case full of WW1 medals, and a display of
relics from the Tan War. The widow said her father was with the
IRA in the War of Independence, while his brother fought for the
British in the Great War. I gazed at remnants of other people's
lives, dual and parallel visions of Irish history.

Then I moved on to my more usual prey, the shelf of

secondhand paperbacks almost hidden at the back of her shop. Mostly old rubbish. I spotted a Penguin Classic, *Chaos And Night* by Henri de Montherlant. Because it was a Penguin Classic, and all books in that series were deemed worth looking at, I bought it from the old woman though she was dubious about selling it to me. Maybe she'd read the book herself, been enchanted by a nasty piece of work which says that the United States is the canker of the world, on the one side good while on the other side evil, and that the dome of St Peter's is the candle-snuffer of Western thought.

Back in Ballybunion I holed up in my bedroom and ploughed into *Chaos And Night*. A sad arid tale of an old Spanish anarchist bullfighter living out his final days, bitter and sterile, in Paris. I thought I felt in my bones the solitary life of Paris as I childishly compared de Montherlant with the other French writers I was reading, Sartre and Flaubert.

Last week I came across *Chaos And Night* again in a secondhand bookshop off the George's Street Arcade—the self-same edition I had bought in Listowel. I was taken aback. A lifetime ago that book obsessed me for three months; when I picked it up again it was like a noxious old friend walking up to me out of my own chaos and night.

I removed the book from the shelf, flicked its brittle old pages, almost cracked its calcified spine. I could hear Rory's tough cogent voice, from back in lost time:

"Don't read that negative shit. The kind of guy who'd write a book like that, he is the very kind of guy who would cut your throat. A book like that will only drag you down. Existentialism is fundamentally reactionary. I've read all these so-called French radicals. This notion that everything is irrelevant because we all die tomorrow morning is bullshit, the perfect trendy reason to do nothing about anything. And you always say that you hate the French anyway."

Standing in the secondhand bookshop, the next door secondhand record shop playing Give Them Enough Rope by The Clash, I felt Rory whispering his resolutely contrary young opinion into my ear anew.

This time I heeded Rory's advice; a teenage boy can endure a lot of existentialism but a middle aged man can only take so much. I put *Chaos And Night* back on the shelf.

YANKS AND PROVOS

It still disturbs me that Rory and I were such good friends, that my life has gone on so very long without him

My phone rings. I don't have a landline in Summerhill Parade, just the mobile on which my *Mannish Boy* publisher phones me about once a week to bully me into finishing *On The Run* so I can get back to making money for her. The other people who call me are Dee, Ma, and my researcher—Ethan—who is in Morocco doing some of the spade work on *Mannish Boy* while I'm literally slumming it in Dublin.

I pick up the phone. It's Nicole, my agent and pal. She has never called me in Ireland but NBC have been on to her. They want to do a talking heads special from Dublin on the peace process. Since I'm here writing a book on the IRA, since my book on the sad tawdry lives of groupies sold a shit load of copies to thousands of Sam Six-pack Seniors out there in Potatoland, since these are such very mediocre times, the people may have heard of me.

"So would you be willing to take part in the show?"

"Yeah, if it's interesting," I tell her.

"Well, look Liam, it *is* interesting," she cackles. "They're offering $3,000 for an hour's bullshitting. Some of these people they've gotten to appear are pretty impressive."

She reads me out the list that's been faxed through to her. The list is impressive, convincing me that I must do the show. It turns out they've got an asshole I know from years back, the son of the former head of MI5 in Belfast, now a big travel writer working out of Donegal. They've got a junior minister from the London government. Joe Kennedy is going to represent America and Irish America's Royal Family. Some lunatic who's involved in the Save Ulster From Sodomy campaign is representing unreconstructed Unionism. (The CIA sure know how to fuck up their ex-pals. There are one or two smart Unionists who can rant and rave about topics other than the price of heifers, saving Ulster from sodomy and the international Papist conspiracy.) The Dublin government will be represented by a guy I knew at Belfield—via Dee—a notorious boy-fucker then but now a Fianna Fáil minister and happily married defender of family values. And Sinn Féin will be represented by Tina.

A taxi picks me up at 11am.

"Now I'm not racist, don't get me wrong, but if you ask me they should fire all them bleedin' asylum seekers out of the country. If we gave them food vouchers to live on like they do in America, they'd be gone. Do ya know, Dublin birds are the best birds in the world? Me brother-in-law is a sailor, been all over the world, and he says to me that the Dublin birds are the best," says my driver as we cross the Liffey by Butt Bridge, pass the U2 headquarters, and head south for RTE's Donnybrook studios. I used to work at RTE all the time back in my salad days.

Yet another rainy day in the bumper to bumper city centre. NBC have hired Studio One from RTE for the whole afternoon and I'm ushered, some important old guy, into a newly decorated reception room where drinks and sandwiches and things on crackers are being served. I recognise the man who is saving Ulster from sodomy, a rednecked Protestant cleric with a neat line in bestselling country and western albums of him singing hymns and spirituals.

Mr MI5 tenses up at the sight of me, insofar as a wobbling mass of fat can tense up. Then he converts to his charming English mode and I make small talk with him, the only person in the room that I know. We talk book publishers and "Do you ever hear from such and such?" Neither Kennedy nor Tina are anywhere to be seen. The London minister is unable to make it and will participate in the discussion down-the-line from London. A PA approaches me to usher me off to Make-Up where I end up sitting alongside the erstwhile boy-fucker. He seems glad to see me—or at least unembarrassed; knows nothing about my progress in life and takes it for granted that I know everything about his historic contributions to Irish politics. He is more or less the minister for prisons, which means he's the guy in charge of locking up Provo and INLA Volunteers after they've been tried by non-jury courts.

"I'm here to defend our policy of letting the lads out of Portlaoise in dribs and drabs," he explains with an impressive tone of whimsy, caked in dark orange make-up, a big white bib hiding his pinstriped Louis Copeland suit. Fianna Fáil has not changed. They're still the moderate manyana party of sophisticated cynicism—with them everything is for the best in the best of all possible worlds. They always land on their feet, never lose any sleep.

The minister is done so he gets up to leave, pulls off his bib. He says he'll see me inside.

"Where's Kennedy and the wan from the Provos?" I ask him before he departs.

"Oh, the two of them are having a private meeting right now, if you don't mind," he laughs. "That's the real axis here now, Liam: the Yanks and the Provos."

Seconds later I'm guided back to the party where a stout pushy blond woman is clapping her hands to get our attention. She explains that we're going into the studio in ten minutes, that they'll film about an hour's conversation with a view to editing that down to nine minutes of TV. Every man for himself, obviously.

We march into Studio One two by two, me alongside Mr MI5. None of us is under thirty. Indeed, I think I'm the youngest person here. Kids are sick of seeing Sixties and Seventies types all over the media, like we were sick of seeing old farts all over our media when we were kids. Just before the cameras roll, Tina and the American are ushered in, introduced to everyone.

When we get down to brass tacks the boy-fucker proves surprisingly lively and sympathetic. Kennedy is animated like all his clan. The Kennedys have a Hollywood background, their members have enjoyed untold Hollywood pussy, and it sure shows. I try to make eye contact with Tina but studiously, like the grand dame she now masquerades as, she manages to avoid either acknowledging me or recognising me. She looks a hell of a lot older, wearing a hideous Lainey Kehoe jumper and average

70

Armani slacks. Bitter and matronly, like she sees a lot less Volunteer cock than was once the case. For her there must be light at the end of the tunnel. Respectability. Comfort. I get so caught up in looking at her that I nearly miss the first question that's thrown at me. My job is to natter on about the things Rory and me often debated in our long-ago flats—the democratic or anti-democratic nature of Republicanism, the differences and similarities between the Provos and the veterans of the Tan War.

"Liam Crowe," barks the presenter, "you've made a lifelong study of the original IRA, the men who achieved Irish freedom in the Twenties. Is there any comparison between their methods and motives and the methods and motives of modern IRA terrorists?"

Like all recording, our feral process seems to be over before it starts. The studio lights turn off, there is an instant diminution of the hothouse atmosphere. By the time I've relaxed, Tina has already bolted for the door—she still moves quick as a soldier. I'm surprised for maybe ten seconds but, casting decorum to the wind, I give her chase. I head for the foyer where, through walls of glass, I spot her marching like a restrained gazelle towards the car park.

By the time I catch up with her, she is taking keys from her pocket and is paused in front of a polished Mitsubishi Galant. Her shoulders hunched tense, like she knows that I am right behind her, that this is going to be unpleasant.

"Tina?"

"Yes?" she says quizzically, turning to look me directly in the eye. "Can I help you?"

"You don't remember me?"

"You were the gentleman on the TV show there with me," she says like a gauche convent girl, her Belfast accent rough and harsh.

"You met me twenty something years ago in Howth with Rory. We were listening to Blonde On Blonde in your sitting room. Then I wrote that thing on Bobby Sands…"

"You have me mixed up with somebody else, mister. I don't know any Rory…"

"Rory died a long time ago. You must know that." I know I sound pathetic saying this to her.

"I'm sorry," she says sharply, opening the driver's door and sitting stiffly behind the wheel. "I'm sorry to hear about your friend." She closes the door, starts the car, reverses out of her parking spot, and grinds to a halt in front of me.

She presses a button and her window glides down.

"I think in any case, mister, it would have been Blood On The Tracks, not Blonde On Blonde. I never once owned Blonde On Blonde." With that she is gone like a whirlwind.

I stagger back into the TV building to rejoin my fellow talking heads. One of the NBC assistant producers spots me and comes over. "What can I get you to drink, Mr Crowe?" she asks, steering me towards the refreshment table.

I order a double vodka which knocks me back into shape of sorts. I sign a chit for my appearance and a taxi delivers me back to Summerhill Parade.

I can't sleep. I toss and turn, chilled by Tina's pure focus. Born out of revolt, nurtured in prison, now an adult monster, a woman of fifty going slow in a hurry. What would Rory think of Tina? What would he think of the Provos? What would he think of Ireland? What would he think of me?

PART 2

RAIDS AND **RALLIES**

PARABELLUM

It snows.

I walk up the steps leading to the National Museum. I turn to stare at the Dáil where Dev and Haughey once held sway, Kings of the Universe for brief moments. Today Haughey in old age, a lion in winter, is hauled up in front of courts on criminal charges. Today there is a different sort of boss, still a Fianna Fáil boss. He used to be an accountant, as they say, and his daughter is in the next Spice Girls, along with the daughter of a national soap opera star.

My journalism years coincided with the scandal-rich Haughey Era, and, doing my job, I hung out in the Dáil Dining Room on exciting days when the destinies of great men were decided. I've walked into the bewitching private sitting room of the snake eyed Haughey—sailor and equestrian—seen him stand before me like an elegant jockey, sipping tea from a bone china cup. Napoleonically quoting Yeats. Yapping sarcastically about contemporary local minor writers of our mutual acquaintance. When he first met me he was arrogant enough to think his man-of-the-people routine would wow a street-oriented one like me. Later he changed his mind.

Haughey has always been in trouble. He's in deep trouble

right now. He spends most of his time opening art exhibitions or making court appearances. Today they seem upset that he spent State money buying expensive shirts. They think he took money from a fat supermarket magnate who was last seen naked-with-whores in a Florida hotel room. Rumour has it U2 were staying in the same hotel, perhaps praying for his salvation. Dublin Babylon. And then there are all these stories about the sex lives of queer boy bands. Dublin Babylon...

Haughey is in his seventies. He built them this awful new country they love so very much. Fianna Fáil have thrown him to the wolves in order to survive. This morning I caught a glimpse of him on the TV news. Surrounded by photographers and TV crews, dapper lounge lizard in a fancy suit, getting out of his black Mercedes for one more court appearance and striding towards the courthouse door. One of the photographers shouts to him:

"Turn back, Mr. Haughey!"

The old man pauses, turns briefly into the glare of a million flash bulbs and Klieg lights, growls:

"There can be no turning back!"

Nothing happening in the Dáil today. No TDs conspiring in front of their Audis and Mercs. Six bored young Guards keep vigil over the front gate, clapping their hands together in protest against the cold. I look beyond the Dáil forecourt to the National Library where the manuscripts of Yeats and Dan Breen and Joyce and Ernie O'Malley and the whole damn lot of them lie in impeccable sterile conditions. Far away from poetry or rancour or battlefield.

I enter the Museum ignoring the star attraction, a kind of touristy show to do with Viking longships, and march confidently into the War of Independence room to the left of the main hall.

The National Museum is old fashioned and nice. I've been to see the stuff from the Tan War many times as a kid, but the last time was around the time of *Against Tyrant's Might*, when I first saw Ernie O'Malley's Parabellum.

This room seems unchanged after nearly twenty years. They've installed a pretty basic multiscreen featuring ancient newsreel footage of the War. A young bespectacled student and his girlfriend—holding hands—sit on a bench in front of the screen staring silently at images new to them that I know off by heart.

I note the clothing of the revolutionary generation, how dapper and clothes-conscious they must have been. It was, of course, a more elegant age but there is a contradictory vanity about all revolutionaries.

The improvised uniform that the civil war IRA hero, Liam Lynch, was wearing when they killed him in the mountains of Tipperary. A brown/orange jacket and expensive looking riding breeches. I walk around the glass display case twice, searching in vain for bullet holes in the costume of a man who died from bullet wounds hours after his capture, surrounded by his enemies, enveloped by the freezing fog of the mountains. His final words before he went into a coma were: "God pray for me. All this is a pity. It should never have happened. I am glad now I am going from it all. Poor Ireland. Poor Ireland!"

The Irish Times reported:

The news of the capture caused great excitement, especially when it became known that Mr de Valera had narrowly avoided capture. Liam Lynch was captured, severely wounded. Several other leaders including Mr de Valera and Dan Breen escaped.

Ernie O'Malley's tiny Harrington and Richardson automatic with *H.&R. Arms Co.* engraved on its side. A four inch Bayard automatic pistol. The long neck on his Parabellum.

I walk cautiously towards the Countess Markievicz section. The comrade with no comrades. She said "I have seen the stars. I will not follow a will-o-the-wisp." I stare respectfully at her Peter-the-Painter gun. Alongside the gun is the print-out of a recollection from a veteran of the Rising:

Madame had her HQ at The Hammam, one of the bigger hotels on O'Connell Street, all through June 1922. My job was to bring intelligence reports to her from across the North Dublin District.

I found her sitting down to a lunch of strong tea, brown bread, fruit and cheese. She invited me to join her. I'd not had good food for two days so I was only too glad to accept her offer. I knew Madame was anxious to hear what news I had, so I made haste with my meal.

"Madame," I said to her, "thirteen Volunteers have been killed this morning by one sniper operating from the Hibernian Tower. We've sent our best men up against him but we can't get him."

The Countess said nothing for ten minutes but relaxed in her chair, sipping tea and staring off into the distance. Then she snapped out of it and began to search around frantically for her Peter-the-Painter. When she spotted it she grabbed her weapon, and looked at me.

"Come with me," she said, making her way to the secret tunnel which went from The Hammam to a building almost directly across the road from the Hibernian Tower. We climbed from the basement of that building to a shabby little office on the fourth floor. Madame was about fifty at this time but as agile as a mountain goat.

She smashed open the office window, got a clear perspective of Hibernian Tower, and began to engage her man. The distance between herself and the sniper was less than a hundred yards so she was full of confidence.

"Peter-the-Painter," she says to me, "is accurate at ten times this distance."

Despite this she was unable to get her man. Still he fired and still she engaged him. After two hours we were joined by some of the lads who pleaded with Madame to withdraw for her own safety. Insofar as she was working out his exact position, he was working out the same thing about her. She sent them away and two hours later they came back to make the same appeal but again she refused to budge. These two kept firing at one another until evening time. At about half six we realised that he was not returning fire.

"He's dead now," she said to me after half an hour of no response. We went back to HQ in silence. The Countess collapsed into a beautiful old hotel armchair where she fell into a deep sleep.

I feel I have my finger on the pulse of what is going on inside the museum. The real world of Ireland today is beyond my reach. I've been silenced by my exile and age, by the fact that Ireland is now out of control. Not that I ever wanted to control it—indeed it was always the aspiration of my generation that the place should spin out of control and splatter itself all over the world; a multicoloured, kaleidoscopic contributor to the chaos of the world, itself at the eye of the modern storm, but certainly not calm.

FINGERPRINT FILE

During the summer of '75 de Valera, Tan War veteran and Fianna Fáil founder, died.

I was a year ahead of Rory at St Fursey's so I went on ahead. Rory stayed on in Waterford for one last year, deeply disinterested in an education that offered him nothing; he was already over educated. He got stranded down the country, where I came from, and I ended up in Dublin where his folks lived.

At UCD I fell in with a bad crowd and laughed and drank with them, most of them precocious and friendly members of a Trotskyist group called People's Voice that I got to know through Davit. They were involved with radical life off the campus and active in the Student Union within the university. Wonderfully promiscuous people, organising lots of demos, occupations and opportunities for us to chain ourselves to strategically located civic buildings before throwing away the keys. I used to sit in the Student Union offices selling condoms, illegal in Ireland at that time, to surly would-be weekend lovers, annoyed at having to buy such intimate personal things from a sniggering smartass like me, their anger quite understandable with hindsight.

I loved the life I was leading which was a nuclear explosion all around me and an acid trip deep inside my brain. Things were happening for me in all parts of my life, from my body to my mind. Irish culture was undergoing the most profound conversion, the old certainties of Sixties liberalism giving way to angrier more artistic stances—punk stances—coming out of New York. Dublin was alive with people obsessed with William Burroughs, Joseph Beuys, Patti Smith, that kind of shit.

This girl I knew socially—Dee Hutchinson—was Ents Officer with the Student Union and the leading force behind People's

Voice on campus. I'd hang out in Dee's office during daytime hours, using her phone to call my friends all over the country while Whips and Furs by The Vibrators or Live At Budokan by Bob Dylan blared out of her stereo. Dee painted her office shocking pink and she had long mousy blond hair.

I'd use Dee's phone a lot to ring Rory in Waterford. With me gone from St Fursey's, he was feeling sort of isolated and sorry for himself. Nobody liked him because of the politics he wore on his sleeve and because of his forbidding manner, which belied a boyish sense of humour and a love of malicious pranks.

I'd get keys to the Student's Union off Dee and sneak in there after working hours to phone Waterford, interrupting his evening study period in St Fursey's. I would call the school, pretend to be his father, and have Rory delivered from the study hall to the coinbox situated in a small room near the front hall. Those calls would often last for an hour or more and the conversations were sometimes rough going. Me a whole lot more relaxed than him. Him standing in a freezing boarding school hallway while I listened to punk rock albums, staring at Ents gig posters.

School was doing Rory's head in. Life was a series of remorseless accumulations. One thing would irritate the shit out of him until the next thing came along. He was buffeted and laughed at by the Regular Guys who controlled social life in St Fursey's.

He was the restless kind and the restless kind never enjoys true peace of mind; sex never comes easy or does them much good when they do get it, and very often drugs and alcohol don't improve their situation a whole lot either. I advised him to cut out drinking and to drift in the direction of drugs. He didn't like drugs very much, said dope made him nervous, and he dived towards the booze.

Nobody gave a shit what we said to each other on free phonelines. My hair grew longer and longer and I spent too much of Ma's money on what I thought of as cool records. My best friend was this Dee girl whose father was a rich doctor. She lived in a flat near her parents place in Donnybrook, two doors away from the Minister for Foreign Affairs. One afternoon about two months after my seventeenth birthday I was in her folk's colossal and ornate back garden, attending her nineteenth birthday party. All her other guests were upper echelon rich kids and card-carrying Trotskyists.

Sammy Steinhouse, the cold effeminate son of a UCD geography professor, was swinging on a kid's swing in the garden.

"Sammy is reliving his childhood," I quipped to Dee.

"Sammy never had a childhood," she said, sipping a can of beer with ice-blond elegance and poise.

It was a great source of scandal in my circle that Sammy's mother—a PA for RTE—was having a long-term affair with the Head of Programming at the station. As a result of this adultery Sammy later got a job as a presenter on RTE Radio. His little brother, at that time an angelic pubescent kid with mischievous street urchin eye, grew up to be an also-ran TV producer. I thought it significant that neither of them went into academia.

Dee's offhand manner and patrician good looks were a source of controversy at Belfield. All the guys said she was a real cunt, people either thought that she was boringly ugly or stunningly sexy. I always thought she looked vaguely oriental myself. Maybe it's just that she is cold and inscrutable, that I'm as partial to stereotypes as the next man. She had a nasty tongue in her then and I reckon she was way more intelligent than most of the men she parried with.

I saw more and more of Dee as the weeks drifted into months. One day I was in her flat, which she now shared with her activist boyfriend Tom, a very smart writer. We'd been smoking grass while listening to punk and funk. I got so stoned that I thought Dee'd gone out to the shops whereas in fact she'd gone to take a shower.

I walked into the bathroom for a piss to find her standing naked in front of me, a beautiful thin ripe cherry girl's body, real relaxed and casual. I wanted to look away but I just kept on staring.

"Sorry," I said as I withdrew.

"It's OK," she said neutrally.

The two of us were actively involved with Palestinian and Arab issues. For three years we got sent by People's Voice to represent them at meetings held in Trinity to commemorate the coup which had brought the Al Baath Arab Socialist Party, featuring Saddam Hussein, to power in Iraq. We'd sit through awesomely tedious speeches about the achievements of the Al Baath Arab Socialist Party in the areas of irrigation, telecommunications, and health care. Afterwards there would be very strange parties at The Libyan Centre where Dee'd be the only woman present, during which lots of Coca-Cola and lemonade would be consumed. After one such party Dee and me went to the TV Club on Harcourt Street—the home of With-It Dancing—to see the Velvet Underground's John Cale perform solo. There were a hundred people in the 800-capacity TV Club. Cale was going through his drinking period, authentically Welsh and stout in fine black leather trousers. Me and Dee got very drunk too and ended up in bed—for the first time—back in Donnybrook.

"A very small step for mankind," she said the morning after. "But a big step for your dick."

We lived together on and off for a few years. When we had a child and got married, we grew apart, divorcing not long afterwards. She moved to America with me. We've done nothing to each other that time will not erase.

Because of the company I was keeping, that was a good time in my life. Now I wonder what I was really doing. I was determined to have a brilliant life, to become an eminent academic, or maybe to become famous for something else like writing or even playing the guitar. I spent Ma's money hanging out at the punk-oriented Advance Records just off Stephen's Green (owned by a cousin of the drummer in Thin Lizzy). Buying American import punk singles. Picture discs. Coloured vinyl. Shape discs. Anything. Everything.

Like most guys of my age I was principally interested in doing nothing and in having an easy time. I suppose I had it in mind to eventually find a partner, a mate, but the one thing I had worked out for certain was that in this life there are no real partnerships. My mother, embittered by her marriage, told me to enjoy myself while I could, that I'd be dead long enough. You come in alone and you go out alone.

DARK SPACE

Somewhere a lonely radio is blasting out Pretty Fly For A White Boy by The Offspring. I stand in front of the ruins of The Project Arts Centre, a temporary Seventies structure that remained in use until the Nineties. The ruin is covered in semi-hip urban graffiti, ads for gay clubs, all manner of cultural detritus. A notice says that Project activities are continuing in some theatre elsewhere while the new Project is being built on this site. The notice also says that the new building should be completed by June, 1996. There is no sign of any construction going on.

Across the street is the Clarence Hotel, owned and designed by U2, where Hollywood movie stars, fading rock stars and suchlike gilded folk stay when they grace the city of Dublin with their presence.

I was in The Project in 1978 while this particular incarnation of the place was being built. All of the insides were gouged out so it was a safe site for a small punk rock festival, Dark Space, which ran for 24 hours. I didn't have enough money for the ticket and neither did Dee but when we were taking a bus into town she found a wallet holding thirty quid on the seat in front of us. We got off in Stephen's Green, went to a kids' pub where the barman dealt us acid, and headed for Dark Space.

Johnny Rotten formed his new band, Public Image, the week before so, being kind of Irish, he was coming over to our backwater to launch himself post-Pistols at Dark Space. This was indeed big local news so every self-respecting trendoid in Dublin came out in all his or her finery. Because of the acid, I lost track of Dee when we got inside The Project. As the name implied Dark Space was kind of murky and shadowy, meagre illumination provided by projectors and lighting rigs on three different stages where bands played. The first thing I stumbled into was a band of transvestites called The Virgin Prunes who later went on to enjoy European artpunk credibility. Huge in Italy, I think, was their claim to fame.

At the end of the Prunes set I wandered aimless as a feather in the wind, so that it seemed to me that hours had passed. I looked to my left and there, standing right alongside me, was Badger McCarthy, erstwhile captain of the St Fursey's Gaelic Football team. As stocky, pushy, physical, and as space-consuming as he had ever been, only now he had ginger hair all the way down to his shoulder blades which didn't suit him at all. Badger sported a black leather jacket, a Ramones teeshirt, and extra-large bondage trousers. I hadn't seen him since before I went to UCD.

Badger didn't look a day older or happier. He wanted to talk with me but at the same time he kind of glowered at me like I was in some way dishonourable or, within his terms of reference, disreputable.

"This is fucking great, Badger. What d'you think?"

Badger thought it was great too, and we walked into the scoured-out foyer of The Project where they were showing Reefer Madness and Robert Mitchum movies.

"What're you doing now, Badger?

"I'm an anarchist," he growled defensively, like I was a police informer.

"I'm an anarchist too, Badger," I grinned, Easy Rider style.

I wanted to have a piss so I asked Badger where the toilet was. It turned out that I had to climb a ladder to the roof and piss off the side of the building into a courtyard below. Three others were pissing at the same time.

"Where d'you think the chicks are pissing?" one of them asked me, perplexed and obviously as out of it as myself.

When I clambered back down into the foyer there was no sign of Badger but, following the noise, I headed for a small side stage where a band had just kicked off.

I'd been looking at the band for about ten minutes—I recognised the singer, used to see him wandering around the corridors of Belfield during the first lonely weeks of First Year—when I looked to my side and there was Badger again.

"What d'you make of this crowd?" I asked Badger, pointing at the stage.

"They're alright," he mumbled, glaring first at me and then at the band. Which of us was doing something wrong? The boy singing onstage or me looking at him? I disliked Badger's assumed air of superiority.

"The boys sound a bit like Lou Reed to me," I said. "What're they called?"

Badger hadn't a clue who they were but he helpfully consulted the Dark Space timetable.

"They're called U2," he said crisply, folding his programme, putting it methodically into his back pocket, everything about him suggesting that I should have had a programme of my own. I watched the band ten more minutes and quit the scene without saying goodbye to Badger.

I dismiss memories of Dark Space and walk past The Project's remnants towards the Connolly Bookshop, owned by the Communist Party. Called after Pearse's Socialist collaborator in the Easter Rising, James Connolly.

This was a favourite haunt of Rory's, not least because the old guy who served behind the counter was often Michael O'Riordan, Leader of the Irish Communist Party. The man who went to Moscow every year to collect fraternal funding and to have fraternal meetings with Brezhnev. There was no elitist bullshit about O'Riordan. He was present in the shop to meet the people and to spread the word.

"Interesting fucker O'Riordan," Rory said one Saturday when we left the Connolly Bookshop. "Very active in the Spanish Civil War as a Commissar. But he actually boasts proudly of executing Anarchists who refused to take instruction from the Commies! Bloodthirsty fucker. I like him and I don't like him. He's OK on the North."

I step inside out of the present. The Communists are obviously still in charge although O'Riordan may have moved on to the next dialectical stage. Where once the shelves burst with new and cheap Moscow editions of Gogol and Tolstoy, Marx and Lenin, Brecht and the Harlem Renaissance, now those selfsame tomes are joined by hundreds of secondhand books and almost anything else that might sell by way of history, Irish interest, or literature. Even the Commies have been forced to embrace the free market. A guy in his early thirties who remembers me nods a greeting. I nod back.

"How're ya doing Liam?" he asks in his amiable sing-song Dublin accent.

"I'm doing pretty good," I reply. I smile.

He must have been a kid the last time I saw him. A windbag with a lethal Cork accent is discussing the Banana Campaign—whatever that is—with a chubby young guy from the Caribbean in a lime green padded anorak who is apparently the leader of the opposition on whatever island he comes from.

I leave the bookshop and retrace my steps in the direction of Temple Bar, the tourist attraction part of town where Ireland lays down on its back, spreads its legs, and welcomes all comers. Particularly English boozers who occupy Temple Bar most of the week, having rediscovered a congenial part of their ex-Empire where a man can still shit and piss and puke on the streets to his heart's content.

"Fuck it!" I say to myself out loud, as I head back towards Summerhill Parade, *On The Run*, and the future.

FAITHFUL DEPARTED

The winter of '75. A cold and heartless winter. They arrested Patty Hearst on armed robbery charges. Carlos the Jackal took eleven oil ministers, and about sixty others, hostage at the OPEC headquarters in Austria. South Moluccan guerillas seized the Indonesian consulate in Amsterdam. A psychiatrist persuaded the fighters to give themselves up, but not before both hostages and guerillas could be heard singing Happy Birthday inside the consulate. Tangled Up In Blue and Idiot Wind by Bob Dylan were the songs on my radio.

While I was getting on with my pseudo-cool dude life in Dublin, Rory got picked up on the Waterford docks one tragic night by the Guards and plunged into big shit trouble to do with himself and his politics.

He phoned me from a coinbox on the Waterford Quays at about eight the following morning, immediately after they let him out of hospital, and told me all about it. He was supposed to go straight back to St Fursey's but Joe Spunk didn't send a car to pick him up, and the Guards didn't bother driving him back there. He was sixteen then and to be sixteen in Ireland in 1975 was to be a boy still; because he was a boy they expected him to obey orders and return to captivity to await his fate. His enemy's indifference made him the winner.

"I was out on the town with Johnny Phelan. We met these German sailors…" he began his account laconically.

He'd been down the docks at night with Johnny, lots of brandy in the two of them, when they met these bell bottomed German sailors who brought them onto their ship where heavy drinking ensued into the early hours. Rory woke up on a footpath before the dawn, do-gooders poking at him, asking "Are you alright son?" while one of their number went to a phone box to call for an ambulance. He blacked out again, and the next thing he knew he was in that ambulance, being hauled off to Ardkeen Hospital. The big problem was a small notebook that the Ardkeen nurses, looking for ID, removed from his pocket while they were reviving him.

He kept this little notebook, which I knew all about, containing the names, phone numbers, and home addresses of all the judges in the Waterford district. Alongside each of the judge's names Rory had written notes on their track records for sentencing Republicans who ended up in front of them. Where he had access to such information, Rory also inserted into his notebook personal details such as the schools their children were attending, where their wives worked, what golf clubs the judges were members of, habits and movements, stuff like that. There were other notes on the home lives and schedules of important local politicians.

In his classic book of guerrilla war Che writes that the backbone of any revolutionary movement must be the remorseless gathering of intelligence. On top of the revolutionary justification for his researches, Rory was motivated by a less worthy puritanical streak ("Those fat bastards living high on the hog out playing golf and getting their cocks sucked while the Volunteers end up doing fifteen years in Portlaoise"), a voyeuristic streak, and a complete hatred of his own class.

"Someone in Ardkeen sent for the pigs and they questioned me for half an hour, saying they'd be back later," he boasted from the phone booth. By this time he'd given me the number of the coinbox in Waterford and I'd rung him back. "Then first thing this morning the ward sister, a big stupid bull dyke from Kerry or some fucking place, comes in and says I can go back to St Fursey's. They'd just given me a breakfast—breakfast after a fashion—so I got dressed, legged it and here I am."

He was matter of fact about his situation, not freaked out but painfully aware that he was now in a dark spot, under serious pressure.

"So what do you think will happen next?" I asked from my Donnybrook student home—lime-green walls, canary yellow walls, no curtains but window panes painted black—where the whole thing seemed very remote and unreal, a true life adventure experienced at a great distance in the very early morning.

"They'll have been up to the school by now and gone through my locker and they'll have found all sorts of shit there. The fucking *Republican News* and other notes I've been keeping on local assholes..."

"Shit, man." I rubbed my eyes, still trying to wake up.

"Exactly. All the dirt on the ones who deserve a bullet right away," he laughed drily.

"Maybe you should go back and suss it out," I said. "Or ring in and see what the vibe is. Maybe they'll just let it pass."

"They don't let nothing pass. They're pigs and I'm a

revolutionary: they exist to wage war against people like me."

Rory was exaggerating, of course, but there was something to his analysis. He was always an astute and crafty man, even then when he was a lad under the most tremendous pressure. His intelligence was never in doubt. It came from his Grand-dad. I'm not sure that he was in such enormous trouble but, certainly, he was about to make his first appearance on The Man's shitlist. He said the information he collected was regularly passed on to people further up the chain, via Tina. This was no child's fantasy that he had wrapped himself up in. I was proud of him but I was seventeen so I didn't have much to offer by way of practical support. There was silence on the line for a few seconds, the silence of solidarity.

"I might ring the school, just in case," he said, suddenly sad, young, insecure, aware of his situation. "But I'm going to fuck off in any case. At the very least I'll be thrown out of this fucking dump and sent home and my old man will give me a mountain of shit about it...watching my every move...I can't handle that...the fucking awful thing about this is that I feel like a complete fucking jerk, I feel like a child. The whole thing was so stupid of me."

"Yeah. You drink too much. You should cool down and take it easy, get a girlfriend, smoke a little...anyway, enough middle class advice. What do you think you'll do now?"

"Oh, I'll fuck off to London for a while until it cools down a bit. Do me no harm anyway." He coughed phlegmatically.

"But the pigs won't charge you with anything just because they found you with some incriminating lists in your pocket."

"This I know," he laughed. "But they'll be tracking me, keeping me under surveillance, giving me shit all the time...I guess this is as good a time as any to break with this stupid childish life I'm forced to live. It's OK for you up in Dublin smoking dope and fucking around. I feel so stupid down here locked up with all these football morons, all these fucking sheep-shagging West Waterford farmers, when I could be doing something important in Belfast or somewhere."

"Got any money?" I had a little in the bank I could give him.

"I've always had money put away for a rainy day like this," he said sarcastically. "First thing I'll do today is wait for the banks to open and then I'll go get cash. I have my bank book with me. The pigs didn't take it."

Rory had a lot of shit circumstances in his life in those days but his folks never left him short of money. He said it was guilt money. Only he would have kept his bank book permanently in his jacket pocket for a rainy day.

There was more silence on the line for a moment. I was wishing him well in my heart.

"So you'll go to London like many a man before you and work for the Saxon Shilling, my friend?" I said when we'd been silent long enough.

"I won't like it," he said petulantly, like he'd been accused of some political failing, "but I'll survive in hostile territory. I've got to learn how to do that sometime."

"I'm sure you'll survive." I felt nervous for him, but I did think he'd make it.

"Anyway, no harm taking a long hard look at the enemy in his own environment...I don't know when I'll get to call you again," he mumbled, confused and tired. "It depends what speed I'll have to travel at. But you know I'll keep in touch."

He rang Fursey's and whatever priest answered the phone put

him right through to the venerable Father Joe, who sounded concerned, paranoid, and agog.

"Don't worry about a thing Rory," he shouted in his camp, booming, West of Ireland brogue, "you'll find things exactly the way you left them here at St Fursey's. These things happen with boys all the time, and I can't condemn a man for a minor transgression. You should take a couple of days off and resume your classes when you feel up to it."

All of this sounded deeply suspicious to Rory. Father Joe was a ferocious tartar and also, as luck would have it, an involved Anti-Republican. During the Tan War his grandfather had owned the only grocery store in Mayo willing to supply provisions to the Brits. Joe's father had been on the pro-British side in the civil war. Spunk despised the IRA with all his might. He was forever being quoted approvingly in *The Irish Times*, happy to denounce the Provos at any hour of the day or night. He sometimes appeared on BBC TV shows, more or less calling on God to strike down every Provo known to man. A presentable dry-cleaned Catholic who was willing to say to the people of England: "Please forgive us. We're nothing but savages over here."

Rory used to say that Franz Fanon had a lot of things to say about people like Joe Spunk.

Joe's other good news was that Séamus was on his way down from Dublin that very afternoon. This was enough for Rory—the mere mention of his father was like a red rag to a bull. Rory told Joe he'd be back at Fursey's in about an hour, put down the phone, and went straight to his bank. The guerilla fighter cleared all the money out of his account, and moved quick as a flash.

He went across the rickety old suspension bridge over the Suir and into the CIE bus and train station, where he bought a ticket on the first bus out of Waterford. Two hours later he was in Clonmel where he got something to eat, bought himself a hat and jacket, and caught a train to Rosslare. You didn't need a passport to get into the UK if you were Irish. Rory took the next ferry to Wales, where he got another bus to London. He had a cousin living in a big London squat, the same cousin who gave him the bomb making plans that led to his being banished to St Fursey's, the same cousin who'd told him about Kino. He'd rung the cousin's parents from the CIE station in Waterford—before the shit could possibly hit the fan with his family—and got a London work number on him.

Two weeks later I got a Dali postcard with a London postmark; a series of long letters came in the months that followed. I'd never been to England but Rory wrote detailed analyses of various aspects of the English character, critiques of English politics, and cheery tales of squat life. The letters were written in an adolescent "comradely" style, reminiscent of Che's diaries, and the more human aspects of them spoke of loneliness and depression.

He didn't come back home for two years. During that time he lived in three different squats. From the second squat he wrote to me:

You'll find this hard to believe but I've actually succeeded in getting myself a girlfriend. Even me! She's a Spanish girl and I think you'd really like her. Her parents are small hill farmers from Andalucia. Her grandfather was an Anarchist during the civil war, active around Barcelona in the Red and Black Column. When the war finished he was arrested and put in prison. As soon as he was released he joined the clandestine struggle against Franco, helping organise the resurgent Peninsular Libertarian Movement. He was arrested and shot by a military tribunal in 1947. I met her at a club in town one night and she brought me back to her squat. I don't have to tell you what happened next! She is filling my head with anarchist ideas and I'm telling her all about our struggle, mutual education of every kind!

Eventually he moved into a rented house in Stockwell which he shared with three other hippyish Irish guys.

I'm not exactly moving in what you might call revolutionary circles, but these are good guys. One of them says he wants to become an artist but I don't know. He does these kind of fantasy drawings, androgynous human beasts with wings. Another one of them comes from Kilkenny and thinks he vaguely remembers you. The third of them is a right old bollocks, but my Dad was always saying I don't have enough give and take in me so now I'm learning a little about give and take. Amongst other things.

He worked as a labourer, making good money. His letters grew vague and short as he plotted his return to Ireland.

When Rory got back, he was a man. At school he'd been tall and strong, but still gawky and awkward. When I encountered him in Dublin post-London in 1977 he was a big strong six foot man with broad shoulders, muscled legs and arms. His black hair was very long, he wore it in a ponytail, and he had the sort of trendy London clothes that made me feel jealous because I had to buy my threads locally. Which meant provincially. He had seen life, tasted good and evil in their bedrooms and their bars, and he wanted to commence his work as a member of an IRA active service unit. Rory was ready.

I didn't see too much of him after his return because I was on a bit of a sexual binge, seeing several different sex partners, putting in a lot of time with this American girl living in Rathgar. She'd introduced herself like this: "Hi! I'm Betty! I'm a square from Delaware." I didn't find this irresistible but her obvious availability was unputdownable. It was just a phase I was going through, a dark depression from which I could get no relief. I was being unpleasant to everyone, I think I was lucky not to catch something unpleasant.

Rory was very busy too. His was a more dangerous game. He was pushing himself into the inside of the Provos.

His life was now recklessly complete but London, somehow, had taught him some complex smarts. He'd grown subtle enough to convince his father and everyone else that he'd grown up and forgotten about the Provos. By way of reward Séamus, through Knights of Columbanus/Fianna Fáil connections, fixed him up with a good office job in one of the multinational oil companies. Rory was happy there at first; he signed a stack of forms every hour, he got well paid, and everybody thought he was just a regular guy from Howth. He was drinking a lot after work, nasty work drinking, not the kind of party drinking I sometimes did.

Most weeks he undertook some sort of covert activity. He was heading north for bombing raids. He was robbing banks. He'd go on training and instruction courses in the Dublin Mountains every weekend, saw active service regularly. Sometimes he'd drop around to see me after work and we'd go on a drinking spree he'd pay for.

These were very strange and fevered nights for me because I realised, gradually, that I didn't enjoy them at all. I'd begun to drift away into a decadent world where alcohol was not a cool drug. I was all the more intensely a Republican, but I was also checking out punk rock in great depth. Everything that particular revolutionary creed suggested by way of diversion was researched and acted upon. Punk rock got me addicted to speed for eight months.

SINN FÉIN

On the 2FM news they report the arrest in Kerry of an IRA man, wanted for killing an SAS man in Belfast twenty years ago. The next item concerns the forthcoming MTV Awards in Dublin. One of the organisers says "Get those aftershow tickets now!" The news ends. Cut to Marilyn Manson singing a hideous Eurythmics song. I head out. As I lock my front door I notice a fresh graffiti on the wall across the street: STOP HISTORY.

It takes fifteen minutes to walk from my house to Parnell Square where I enter The Garden of Remembrance, a much-vilified Sixties architectural masterpiece celebrating the struggles of the heroes of the Tan War. In the Sixties when he was a blind old wreck, and President of the country, Dev used to lead massed Fianna Fáil worthies, bishops, and army brass bands at Garden of Remembrance wreath-laying ceremonies. By the Seventies this national piety was a source of youthful contempt and the only times I ever visited The Garden of Remembrance were to score dope.

Today there are a few junkies gathered around the entrance but the garden has a more upbeat aspect than I remember. I walk past the crucifix-shaped pool, tiles flaunting symbols of Celtic mythology on its floor, and up the steps leading to a huge bronze sculpture of figures who are half-human, half-swan: the Children Of Lir. Gangs of French and Spanish schoolkids sit around in little clusters, their feeble pop music emanating from ghetto blasters. Well-heeled suburban children of architects and dentists, over here in Dublin living out watered-down fantasies about being on the road.

Behind the sculpture is a longish text in Irish which explains what the Garden is about but my Irish is not good enough to read it. A small plaque to the left has French and English translations:

In the desert of discouragement we saw division. In the winter of bondage we saw a vision. We melted the snow of lethargy and this we left for you as our inheritance.

I used to know Parnell Square and its environs intimately because that's where the Sinn Féin HQ was located. The year I left college, I joined Sinn Féin, which Rory referred to as a 'talking shop full of old women and wankers'.

He hated them, said that the Republican movement was not supposed to be democratic, that therefore he didn't see what purpose a political party served other than to expose idealistic innocents (such as myself being the kind/unkind implication) to the hostile attentions of the Special Branch. His other big problem with Sinn Féin was a more conventional ideological one; the leadership of Sinn Féin were old-guard Catholic nationalists—Sinn Féin meetings began with a Decade of the Rosary in Irish—whereas the young bloods in the Provos were dedicated internationalists and leftists.

He was correct—Sinn Féin was a farce, a black-humoured Irish farce. The chairman of the UCD branch of Sinn Féin was a chubby mammy's boy called Vincent who kept loose women at a good distance. Vincent's misogyny, like most misogyny, was comic and clichéd. Once, before he knew how close I was to Dee, he remarked, seeing her shimmering sultry form queuing at the counter of the Belfield canteen: "I'd say now you'd get a right dose of the claps off that wan."

I attended a secret Sinn Féin meeting in Pearse House, a murky Georgian dump just north of Parnell Square. The unnecessary risks and problems I exposed myself to by being politically active reached out to surround me. This "secret" gathering involved student Republicans from all over Dublin meeting up with a distinguished representative of the IRA's Army Council. Sinn Féin owned a lot of property in that part of town, some of which had fallen into their hands as long ago as the Tan War. Covert revolutionary actions have taken place on those piss poor streets for centuries.

Pearse House went back to the earliest days of the struggle. Sinn Féin rumour had it that it was purchased with money raised from the sale of the Russian Crown Jewels. But others said Dev never actually sold the Russian Crown Jewels. Still others, of course, said that there never were any Crown Jewels. Proponents of this last theory were invariably supporters of Fianna Fáil.

A smelly premises, where various propaganda and organisational arms of the Movement maintained offices, Pearse House was a shambolic mess. The ground floor and the basement were used for small private meetings of various sorts, both local and national. We were chalked in to meet the Army Council man in a dank and miserable basement room. A hundred watt bulb hung from a bare wire protruding from a smoke-stained ceiling badly in need of replastering. There were thirty chairs in the room, about sixteen adolescents sitting nervously in some of them, the only warmth coming from a one-bar electric heater which threw out heat you'd only catch if you sat on top of it.

My UCD companion for the evening—I was supposed to watch her and she was supposed to watch me—was a girl I knew vaguely but didn't like very much, a buck-toothed archaeology student from Derry, usually seen in Mother of Ireland shawls and long tweed skirts, who always implied that she'd seen active service back home, was just slumming it in our sedate circles until she could get back to the war. It subsequently emerged that she was a police informer, that this was the real reason she'd quit Derry.

Us students all nodded nervously to one another, all wannabe revolutionaries, the very fact that we were students meaning that we were mostly middle class kids on weird trips. In the late Seventies other teenagers were getting into bisexuality or Lou Reed or heroin. We were getting into the Provos. That didn't mean that we particularly enjoyed the shabby and spartan atmosphere of Dorset Street. No doubt we all shared a cheap thrill at the thought of our anticipated meeting with a man who sat on the all-powerful Army Council, this infamous committee of Provo elders who decided who got shot, who planted the bombs, what was going on.

Sitting close by me to my left was a boy who looked to be seventeen, very thin, wearing frayed denims and the jacket from a pinstripe suit that had seen better days. His beautiful poet's face was restless and internalised. While he waited for things to kick off he paid no attention to the rest of us but buried himself in a Graham Greene paperback. He held the book in his left hand, his left arm resting on his knee, his right hand holding a Benson & Hedges cigarette which was the only thing distracting him from his reading. When he saw that I was watching him he squinted in my direction, acknowledged me vaguely, and returned to his reading.

Three rows behind me three longhaired guys—two from Dublin, one from Donegal—were denouncing the Irish government as Brit collaborators. The Donegal lad, the tallest and best looking of the three, a rural Irish vision of the New York Dolls' lead singer, was busy shouting the loudest.

When I turned round to look at him he leered at me, fixing me with a bargain basement Jagger pout. I nodded back before averting my gaze. I thought these were most unusual potential guerrillas.

Over an old blocked-up fireplace hung a fine yellowed portrait of Patrick Pearse, the blood-sacrifice poet and educationalist who really got the freedom ball rolling with his reckless self-sacrifice during the 1916 Rising. I had great respect for Pearse's extremism, though less for his mystical zeal-of-the-convert Catholicism. Pearse was a boy-lover, an obsession liberally confirmed and illustrated by his poems, addressed to young boys who attended his Irish-Ireland school:

Raise your comely head
Till I kiss your mouth:
If either of us is the better of that
I am the better of it.
There is a fragrance in your kiss
That I have not found yet

In the kisses of women
Or in the honey of their bodies.
Lad of the grey eyes,
That flush in your cheek
Would be pale with dread of me
Could you read my secrets.

The man from the Army Council stormed into the room while I was preoccupied daydreaming about Pearse. Army Council was a bullish greyhaired dude in his late fifties. None of us kids were supposed to know who he was in real life but I used to see him all the time around Grafton Street, where he went for a stroll every lunchtime, escaping from his big job in the Department of Justice.

A puritanical Kerry-born civil servant who'd played the Fianna Fáil game to the hilt, he was big in the Irish language and folk music movements, the senior adviser to the Minister for Justice, perfectly placed to pass on vital information to the Movement. A onetime star of the Gaelic Athletic Association—he'd played football for Kerry in his youth—he still held himself impressively like an athlete.

He moved fast like what he did was very important, as if all would be lost if we took the time to breathe. In this man's world, everything was still to play for. An old man in a hurry, the most dangerous sort of man.

He wore the regulation Louis Copeland suit of a government apparatchik, an expensive grey silk item cut perfectly to his muscular frame. You could tell from his language-revival disdain, from the deliberate way he pronounced "girl" as "gerrul" and "film" as "fillum", from his cold slow-moving grey blue eyes, that he didn't approve of the way most of us kids dressed, behaved, talked, or thought. His tight-cropped hair gave way to a literal red neck which rubbed against his tight-fitting shirt collar.

He gave us a long lecture on conspiracy, secrecy, and how to deal with the Special Branch.

Mr Army Council guy left before us, his farewell message delivered in Irish, a language I have scant knowledge of: Beir Bua agus Beannacht, A Cháirde Gael (Victory and Blessings, Friends of Ireland). When our turn came to leave the building we were given a brief—more trenchant—pep talk by a more low level Provo on how to avoid the Special Branch who, we were now informed, were lurking right outside the front door ready to question us.

This bad news bore out Rory's contention that the only thing to be gotten from joining Sinn Féin was trouble and a Special Branch file. We were told by the Provo—a nice working class Dublin guy who looked poor—to hang back in the arched doorway of the building until a bus pulled up at the bus stop just outside the door. We were to wait until the commuters queuing to get the bus were all on board and then—just as the doors were about to shut—we were to leap from the darkness, averting the eye of waiting Special Branch men, into the darkness of the night and out onto the bus. I thought this was a stupid plan—it all seemed a bit comic and paranoid until I had to do it myself; when push came to shove it scared me. While hiding and waiting I could clearly see the Branch men parked right across the street in two blue Ford Capris. Four in each car, eyeing us cowering kids like jackals ready to strike. Brendan Behan used to say that the Irish cops were lured down from the sides of the Kerry Mountains with hunks of raw meat.

When the first bus came I disobeyed wise instructions and leaped into the centre of the crowd of normal citizens trying to get on the bus. This seemed to be good strategy because, by the time I was sitting comfortably in my upstairs seat, some of my straggling comrades were surrounded on the footpath by Branch men with pens and notebooks in hand. The Graham Greene reader, still in his literary daze, stared at me absent-mindedly from the middle of this scrum, making me feel a little treacherous and sorry for him. I had no idea where my bus was taking me so after a few stops I jumped off at the side of Trinity College where buses left for Donnybrook, where I lived.

I was waiting for the Donnybrook bus when I was joined by two Special Branch guys on foot. They'd tailed me from Parnell Square in their Capri. They questioned me for about half an hour. Who was at the meeting? What transpired? Where did my parents live? What did my father do for a living? They were full of peasant disbelief when I told them my parents were divorced. In the Ireland of those days such behaviour was a symptom of progressive freethinking, not of personal unhappiness. There was no divorce law then; Dad and Ma had to travel to England to get theirs.

The Special Branch eventually let me go and a Kilkenny cop called around to see my mother a week later, putting the fear of God into her by telling her that I was in the IRA and would be killed by them if I ever tried to leave. I had Ma on the phone after that for weeks, frantically imploring me to get out before I was shot.

Rory frowned when he heard about all this high drama. This was not his style. He said I was being used, and used for no particular purpose.

"Look at the shit all this has gotten you into. And what for? So that your name ends up in the Special Branch files and your mother gets those pigs calling around to her. Sinn Féin just want young guys in the party to make them feel good about themselves. I mean, do you really want to help us? Or have you just decided to adopt a kind of punk rock stance?"

"No! Fuck you! I want to help," I shouted, meaning it and knowing where the conversation was going. "I believe in this stuff. I believe in…what we're all doing."

"Because they've been asking about you, if you're trustworthy. I've told them that you are, naturally."

"And?"

"And we need a place where we can meet up before going on jobs. A safe house. We need a place to store our guns and bullets."

"And you want to use my flat?"

"What d'you think?"

"No problem."

I didn't stop for a second to think about it. It was the right thing to do. The English took our country at gunpoint and then they feigned amazement when we decided to grab it back off them at gunpoint. That was how I felt about the state of Ireland right there and then. And that was what I said to Rory.

He was happy with me and, I guess, I was happy with myself. It was the least that I could do.

THE WIND BEGAN TO HOWL

People's Voice brought over this old American radical, George Spears, who as a student had been one of Trotsky's bodyguards at the time of his assassination in Mexico City.

Spears had written a book about the assassination and several other hefty books on American foreign policy that I was given to read. The veteran revolutionary was due to speak about the Fourth International at a public meeting on UCD campus. A rival Trotskyist outfit, the one backed by the English actress Vanessa Redgrave, claimed that our hero was in fact a CIA agent who'd been planted in Trotsky's inner circle in Mexico, and had played some part in Trotsky's death. Rumours were going round that the Spears meeting would be disrupted, so I got drafted in as one of several bodyguards for Spears. This sounded cool—bodyguard to Trotsky's ex-bodyguard.

I had dinner with Spears at his crummy Gardiner Street hotel, shared the taxi with him to Belfield, and sat in the back row of the lecture theatre while he spoke brilliantly and vigorously about Trotsky's vision of permanent revolution, his legacy of disturbance and subversion.

Spears was getting on but he was still sharp and craggy. He was disgruntled with life; he'd have done a whole lot better for himself if he'd stuck to the straight and narrow.

I liked the Trots because they liked Al Green and Blondie. I liked the Trots as individuals. You could dance at their revolution.

Comrades though they were, I couldn't tell People's Voice—not even Dee—what I was really up to with Rory.

I assume they all regarded me as a bit of a bar stool radical. They offered a somewhat conditional theoretical support to the armed struggle; I was the boy going home in the evenings to take out from under his single bed an old brown leather travelling bag full of oilcloth-wrapped sawn off shotguns, jet-black revolvers, bullets of various shapes and sizes. There was one sawn off I regularly unwrapped and fondled—an altered cold, clean, heavy, magnificent, and elegant weapon. I'd speculate as to how many people had been killed or maimed with it. Aside from worrying about my own security, I had no interest in the upshot of my attitudes.

I gave Rory a set of keys to my home. He would call me the night before his Active Service Unit needed to use it.

On those days I'd vacate by two in the afternoon, go to the *Anna Livia* offices or to a movie in town or kill time reading, posing, and drinking coffee in the Grafton Street Bewley's. I'd keep away from home until late in the evening because it was important that I not bump into my houseguests accidentally. I wasn't just a fellow traveller, I was aiding and abetting these guys, so it was vital that I didn't know them or they me.

When I finally did get home everything would be much as I'd left it. They usually left £20 on the kitchen table for me, presumably deducted from the proceeds of whatever heist they'd been up to that day. There would be a black plastic rubbish bag in a corner of the kitchen containing a pile of empty beer cans and the remains of four Chinese takeaways. The brown travelling bag would be back under my bed, like it always was.

This subversion went on for nine months, a cold clean revolutionary activity. Some evenings I lacked courage, convincing myself that some small blue car parked across the street from me contained my nemesis, Special Branch men all set to invade my home, find the guns, demolish and dissolve my fine lifestyle. The Volunteers—sharp, focused individuals—knew that their routine was becoming too cosy and that anybody, such as one of my prosperous neighbours, might have spotted them for what they were. Donnybrook was bohemian, but not that bohemian.

THE TAUT AND TAME

I first met Jim Devoy in 1977 while he was DJing for a pirate station called Radio Free Dublin which operated from over a whorehouse on Stephen's Green, and I was at UCD. Back then he did rambling open ended shows running nonstop into the middle of the night. Sometimes I'd walk into the studio at 4am and broadcast my personal bullshit to whoever was listening. When Jim felt like signing off he'd do so, and close the station down by switching off the transmitter before locking the door as he left.

RTE started their pop station to defeat the pirates, hiring Jim to play heavy rock for them. He broke U2 in Ireland which gave him a global reputation. I can't say that I was too impressed by this achievement but then Jim liked the Beatles and I carried a torch for the Stones. His global reputation has resulted in several TV series for VH1, coffee table rock books, and a home in Howth that once belonged to Phil Lynott.

Jim was nice then and is nice now, so his invitation out to Donnybrook won't be denied. Now Jim broadcasts between seven and ten, six evenings a week, and we end up face to face in the studio again, still bullshitting about music.

His long curly black locks, he tells me, disappeared years ago.

Now he sports a flashy flattop. He looks good for his age—like you do when you have money. I don't get a chance to chat with him before I go on air. For ten minutes I stand in the production booth looking at Jim working and then I'm ushered politely into the studio while he's playing Pavement. He stands up with his headphones on and puts his arm around my shoulder.

"Hey Liam, we're going to go to travel and then I'll talk with you."

But when he goes to travel after Pavement his producer steps into the studio and goes through a list of gigs Jim has to announce before he goes to me. So after travel it's Rage Against The Machine, gig listings, then cut to me. Jim liked slightly better music once upon a time in the West. That's what comes from staying in the same job forever, and from being able to afford Phil Lynott's home.

"So now we've been joined by Liam Crowe, onetime Dublin journalist and troublemaker. Liam is best known these days as the author of *Punk Rock Girls*, a brilliant study of the evils of sex and drugs and rock'n'roll. Liam is back in Ireland right now writing a book about the IRA. Liam, welcome to the show."

We talk a while about punk groupies. Jim asks me about whatever happened to punk rock.

"It kept going, Jim," I explain patiently.

Then we talk about Brian Jones, and how that book is going. The name Dan Breen is never mentioned, and that project is gently glossed over.

"Which leads us neatly to what brings you out to the studios this evening, Liam. You've been listening to the new live album from The Rolling Stones, their fifth live album, No Security."

"Well, Jim, they do a filthy version of Gimme Shelter, that

110

great tribal summoning up of the diabolic spirit of rock'n'roll. Jagger has never sounded better. Perhaps this is the definitive version of this song."

"Really? So you don't think the Stones did all their really relevant work over twenty years ago?"

"No, I get that argument but a lot of the time it's just a methodology for dealing with them. My best friend at school in the mid Seventies used to say that the Stones were once a *tour de force* and that now they're forced to tour. And that was twenty years ago he said that! Smartasses have reckoned the Stones are past it for the longest time. I think musicians go someplace special when they get older. Greil Marcus, a critic I have little in common with, once commented on the cynical snarl that's snuck into Jagger's voice over the years. I think this was fair comment on Jagger's Eighties work, when his voice was letting him down, the Stones were in various states of disintegration, rock music was going through a pretty sick phase in general. There was a global conspiracy by the record labels to kill off rock music, which they found troublesome...messy...inefficient. But since they got back together Jagger has just gotten better and better. Now he sounds so black-hearted, treacherous, and true."

Jim plays the new live Gimme Shelter, more to oblige me than because he thinks it's any good. I'm glad to get such a piece of music played for the people out there in radioland. Jagger singing about being young, foolish, lucky. But the track is eight minutes long and Jim can't handle it. He cuts after five minutes to The Taut And The Tame by Tortoise. At least Jim still has one good record.

DUCK FOR COVER

I left UCD in 1980 and drifted into journalism. My first big article was on the significance of JR Ewing, the anti-hero of Dallas. By the end of the year the Sixties was profoundly over—Reagan was President and John Lennon was dead. The soundtrack to that period in my life was The Ramones, Thin Lizzy, and Blondie. I had a sense of kicking out the jams, of being in control, or out of control.

I was still living in up the road from the Belfield campus in Donnybrook, an upmarket inner city suburb full of leafy avenues populated with beautiful provocative rich kids some of whom visited me in my flat to share intimate moments. Donnybrook was home to actors who worked nearby at RTE, writers published in Penguin, ageing mistresses of long-forgotten important men, UCD academics and suchlike. I liked it specially in the autumn when Morehampton Road, the majestic tree-lined artery connecting the city centre to the elite southern suburbs, converted itself into a wild valley of brown leaves falling to the ground every time the wind blew.

Just out of college, I had big-stuff ideas about myself and my Breen book. I wanted to call it *On The Run*, and had an artless New Journalism idea about what kind of book I was going to write. Liston had a better idea, he wheezed at me: "What the nation wishes to read is a simply told tale of an Irish hero." He wanted to call it *Against Tyrant's Might* because he'd just discovered this doggerel which excited him:

In the hardest fight
Against tyrant's might,
Your place was the battle's van.

All respect to you
Who were staunch and true,
And who proudly lived 'the man!'
You kept in sight
In the eclipsed light
The cause of Rosaleen!
When the sun shines high
In proud Freedom's sky,
She'll remember Daniel Breen!

Rory was amused by my dilemma: "That fucking poem is so truly awful that you're going to have to go with it. Probably written by some child-molester priest. Look at all those exclamation marks. I hate exclamation marks. Always a sign of a bad writer. You'll be a hero with every gobshite in South Tipperary and West Waterford when this thing hits the streets."

He was right. *Against Tyrant's Might* sold 5,000 copies in three months, 2,000 of them in South Tipperary. I think Liston, who certainly knew what he was doing when it came to book publishing, secretly reprinted the book in Finland thereafter. In the early Eighties I came across copies printed on paper different from the cheap pulp edition I was supposed to know about. When I got my first royalty cheque I tore open the envelope, thinking there might be enough royalties for me to buy a new turntable. There was just about enough to buy me a new stylus.

But at least the book established me as a writer of some sort. Nobody—except myself—seemed to notice how shoddy a book it really was. This taught me a lot about the writing game, the book reviewing game, and the process of reading. I got work reviewing Irish history books for *Hibernia,* a fortnightly journal of liberal opinion. This led to book reviews with a few of the nationals and author profiles for *Anna Livia*, a leftish fortnightly listings magazine whose editor eventually gave me a music column inside the back cover, a desk, and a phone of my own. It never quite amounted to being a job but I had regular money and someplace to go every day. It also gave me fun. I managed to libel both Graham Greene and the Attorney General within four weeks of one another.

The sort of left-wing cause that went down well at *Anna Livia* was the cause which was long ago or far away. It was hunky dory to support the ANC in South Africa, the Sandanistas in Nicaragua or the PLO in Israel but the Irish situation, *Anna Livia*'s editorial line had it, 'was different'. Freedom fighters over a thousand miles away with non-white skin were progressive forces, white freedom fighters who spoke English and lived an hour's drive up the motorway from Dublin, listening to Thin Lizzy and Horslips, were anti-democratic and reactionary elements.

The best thing about *Anna Livia* was its location, the top floors of a converted Victorian woollen mill overlooking the Liffey about five minutes walk from the city centre. The downstairs hosted a hippy restaurant which was a regular haunt for *Anna Livia* groupies and British intelligence types. Most of Dublin's disgruntled activists (feminists, working class intellectuals, Animal Liberation types, hooligan socialists) passed through *Anna Livia* at one time or another in any given week. A lot of corrupt people kept sly eyes on us.

I'd sit at my desk, overflowing with freebies and press releases, looking out my window at the filthy regal Liffey flowing neutrally under the Halfpenny Bridge, a famous and overestimated Victorian pedestrian bridge. It was especially postcard-charming to sit at my third floor eyrie in the summertime, my window open, watching the fresh faced teenage couples, the juvenile prey of Ireland, stroll arm in arm across the river. When I was stoned I felt like I was a part of something, like I was somebody.

I was doing good as a music writer. When the Stones played outside Dublin I was sent off—without anything having been organised—to get an interview with Jagger. I weaselled my way onto the festival site and quite by accident bumped into Jagger walking down a grassy incline. I got about five minutes of pleasantries out of him about how thrilled and delighted he was to be in Ireland before a minder rescued him from me. I missed a career beat when I failed to take proper note of U2, a phenomenon destined to happen whether my generation wanted it to happen or not. In politics I admired the difficult, the contrary, the brave. My taste in music followed a similar graph: I was more attracted to perverted supernovas and their demented B-side mentalities. I got very caught up with Velvet Underground obsessions, the darker side of the New York punk revolution. Bullshit music had to be jettisoned in the interests of good taste and, just as important, of looking good on the streets.

The first book was still in typesetting when I began writing a second book for Benbulben. This time it was a life of Seán McBride who, unlike Dan Breen, was still very much alive. McBride was the son of Maud Gonne McBride, who was once considered the most beautiful woman in Europe, famous for having been the central sexual obsession of Yeats, his "burning cloud". Maud Gonne—more interested in politics than in poetry—rejected Yeats, remained a hard-line Republican all her life, an elegant thorn in de Valera's side. Into her eighties she was still picketing prisons and organising rallies. She was too famous and too important for Dev to ever do anything about her other than refer to her, icily, as Madame McBride.

Seán McBride led the IRA during the early Fianna Fáil years. He subsequently became Minister for Foreign Affairs in a coalition government, founded Amnesty International, and won both the Nobel and Lenin Prizes. He maintained subtle but firm links with the Provos up until the end of his life.

"Seán McBride, now, for all his great distinction and noble demeanour," huffed Liston at me in his Ballsbridge bolthole, "is a magnificent man. A flawless Irishman. You'll get on like a house on fire, now, the two of ye."

I was given the job of writing a brief life of McBride. Not the authorised biography, which was assigned—not to be written until after the old man died—to a distinguished academic biographer who was granted exclusive access to McBride's papers. My hack-like task was to bang off a sort of footnote-free stopgap which would make the enduring old schemer look good. Something he richly deserved to look.

I got to meet him six times to research the book. These meetings with McBride were a source of awe to my pals, like I was going to meet the Pope. Only he was the pope of politics and not the pope of wishful thinking. Dee said I was meeting one of the most important men in the country (true), and that knowing him would change my life (untrue). She had a hundred questions she wanted me to ask the ancient relic.

Because of the book Liston had commissioned me to write, I kept diligent notes on our meetings in addition to taping the six conversations. I found those notes in a box in my room in

Kilkenny last week, and am impressed by the relatively low level of bullshit they contain. Richard Hell has this punk rock song about running into, on the street, the Richard Hell who existed ten years earlier. In the song, Destiny Street, he knows what he thinks of the younger him, but wonders what the young Hell makes of the older guy. The notes on the McBride meetings are the only extant writing, other than *Tyrant's Might* and journalism, that I have from those days. The Breen book and most of the journalism are complete shit.

This is the note I took after my first meeting with McBride:

I get a pep talk from Liston first thing in the morning. Patriotism...Ireland is the best little country in the world...a bonnie fighter...my duties as a writer. I think he has mistaken me for a boxer. He thinks I need to be worked up and motivated. His talk has the opposite effect to that which he intends for I despise nationalism, chauvinism...anyway, in honour of the great occasion I abandon my usual cleanest dirty shirt routine and wear new black shoes and my nice Italian suit that Ma gave me last Christmas. Ma always said I was headed for greatness and here I am heading up Clonskeagh Road towards a great man.

A very hot uncomfortable South Dublin late afternoon. I turn right into the grounds of ——— House. A tree-lined avenue gives way to a rose garden and a small mansion, where The Most Beautiful Woman In Europe held court and twisted Yeats around her little finger. Where IRA men, in between the Tan War and the Provo revival, met and fulminated. I walk towards a house where, in part, the history of my country was played out by major players.

They're expecting me, they've spotted me walking up the avenue. The front door opens and a teenage girl comes out through it, walking talking proof that her great grandmother, Maud Gonne, must indeed have been the femme fatale of her epoch. This is certainly the loveliest ethereal girl I've ever seen, and I think I've seen a few. She is very tall and strong-boned, long blond hair, eyes so cold I can't tell if she's stupid or bright. If the circumstances were appropriate I'd have said that she had perfect blowjob lips, but that's the kind of thought I have to push to the back of my mind right now. She tells me her name is Eva in a sweet patrician accent, that her grandfather is looking forward to meeting me. She guides me through a large silent hallway. To my right a sitting room converted into McBride's bedroom. I can see a clothes rack bearing about thirty Fifties-style suits, silk shirts, linen shirts, and a variety of ties. I'm facing a wooden door behind which McBride lurks.

Just before she opens the door Eva says: "Grandad enjoyed your book on Dan Breen. He said it made him laugh." Presumably making the great man laugh is deemed to be a good thing.

She pushes the door shut behind me. I miss her already but now I'm in a seriously big room so at first I don't see the small old man standing behind a huge potted shrub, staring out his window into his back garden. He turns, smiles at me, walks towards me with his right hand extended for shaking. I've never been really comfortable about shaking hands, I have a weird glitch about that. McBride moves well for such a real old man. His rice paper skin corpse-like but his eyes mischievous and very young indeed. The room is dominated by a fine, much-reproduced in coffee table books, painting of Maud Gonne, the patron saint of us unreconstructed, recidivist, Republicans. The Nobel Prize plaque rests on the marble fireplace.

This is what I wrote about my last audience, dated a couple of months later:

He never gets tired, driven by a real fanaticism. I've never met anyone so extreme in my whole life. He tells me the books editor at *Anna Livia* is a British spy.

"Yes she is," he says with some satisfaction, "Oh yes, she is. And a lesbian too by all accounts!"

His left hand resting in his trousers pocket, while he gesticulates wildly with his right. Did I know about the homosexual scandal involving Thomas McGreevy, pal of Beckett, the former Director of the National Gallery, "rather overestimated poet and underestimated hypocrite" and the Swedish Ambassador? It seems these gentlemen, and several Fianna Fáil worthies, shared a rent boy whom they "passed around like a plate of biscuits" until he got out of control in 1957. He tried to blackmail McGreevy, threatening to go to the English papers. For his trouble, the boy ended up in the Liffey.

"Fianna Fáil are hilarious," said the man who came within a whisper of destroying de Valera. "I like them a great deal because they're the best of a bad lot. They're responsible for the mess we're in today with the North, but they're also responsible for fine young men like you who may yet turn this country into the sort of place the founding fathers dreamed of."

The slacks-wearing Beatles-admiring provincial circles I'd moved in at school were a thing of the past and I was obsessed with swimming out into the sea of city life, applying cock to cunt as if to the manner born. My accent changed. I lost the colourful cracked brogue that goes with being from Kilkenny, swapping it for a kind of strange neutral thing that I still talk with, my awful shallow South Dublin tone of superiority and calm arrogance.

I followed Rory's advice and quit Sinn Féin. I hung out with the rich kids and the People's Voice Trotskyists who took drugs, threw wild parties, and were often the selfsame rich kids. They had the best brains at UCD as well as the tightest asses. I think I more or less agreed with everything they had to say about politics.

As the Eighties began, as punk rock—all art, anarchy and ass—gave way to a more mature radio-friendly New Wave, I disconnected from the American scene for a while. The electronic music of Germany was the next vogue, one that I checked out with dodgy National College of Art & Design types I'd met through People's Voice. Now we were finally, inevitably, dancing hedonistically at our own revolution.

I got a strange conspiratorial phonecall at *Anna Livia*. Some old comrades from Belfield—who now styled themselves the Irish Revolutionary Challenge—wanted to meet with me. They had something crucial they needed to discuss. Hesitantly—they'd split from People's Voice at the end of our UCD period amid great acrimony and accusations that they were CIA agent provocateurs—I agreed to see them one night at the Quaker Meeting Rooms in Eustace Street, a building owned by the Quakers, made innocently available to radical political groupings for committee meetings and suchlike. When I'd first known People's Voice they used to hang out there.

The leader of Revolutionary Challenge arrived first by herself, a short dumpy redhaired girl who put out her hand and introduced herself to me by her revolutionary pseudonym, Tuma. I knew of course that she was really Helena Hurley, the brilliant law student daughter of the Attorney General for Kerry, but I didn't say anything.

We were joined by three nervous looking lads in their early

twenties that I was on nodding terms with: Maurice Lynch the President of the UCD Archaeology Society, Noel Dwan the son of a Fianna Fáil hotel millionaire, Conor Edwards the campus acid dealer.

Tuma Hurley explained what they were up to.

"The Republican movement and its various splinter groups are in league with international capital. Only through outrage...destructive, not constructive, terrorism can we change anything, do anything to disconnect the State/Church control over the people."

Which translated into a simple plan—involving me. I was to seek an interview, on behalf of *Anna Livia*, with the recently retired Government minister and intellectual, Conor Cruise O'Brien. There was a good chance that I'd be granted such an interview since *Anna Livia* was vaguely in league with the Labour Party, of which The Cruiser was a member. Also they were totally in love with The Cruiser's remorselessly bitter war against the Provos; he argued in favour of locking up the lads without trial from a leftist perspective. And The Cruiser was vain and I was a happening hack.

"All you have to do is arrange to meet him someplace other than in his house. He has security on the house. He'll probably want to meet you in a pub somewhere. He likes a drink. You just have to meet him," explained Tuma, "and we'll do the rest."

"Meaning?" Though I knew what she meant.

"Why...we'll assassinate him. Proving that people like him can run but they cannot hide," she said, beads of sweat developing on her young forehead.

"What about me?" was my rather hangdog response, the universal response of all men to all situations. I had about as much time for O'Brien as Tuma had, and everyone knew he'd set himself up as a target with his outrageously outspoken stance. "What if you miss him and hit me?"

"You duck," Tuma said calmly, as if the very moment of violence was upon us. "Say, if the meeting is in a pub, you duck under the table. When you duck we'll take that as our signal and open fire."

THE FINAL QUESTION

An ageing glam rock star is being tried for downloading kiddie porn from the Internet. The Dublin government announces a six billion pound spending spree. Unheard-of generosity as recently as three years ago.

Dublin is plugged into twenty channels of TV junk but Dublin—when it gets right down to it—is totally unplugged. Leaves me nonplussed. They're not spoiled for choice in life but they're spoiled for choice in TV. Dublin was once a nice provincial backwater with a small community of working artists, a lot of failed artists, and lots of vagabond bullshit personality. Now the gossip is all about the sex lives of the boys in Boyzone. I left here in my prime when all my friends were twenty-whatever. I come back here "looking good for my age" and they're all cruising forty—they don't recognise me and I don't want to know them. There is tremendous money here, but where is it coming from and where is it going to?

From time to time I see some archetypal middle aged balding fellow staring resentfully at me on the street. Why is he staring?

I ask myself, and then I realise that he is one of my journalism readers from back in lost time.

One day last week there were two of these characters sitting at the next table to me. I was in Café En Seine having a hot whiskey to help me forget about the wind and the rain when I noticed them looking at me sideways, all frantic gestures and facial tics. They talked about me for ten minutes. I overheard one of them say to the other:

"He has stood the test of time rather well."

The same, I felt like quipping, could not be said of themselves.

The troublesome cancer of ideas has been excised from the Irish body. Catholicism, communism, republicanism, existentialism, they're all gone down the tubes to be replaced by the idea that there is nothing more important in life than money—the making of it and the spending of it. As with cancer, to cut out an idea you have to cut out most of the body flesh that holds it in place. You lose a lot of muscle when you lose an idea. Dublin lacks muscle.

But I'm here now—I'm the man I am now, not the cardboard cut-out I was then—therefore I have the TV and the central heating on all the time to protect me from a cosmopolis whose real poverty howls all around me; whose drug dealers will be shot on sight and whose child molesters will be molested without due process.

I sit now with my back to the TV, hunched over the computer writing an intro to *On The Run*. The book is ninety percent done, and with it my time back in Ireland.

Every biographer's problem is to ask: What is the Fair Question? Or perhaps even: What is the Final Question than can be asked about a man's attitude to the main task that he undertakes during his lifetime?

If this question expects too much of the victim of biography, then the biographer is being unfair to his subject. If the question asked expects too little, the biographer is being unfair to his reader. In either case the biographer will fail to locate the heart of his chosen man or woman.

Dan Breen used crude methods to achieve sophisticated ends. The democracy we enjoy in Ireland today is not a dubious one—for all its imperfections, this is a truly free country. My last book on Breen used the life's work of a sophisticated man to deliver a crude message—that there *were* some similarities between the aims and methodologies of the Old IRA and the Provos. This time I think I've gotten the balance right—I've kept politics out of it.

I don't think Breen would be terribly impressed by the achievements of Gerry Adams and his ageing Provos. History may well prove them to be no more than an opportunistic criminal gang interested in self-aggrandisement, drug running, protection rackets, punishment shootings.

The question is not whether it is legitimate to use violence to achieve political ends. Two World Wars, the Gulf War, the Kosovo War, were all deemed legitimate. The question about the Provo leaders is very simple—did they ever have any political agenda other than getting themselves into power?

I travel to Tipperary to investigate a substantial but unsubstantiated black rumour: a story that in 1920 thirty IRA Volunteers were executed by Breen's Third Tipperary Brigade during an internecine feud to control IRA arms in Munster. I find no proof that it is true. But then how would I? Everybody is dead and a secret army leaves scant documentation behind it.

I hear about one old man—he took the anti-Republican side in the civil war—who might throw some light on the rumour. When I ring him his wife answers the phone and exhaustedly says:

"Mr Crowe, Ger would be only too happy to talk to you. He loved Dan Breen and he enjoyed your book when it first came out. But he is lying on the flat of his back in the other room, now, dying of cancer. He's not going to make it through the night, Mr Crowe. So he can't talk to you. Ger would have loved to have talked to you but he can't. Please say a prayer for him, that he may be released from his suffering."

It's not Liston's fault that I wrote a mediocre book the first time round, or Rory's fault or Dan's fault. It's my fault. When the Final Question was put to me, I ignored it.

BLUES FOR NOTHING

When Bobby Sands lay dying in the last days of his hunger strike at the H Blocks in 1981, I was at the height of my powers as a Dublin journalist. I was getting articles published in two Sunday papers, three daily nationals, three magazines, and I was in and out of RTE five or six times a month. Work was drifting in from London and New York too; I'd done a fair bit of stuff for *Sounds* and I was just cracking *Rolling Stone*. I had some kind of professional status.

Rory phoned me to say that Tina'd been on the phone to him. She was now working for the Provo newspaper, *An Phoblacht*, and they were planning to publish a book of the Sands prison diary, written in microfilm-tiny block capitals on single sheets of toilet paper smuggled out of Long Kesh by wives and activists who were getting into Long Kesh on visits. Sands, recently elected an MP, could die at any moment, Rory said, and they planned to publish his diary the second he died. And could I write something about it if they got me an exclusive advance copy? I said I'd review it the day of his death for the *Irish Press*, the official Fianna Fáil organ owned by Dev and his American backers, its murky finances yet another alleged beneficiary of the great Russian Crown Jewels.

Rory was a bit ambivalent about the Hunger Strike. A sacrifice of good men, he reckoned, and a good way of getting rid of gung-ho radicals. He saw it as a Sinn Féin political strategy to mobilise a mass movement.

"Once you have a fucking mass movement," he said as he drove me out to Tina's place in Howth, "you have the fucking masses on your back and you're answerable to them. And all the masses ever really want is tight pussy, new shoes, and a warm place to shit. Suddenly your life has no meaning. You're destined to be the victim of opinion polls and editorials. Whereas once your revolutionary movement was young, tough, virile with a killer instinct."

I'd not met Tina since college days, and it was weird to drive down her same street after all those years, Rory a real IRA man, me the big shot journalist, Rory at the wheel of his own car, history being made. Music having changed beyond recognition. Myself having mutated so radically that I hardly discerned myself in the mirror.

Tina had changed very little. She was still a stocky, rough, Belfast diamond. Her home looked more prosperous and modern, like she'd started buying style magazines or had inherited a fortune. She didn't seem to listen to music much anymore, it was almost as if the same records lay in the same pile in front of the same stereo. Three German 'students' were staying with her, lithe longhaired blond giants who, Rory reckoned, were Red Brigade boys.

The sitting room, once neat enough and much like any young woman's sitting room, now overflowed with photocopies, pamphlets, files; the meat and potatoes of activist life.

"And, Liam, you can write it, now, for the *Irish Press*?" Tina asked anxiously and efficiently, handing me the uncut and unbound printed sheets of *The Prison Diaries*. I noted that the back cover blurb read: 'Bobby Sands gave his young life for the cause of Irish freedom.' As it turned out, poor Sands lived on for another week, his young strong body resisting martyrdom to the last.

"Yes, Tina," I assured her, for I was on top of my gig. "I've already spoken to the News Editor. It'll go in the day Bobby dies."

"About those German students…Tina's real job," Rory explained as he drove me back into town with my exclusive advance copy of the diaries in my bag, "is now to liaise with the international revolutionary community…whatever the fuck that is…a gang of head-the-ball hippies from Belgium or progressive governments like Libya or Cuba who fund us or give us weapons."

"So she's in charge of the new Russian Crown Jewels," I quipped.

"Exactly!" Rory laughed. "God, I'd forgotten all about the Russian Crown Jewels. Poor Pádraic. I still think about him."

"I think about him myself sometimes."

Various highly regarded Irish poets and authors are now credited with having written the Sands diaries but maybe he wrote them himself. Revolutionaries do have their own unique eloquence, like hustlers and farmers. When I started on *Against Tyrant's Might*, everybody assured me that Dan Breen was illiterate. In fact he was a writer of vigorous and elegant letters. So sharp and razor-like that they had to silence him with the accusation of illiteracy. British intelligence usually tries to present extremist Republicans as if they're rough-hewn or primitive. A bullet had shattered Breen's right hand during the Tan War. As a result the hand only operated like a claw. When he wrote he held his pen in a claw-like grasp; his penmanship was crude but vigorous.

In ancient Ireland when neighbouring landowners had a dispute the aggrieved party would take himself to the border between his own and his enemy's land. He would plonk himself down on that border and refuse to eat anything, go on hunger strike until either he died or the righteousness of his case was acknowledged by his enemy and his community. Bobby Sands, and the other young hunger strikers who died horrible deaths after him, caught the attention of their community. Out of that attention grew the mass movement which gave rise to the ascendancy of Gerry Adams.

Rory let me off in front of Trinity College because he had to go on somewhere else. He was all kind of dolled up, with a snazzy new black leather coat and an expensive looking hairdo. He said he was going to meet some pals from work but I knew he had no real pals at work—even if he was meeting such creatures there was no need to dress up for them—so I reckoned he was meeting up with a woman. I didn't really want to raise the topic as he remained pretty tight-lipped about sex matters. I knew of various liaisons, but copulation was still a blushing matter—or so I imagined.

I caught a taxi to Donnybrook, began reading the diaries in the taxi and finished them within an hour of getting home. It was a simple valedictory, painfully lucid and honest. About to be published for the edification of the masses, the diaries seemed to have been written for no particular purpose. Bobby Sands was just a poor Belfast kid who got caught up in the history of his own country. He was willing to starve himself to death because he was a righteous fundamentalist. My reaction to reading his journal was one of pity.

I stayed awake until five in the morning writing a party-line review. When I got up in the mid-afternoon I photocopied the review for Rory and delivered the original to the News Editor at the *Irish Press*.

The next few days were tense. Like the rest of the country my entire attention was focused on this young man dying slowly and voluntarily two hours north of the fleshpots of Dublin.

I got a letter during the week from Liston at Benbulben, terminating my contract for the McBride biography. I never quite worked out what the problem was, but it left Liston good and sore. Tom Flannery at Benbulben muttered something about McBride and Liston having had a blazing row which saw Liston badly hit below the water line.

Despite his handsome strong broad-shouldered man's body, martyrdom came Bobby Sands's way. Then I saw my part in turning him into a Republican saint take shape. Last thing before I went to bed one night I heard he'd slipped into a coma and was due to die at any moment. Waking at six thirty the following morning, my brain knew what the news was going to be. I turned on RTE radio and they were broadcasting It Says In The Papers.

Sands had died and about forty seconds after I turned on the transistor the presenter said:

"And in the *Irish Press* Liam Crowe writes that Bobby Sands's diaries are an honest and remarkably cogent valedictory which will be acclaimed in the annals of prison writing, comparable to the writings of Black Panther martyr George Jackson."

I didn't get out of the bed for an hour, but tossed and turned under the sheets, holding my head between my hands while the radio reported a country in trauma and on the verge of disintegration. I felt that I was in on the birth of something huge, something like the diabolic second coming Yeats wrote about in his poetry.

When I finally got organised I walked out to Morehampton Road and bought five copies of *The Irish Press*. There I was on page one, my first front page exclusive. Me and Bobby Sands.

Within weeks of his death anti-Republican graffiti around Dublin said:

WE'LL NEVER FORGET YOU, JIMMY SANDS.

WIRED TO THE MOON

It takes weeks to organise. First I get on to Dundrum and they say that if I want to go see Johnny Whelan I must first get permission from his mother.

So I ring the mother. A leathery old agricultural matriarch, Mrs Whelan continues to be broken hearted by the fact that

Johnny, her blue-eyed boy, grew up to be a murderous lunatic. Having obviously heard about my adult doings and not liking much of what she's heard, she is not anxious that I should get to visit Johnny.

But Johnny and me were good friends so my rationale for wanting to go see him, that we were old school pals and that I'd just love to see him, holds water. Rory was also kind of attached to Johnny.

Dundrum is a hospital for the criminally insane set behind high stone walls in a grim Dublin suburb, all Sixties malls full of young mothers psychoshopping.

Johnny was the best looking boy at St Fursey's. When I headed for Dublin to do Arts he went south to Cork to study Agriculture. His parents—big shots in West Waterford Catholic society—planned it so that he would be one of the new generation of Irish farmers. No more pigs in the parlour. (I speak metaphorically. Johnny's folks were rich educated people.) Johnny would guide his father's farm into the subvention-heaven of the EEC and then on into the new millennium. Before it all turned sour there were two Mercedes (one for Johnny, one for his father) and a Volvo (for the mother) in the farmyard.

This farm running fell completely onto the shoulders of the six foot blond athlete when his father keeled over unexpectedly from a heart attack. Johnny was twenty-four at the time, engaged to a Cork city girl and a player on the Waterford senior Gaelic Football team. He'd never experienced the type of freedom I knew. He went from school to college to responsibility.

I saw him from time to time in the early Eighties but he disappeared into farming while I disappeared into journalism, marriage and America, all in that order. Johnny got married too.

As the afternoon traffic loosens up and allows me to turn left into the hospital's gateway I'm playing a Thin Lizzy greatest hits tape, which is not Thin Lizzy at their angry best. A security guard, he can't be more than eighteen but his skin is creased and wrinkled unattractively, looks me up on a clipboard, looks me up and down, and asks to see some form of identification.

Who knows what sort of boy becomes a young man in uniform? This one points me in the direction of a visitor car park and the limestone building beyond it.

Nobody goes to Dundrum of their own choosing—it's like a jail but yet unlike one. Some of the inmates are more dangerous than anything you'd find in Soledad or San Quentin—they're the unhinged. Cases you read about in the papers. A boy who cut up his mother and put her in the freezer. A father who murdered his wife, mother-in-law, and three of his own children, then gave himself up to the Guards. Fellows who think they're Napoleon or Elvis.

Johnny gradually grew strange when he took control of the farm and got married. He got a farm manager about the same age as himself who'd grown up in a nearby cottage. Andy's father had worked for Johnny's father and on and on back into history.

One March morning in 1988, Andy was sterilising the milking equipment when Johnny walked calmly out of his house carrying a small hammer. Johnny was relaxed as he walked towards Andy, who had his back to him. When he came within striking distance he felled the farm manager with a single vicious blow to the head. As Andy was falling to the ground Johnny hit him twice more on the head, before walking calmly back into his house were he poured himself a cup of tea. Then he got into his Mercedes and drove to Youghal.

Johnny's mother, when she discovered Andy lying in a pool of blood, phoned for an ambulance and the Guards. Andy lived on for a while, sentient but slowly failing, providing the Guards with an accurate account of what had happened to him. When he died Johnny was charged with murder. Investigations found no rational reason for the murder. The two men had always been close pals. Ma cut out the court reports from *The Irish Times* and posted them to me. Johnny was declared insane and got sent to Dundrum for life. His wife took their two girls and moved back to Cork where she has a florist's shop.

I turn off Thin Lizzy, think how old fashioned Lizzy must sound to the security guard.

In 1975 myself and Badger McCarthy and Johnny Whelan and Johnny's best pal, John Quirke the School Captain, went to the Ritzy Café located on an ancient narrow laneway up behind Waterford's Protestant Cathedral. The Ritzy Café was as close as it came in Waterford to Frank Zappa's dictum that every town should have a place where phony hippies meet, a psychedelic dungeon growing up on every street. It had a variety of mini-skirted ageing hussies as waitresses. The juke box featured Brown Sugar by the Stones, Proud Mary by Creedence, and us local yokel's heroes, Thin Lizzy and Horslips. The girls served us powdered coffee or watery tea or baked beans or chips or hamburgers.

It was my last day at St Fursey's. I'd just done my final Leaving Cert exam—in History—and Ma was coming that evening to pick me up. Most of my close pals had already left for home. The younger ones—like Rory—had departed before the

Leaving Cert began. On that last day in the Ritzy I was surrounded by people who were not my usual crew. Johnny Whelan I was fond of, and I was glad that him and Rory'd become friends. Johnny and me shared a passion for the first driftage from rock'n'roll's monolithic bedenimed hold on youth's attention—Glam Rock. Johnny reckoned that the first Roxy Music album was one of the best rock albums ever made and that Too Much Too Soon was another one of them. I still agree with him. It is one of the topics I need to discuss with Johnny now.

I hated John Quirke, an athletic doctor's son from Dungarvan. The School Captaincy had usually been given to some Mammy's Boy under the thumb of Father Joe. In 1974 Badger McCarthy and Rory organised a lock out strike at St Fursey's, demanding democratic reforms. We locked out the teachers and staff, and occupied the classroom building. This got horrendous amounts of publicity in the national papers, and confirmed Joe's belief—which went back to the skinhead incident—that I was a regulation asshole.

As a result of the publicity we won the strike. One of the democratic reforms introduced was a student-elected school captaincy. The first election resulted in victory for Donal Brennan, the sexually dubious lead singer in St Fursey's only glam rock band. Donal got 168 votes. John Quirke, star of the Gaelic Football team, got 129 votes. Most of them from the backwoodsman-like West Waterford sons of rich farmers, who boasted amongst their number Johnny Whelan. Johnny was rough like them but he was both nice and smart, pretty to their simian.

So, much to my amusement, Donal Brennan was begrudgingly installed as School Captain with Quirke as his number two. A couple of weeks later Donal was caught with his arse up in the air in a cupboard and sent home. Quirke came into the captaincy, and Rory said to me:

"This is how democracy actually works. You see how nicely it seemed to have turned out? The queer was the School Captain with his Mick Jagger poster over his bed. But we end up with this vile…woeful…unelected Quirke in any case. While the queer is back in Kerry giving blowjobs to bachelor farmers."

As he stared at me across the table in the Ritzy, I knew that Quirke hated my guts, obviously saw me as dangerous. Badger McCarthy was more to my liking although he captained the football team. His father was manager of the Cork County team but Badger was—like me and Rory—busy being profoundly dysfunctional. A burly bull-necked zealot, Badger agreed with me and Rory on the North, was a big supporter of the PLO. While Badger was sound on all the important issues, he was never somebody that I was especially close to. I talked with him a hell of a lot but it was always about public matters. There was nothing interior about out friendship.

So we were oddly interconnected in the Ritzy. Quirke and Johnny connected to one another through the West Waterford confederacy. Quirke connected to Badger and Johnny through football. Me connected to both Badger and Johnny through Rory.

We ordered Cokes and chips and stuff. Everybody smoking cigarettes. This was a big deal.

"So what are you going to do next year, Crowe?" Quirke asked me condescendingly.

"I'm going to university in Dublin if I get enough points." I think the real idea was to go hang out in UCD for six months before heading to London.

"If you get enough points?" said Quirke, snorting like a horse. "You're not going to change the world then?"

"Fucking world will change itself. I just want to change myself." I laughed roughly. "And you, Quirke? What're you going to do?"

"Oh, I'm going to become a doctor."

"Just like your dad."

"Just like my dad."

Quirke did become a doctor. Now he is a very rich doctor living in Canada.

"And Johnny, what're you going to do?" I asked, turning my attention from the vulgar to the decent.

Johnny gave me a kind of backward country-boy look. You couldn't tell if he approved or disapproved of me. You couldn't tell if he was thinking about what he saw in front of his eyes or if he was thinking about another world entirely. After a few seconds that look disintegrated and he stared right at me, his face shaking with the intimacy of eye-to-eye contact. Johnny'd allowed himself to be fucked by four or five different— impressively masculine—lads in St Fursey's and this always surprised me. There was nothing passive about Johnny, a tough opponent when cornered. Yet when he stared at me that day while Brown Sugar gave way to Lola on the jukebox, all the experience of sodomy was on his face. His torso shook like he was enjoying at that moment an emotional experience of orgasmic proportions. He smiled at me in his contrary way, part farmer, part child of the universe.

"Crowe, what am I going to do? I just want to be left alone," said beautiful used Johnny.

I take Ma's cutting from a 1988 *Irish Times* out of a folder:

John Whelan, 28, of Mahonstown, Co. Waterford appeared in court to answer charges of murder and assault. Mr Whelan attacked and killed Mr Andrew Hackett, of the same address, farm manager on the Whelan family farm.

Mr Hackett, 27, was working in the farmyard when Mr Whelan attacked him with a domestic hammer, causing several wounds. Hackett subsequently died from his injuries. Mr Whelan then drove to the nearby town of Youghal where he was involved in an altercation with Martin and Philomena McGrath in Countess Markievicz Park about an hour later. Whelan pushed in the door of the McGrath's house and dragged fourteen year old Richard McGrath out of the house and assaulted him with a knuckle-duster.

Brian Flynn, defense attorney, said Mr Whelan, his client, was "wired to the moon" all through May, and totally "out of it." His client had spent the last eleven weeks in the Central Mental Hospital Dundrum. At the time of the offences his client had stopped the medication that was prescribed for him. Judge William Kelly said there seemed to be a history of the defendant failing to take his medicine.

Pointing my key at the hired car, I press it and all the doors lock in unison. The thought running through my head is that if only Johnny had broken free of redneck West Waterford, become a Seventies hippy or punk or something, things might have turned out different and special for him.

I'm waiting for Johnny in a smelly red nylon armchair in a tiny room furnished with three such chairs and a yellow formica-topped table. The walls are painted an institutional custard yellow. As least there's not a wire meshed fence and a warden waiting to listen in on every word we say, like in a Jimmy Cagney movie. Johnny, of course, is not a criminal in any real sense. He just killed somebody because he'd come unhinged.

Everything is very orderly in Dundrum. I'm hardly in the room three minutes when the door opens slowly and Johnny walks in, not at all how I expected him to be. For one thing he looks nothing like the forty or so years he now must be. He is still filmstar good looking, his lips still sensual and the upper lip still juts out over the lower one. His sea-blue eyes still arrest me and won't let go. There is silence. He nods at me shrewdly and, therefore, I nod back.

"Liam."

"Johnny!" I'm so pleased to see him looking so good that I stand up and embrace him. He recoils a little and I realise that all this embracing is a very American thing or, at least, a city thing. Johnny never lived in any kind of city except when he was locked up in St Fursey's (I think it was Victor Hugo who said that when you open the doors of a school you close the gates of a prison) and now while he's incarcerated in Dundrum.

I guess I expected him to be pot bellied and balding, his face gutted by lines of frustration and bafflement. I suppose I expected him to be wearing a shabby old institutional jumper and a pair of slacks. Of course I'd ignored his wealth, his good looks, his football athleticism. He wears a light grey top-of-the-range Nike sweatshirt showing off a muscular boyish torso, an ancient pair of Levi's and Nike Air Walk trainers, the type I wear myself back home. I can tell he works out—which is what the vain or smart ones end up doing in any prison—because his body combines adolescent thinness with a well-toned lurch.

While I'm looking at him he's looking at me. I know what I look like. When I'm home I work out every morning in a small gym about a mile from my street. I favour the same clothes as Johnny, casual sports gear. I look tough, tougher than I am. It strikes me that Johnny is intensely poised and self-aware. I wonder if he's having sex here in the prison. It looks that way.

After strained initial small talk it's just like twenty-five years ago.

"I read your book on the punk whores," he says laconically and, perhaps, sarcastically.

"Really? Where'd you get it?"

"I'm in charge of the library here. I saw a review of it somewhere so I ordered it up. Not bad. Why're you back in Ireland, Liam? I thought you'd escaped permanently."

"I'm rewriting my book on Dan Breen."

"Dan Breen? Hah!" Johnny laughs. "And you're not embarrassed to be doing something uncool like that?"

"In what sense uncool?"

"Oh, you know the way things are here now...they've solved their problem."

"That problem will never go away Johnny."

"No. Rory used to say that too. That the reason he liked the Irish problem was because it could never be solved. There'd never be a solution, just endless trouble."

"He never said that to me but it sure sounds like him."

"Oh, it was him alright," Johnny says like a tired old actor. "And how is the Irish soldier laddie? Is he still pumping iron and listening to Curtis Mayfield?"

"You must know about Rory, Johnny...he died a long time ago."

"Oh...yes...of course. He came to see me one time on the farm and it was so nice to see him. My wife whipped out a cream cake and ham and a bottle of...brandy...Hennessy. There was a change in the wind that day."

"When was that, Johnny?"

He doesn't respond to my question but stares at me, happily it seems. Johnny is still agile and sly but somehow distracted or confused. I assume he's on medication.

"When did Rory come to see you in Waterford, Johnny?

"He used to come at the weekends mostly. It didn't hurt too much and he enjoyed it."

"I mean…when did he come to see you on your farm when you were married?" I ask more specifically.

"Oh that. That was just a social visit."

In some ways Johnny is fine. In other ways he refuses to catch my drift.

"Rory wrote to me a few times and then one day he phoned to say he was in Cork and he had a car so could he call out. So I said to the wife Nora, an old school friend of mine is coming, could you make a plate of sandwiches or something? So Nora was delighted because I think she was a wee bit bored with farm life and with her lover man husband. I was never very good at that… and as you know yourself I'm not so big down below. The two girls were really poor Andy's girls. Nice girls. So up he comes in this kind of shabby old car which amazed me a bit because I expected him to have something better. But it was nice to see him anyway."

"When was it he came to see you Johnny?"

"Around the time, I remember it well actually, around the time Thin Lizzy broke up. I remember it because I wanted to go to Dublin to see the farewell concert but Nora said it was about time that I grew up."

Which was around the time Rory died, but I say nothing.

"Do you miss Rory, Liam?" he asks sadly. Childishly.

"Yeah. In ways. I left not too long after he died, '86, and in America you tend to forget your past…which is why I went to America. Not specifically to get rid of Rory but to get rid of the whole fucking place."

"I know what you mean." Johnny smirks and looks around the visiting room. He looks into my eyes, unembarrassed by where life has brought him, perhaps showing a little pride. "Also, Liam, I think you needed to leave Ireland in order to write anything interesting about rock music."

"Yes. I always thought that." I smile. "Rock music…which in many ways is almost dead now. The music we talked about in the Ritzy like…"

"The first Roxy Music album, Liam! The first fucking Roxy Music album. It *was* too much too soon," Johnny laughs, like I'm making him feel better. "But that kind of rock'n'roll…"

"Insightful rock'n'roll that amounts to art rather than entertainment," I break in.

"Yeah, Liam, yeah…that kind of thing." Johnny almost whispers, "I hope I'm not making you nervous, Liam."

"Maybe just a little, Johnny." I can't help laughing. Johnny was always disarmingly frank.

"Don't worry about it." He leans over to squeeze my shoulder. "I'm just as nervous as you are."

He hasn't had this kind of conversation for a long time. But, then, neither have I.

"I can't hear what I'd like to hear in here but I still love the capacity of the music. I have a pile of tapes and some people send me tapes. Badger sends me tapes every month."

"Badger?" I'm surprised to hear his name. "You still hear from

Badger? Do you want me to send you tapes, Johnny?"

"Yes, send me tapes please. I need to get out of here."

"Any chance?"

"Yeah. I've been a good boy. I think they'll let me out sometime. Not too late." He gets up and walks towards the door. "Not too late for anything. I've been twisted all my life. Some part of me. The way I let people like you and Rory dick me…"

"I never fucked you, Johnny. You know I didn't. Rory never touched you either."

"Yeah, sure, Liam," Johnny smiles as he makes to go, like he's just humouring me and I'm the mad one, "I was just getting into my self-pitying routine. Send me a copy of the new Breen book when it comes out. But the tapes the most, Liam, send me the tapes…and what about the last Roxy Music album? What about that? That was a whole other story! Too little too late."

He waves dismissively, sighs and says nothing more, just disappears, pulling the door closed behind him.

NIHILISM

Real IRA activity smashed the fragile eggshell boy inside Rory. It was not the way that he'd expected it to be.

He had been a blue jeans and black leather jacket boy of our time, the Seventies, who went underground to sublimate himself. Gone were the days when he could casually listen to funk music or discuss the American Indian situation with passing strangers. Gone too were the days when he didn't shave and let his unkempt hair fall all over his angry red face. He got a short back and sides, bought Hush Puppies, and dressed casual. He looked strikingly movie star-ish, like Warren Beatty, in his new conservative mode but he didn't look happy and he was certainly not having the sort of life that he had envisaged for himself. He wanted to move to Belfast to fight the English head-on, see his enemy face to face in the rain, but shadowy grey eminencies within the Provo command structure decided he should cool his heels in Dublin and concentrate on bank robberies.

"So I end up," he said on one of our dark drinking nights, laughing but not amused, "going to some shithole fifty miles outside Dublin where we pull balaclavas over our heads, grab the sawn offs, and head into the local Bank of Ireland. When we get inside we scream at the staff until they're all in a state of abject terror. I end up frightening the shit out of some potential heart attack victim bank manager who starts opening and shutting his mouth involuntarily like a fucking fish out of water. I don't want to be fighting these stupid cunts, I want to be taking on the Brits as an equal—a soldier."

"Dirty work but somebody's got to do it," I smartass quipped.

"Not really. Not really," he said, getting serious. "Somebody doesn't have to do it. They get plenty money from America. They don't fucking need somebody with my physical skills and training to do suburban bank jobs for them. Anyone could do it: you just walk in there and intimidate some bald fuck who hands over thousands of pounds to you. That eejit, who may well be a class enemy and a representative of capitalism, is not really my enemy, now is he?"

"In a way he is, and certainly the banks are the enemy," I said, every inch the cool cat in my ragged jeans.

I'd just delivered the finished manuscript of *Tyrant's Might* to

Benbulben. I'd spent the night with Square from Delaware and the morning reading a copy of Kerouac's *Desolation Angels*, so I was in careless form. I was skin and bone and smelly.

Three weeks later I got a detailed handwritten missive from Liston with his suggestions for editorial changes to *Tyrant's Might*, which had now been typeset and was nearly ready to print. Most of the changes were pretty legitimate and anyway I was happy enough to go along with the old boy.

The one big difference between myself and Liston concerned an incident in 1920 when Breen, along with Seán Treacy, shot five English soldiers during an attack on a Tipperary barracks. That night the Brigade held an all night party in the big farmhouse of one of their more prosperous supporters. The same night the Black and Tans, by way of dark revenge, burned about a hundred homesteads across South Tipperary.

One eighteen year old boy was arrested and taken to Tipperary Barracks. When his mother called at the gates of the barracks the following morning she was told her son would be back with her that afternoon. He was. Six hours later they sent him back in a coffin.

I made some remark in my text to the effect that Breen and his gang partied while the "people" in whose name their actions were taken paid a horrific price.

Liston scrawled on the back of one of the photocopied proof pages:

> This personalised commentary, Liam, has no place in a biography of
> this kind, whose ultimate purpose is to celebrate the heroic deeds of
> those founding fathers of our country, to inspire the young to follow
> in their footsteps. Please phone me about this.

When I eventually tracked him down on the phone back home in Galway he was more forthright.

"This sort of attitude is no help whatsoever to the lads, Liam, no bloody help whatsoever. It only makes the lads look bad. Ach! No! No! No!"

While this little disagreement festered I was harbouring one of "the lads" in my home. Tim O'Connor was someone that I knew from my old Medieval Studies group at UCD. A short ratty little Charlie Chaplin dude with a calm reassuring manner, Tim was modest about his serious academic skills; while we were at college he had made a special study of the Cathar and Albigensian heresies. Now he was active in the Irish Republican Socialist Party and, more to the point, in the military wing of that organisation, the Irish National Liberation Army, or INLA.

A Socialist Republican breakaway from the IRA inspired by the thinking of socialist 1916 martyr James Connolly, the INLA acquired a well deserved psychopathic reputation due to the internecine bloodletting that characterised the organisation in its prime. Through Tim, I got to meet the INLA's charismatic founder, a redfaced puritan called Séamus Costello who was a brilliant political and military organiser. Costello was eventually shot through the head at close range, obviously by somebody he trusted: at the crack of dawn on the North Dublin docks he allowed his killer to get in close.

Tim was a serious member of an INLA cell active in Belfield. The big boss of the cell, known as The Nihilist, was a smelly (unwashed, drinking, farting) overweight character who usually lugged around in grey cardigans and food-stained slacks. He was involved in organising anti-heroin vigilante patrols in Dun Laoighre, the middle class south Dublin suburb where he and

Tim lived. The Nihilist's motives were suspect. I think he got involved in covert political milieus to sublimate his sexuality and to enforce a sexual agenda on his comrades. Tim, by way of contrast, was your typical rosy cheeked picture-of-health paramilitary lad; lean, shortish, with tight-cropped black hair and a fuel-injection intellect. We shared a real interest in medieval history, and also in dope smoking and the Rolling Stones.

Tim often crashed in Donnybrook, always welcome, long before he fell foul of The Nihilist. He'd play my twenty-six solo albums by various members of the Velvet Underground while telling me wild but plausible tales from within the uneasy ranks of the INLA. The day me and Liston were shouting on the phone about what I was calling censorship and he was calling 'the larger truth', Tim was asleep in my spare room, three days on the run from The Nihilist who was threatening to kill him because he refused to stop smoking dope. It was a serious threat.

The third day Tim holed up with me, I was away from home most of the morning. When I got back to Donnybrook in the early afternoon I bumped into Dee in front of the post office, shoving a bunch of letters into a letterbox.

"Oh, hi," she said all pleased to see me, "I thought you said you were going to be up town working. Otherwise I'd have called around to see you."

"Yeah, well, I was up town. I had to interview this fuck...this loser who made a fifty thousand pound movie about being on the dole."

"I just met The Nihilist two minutes ago," she gasped. "He was kind of acting all weird hiding in a doorway in broad daylight with this huge overcoat on him. All of a sudden he flung back the coat—I thought he was going to expose himself—and he whipped out this sawn-off shotgun from beneath the coat! I nearly shat myself. He wanted to know if I'd seen any sign of that pal of yours, the IRSP kid? Jim?'

"Tim. His name is Tim," I replied. "Listen Dee, I got to go right away. Tim is hiding out with me. Hiding from The Nihilist. I've got to go."

I gave her a peck on the cheek and went to a phone booth about ten yards away where I phoned my flat to warn Tim.

"Don't step out of the house under any circumstances. The Nihilist can't be more than ten minutes from here," I said.

"Don't come near the place yourself," Tim replied. "He could be watching you right this minute. I'm going to fuck off right away."

Later that year, The Nihilist had his hands nailed to the floor of a Dun Laoighre council flat before being bludgeoned and hacked to death with a hammer and a hatchet. He was twenty-four when he died and I was twenty-three. I went to his funeral with Dee although our sympathies were entirely with his assassins. His death was criminally connected, and had little to do with any political business.

I've never seen or heard of my friend Tim since. I know he had a plan to go live in Holland—he had a fair bit of money put away for that purpose. He said he'd be gone when I got home, that he'd phone me later. Presumably he got to Holland and... whatever.

THE STUPEFACTION OF THE BOURGEOISIE

"I feel like a priest at a pornographic movie," I say to Dee on the phone. We've not spoken for weeks.

She is still a good person; more interesting in ways because the years have been most complex for her. After UCD she became a full-time Trotskyist activist until she moved to America with me. She was on the wing of People's Voice which believed that the Fourth International should throw its substantial intellectual might behind the campaign of the Provos, who were drifting leftwards in the late Seventies.

Our marriage was the end of our friendship rather than the beginning of it. When our daughter Rosa was born we both resented her presence and this self-centredness prized us open and away. Dee worked in women's studies until her father died, the Rathmines family home was sold, and she got a load of money dumped into her lap. With the money she bought a shop in San Francisco where she runs a radical bookshop. Kids have meetings there in the evenings. Anarchists with skateboards. Sometimes I drop in for these meetings and afterwards go eat with Dee and Rosa in their apartment upstairs. But I don't do this too often and can't pretend that I'm a good or diligent father. Dee and me are fine on the phone, uncomfortable when we're face-to-face. I'm always wary with Rosa and she, smart like both her parents, sees this for what it is—indifference.

Dee puts me on the phone to Rosa, who is now thirteen, pretty like her mother and resentful as hell. There's not a lot of positive energy going around in this old family unit experiment. I guess I blew it.

"Dad…" (She calls me 'Dad' reluctantly. I know how she feels; my own father never had much to do with my life.) "Why do anarchists drink herbal tea?"

"I don't know." I'm happy enough that she wants to share a joke with me. "Why *do* anarchists drink herbal tea?"

"Because proper tea is theft."

"Ha! Ha! Ha!"

Rosa passes me back to Dee, not before saying she demands I bring her back some underground Irish vinyl. In this regard, she is my kid. She is an American girl.

"So how goes it with Dan Breen?" asks Dee cynically when she regains the phone. She knows me too damn well not to be intrigued by the fact that I'm going through my back pages.

"Very interesting thing to be doing," I say to her. "Very interesting time to be here too. I hate it. I hate the conceited indifference. I hate this fucking surrender by the Provos."

"Well." I can hear Dee lighting a joint and taking the first puff. In her background I can hear Hole playing; Rosa. "I agree with you that it's a surrender...their leadership has grown old and wants home comforts...but the two of us deserted the place ages ago so I guess we don't really have a vote. Neither are we as expert on the situation as we once were."

"I know this. It's a strange strange feeling...Carly Simon singing Happy Birthday for fucking Adams!" I pause.

"You used to fancy Carly Simon."

"Cock sucking lips." I mimic my student self.

"You remember that old graffiti in the Arts Block in Belfield? *Political parties will come and go but the Provos go on forever.*"

"Huh," I grunt unhappily.

"Huh indeed."

"Also, because of both the Breen book and the Provo thing, I've been thinking about Rory a lot."

"Hardly surprising," she says. She was never a big fan of his. "Did you know he chatted me up one time?"

"Rory?" I murmur. "Really? Sure you're not imagining it? Rory?"

"Yeah, of course I'm not imagining it. Anyway, I think he was kind of in love with you."

I say nothing, laugh to myself. She likes to poke.

"Ah," I explain eventually, "by the time you met him the guy's whole life was turning to shit. I don't think he knew if he was coming or going."

"So you won't be moving back to Dublin then?" She is bored with the Rory subject.

"Oh, God, you sure fucking know why you left, that's all I can say. You let your feet touch the ground and you know why you left," I tell her. "The horrible thought I have about them is not that they keep their deeper feelings hidden, but that these are their deeper feelings."

"What do you think?" I asked Rory on the phone three days after giving him his copy of *Tyrant's Might*. In the end I gave in to Liston, and the book was published with all criticisms of the lads excised. Benbulben sent me six free copies. One each for Dee, my mother, my father, Rory. I still have the other two, plus one I stole out of a library and one a pal bought me in a charity shop.

"Well," he said laughing, "I think you'd have written a much better book if you'd stuck to your guns and included the criticism of the activities of the IRA in South Tipperary which led to the people being terrorised by the Brits. This kind of compromise is hardly going to lead to the stupefaction of the bourgeoisie, now is it? We don't help the revolution by making ourselves and the past generations look like great fellows. That generation of IRA were politically primitive. They didn't fully understand their duties to the people they were claiming to liberate. So they danced and partied while the homes of the working classes were burned to the ground."

"You can't make an omelette without breaking eggs," I said, playing the devil's advocate because in fact I agreed with him.

"Yeah. But we're meant to be Republicans. Which doesn't mean that we're dedicated to a 32 county democratic republic like some would have you believe. It means we're answerable to the people. We serve the people, their betterment, their liberation...them that works the hardest are the least provided. They're not stage props for our egotistical, macho..."

"But...my book?" I interrupted him anxiously.

"Oh, your book is fine. Except for the cover. I'm proud of you. You've written a good book. Now you should write no more books about other people and write about yourself and the world as you see it," said Rory, his tough unsentimental voice full of complex intelligence and simple affection.

The following night we caught a late night Bruce Lee double bill at the Stella Cinema in Rathmines, and went back to Rory's place afterwards to eat something. I didn't get to see him at home very much because he was never there. He worked all day and stayed on the move—with one thing or another—in the evenings. The flat was nice. He had good money from the job and maintained a pretty smart lifestyle. He bought about fifty Nina Simone albums, lava lamps, books when they came out in hardback.

"I think we should stop using your place, Liam. What do you

think?" Rory asked when we'd eaten. Chinese takeaways. His favourite.

"I guess so. I'm indifferent really. It might be an idea to take a break or something."

Two weeks later the bag of guns disappeared and my spare set of keys was left on my kitchen table along with Rory's old copy of Guerrilla War by Che, and £100 in crisp new notes. I was a little lonely for the guns but, on the other hand, relieved that I'd successfully served Ireland without paying a price.

Rory's revolutionary fervour, his purity of purpose, his austere radicalism, all these pillars and many more were about to be rocked by that most counter-revolutionary of all forces, that which festers in the groin, grows between the sheets under the cover of darkness, and twists the minds of men and women most bitterly.

Did Rory fall in love? Or am I just imagining it?

The wind began to howl.

Look what the wind just blew in.

PART 3

ON **ANOTHER MAN'S** WOUND

BUT COME YE BACK WHEN SUMMER'S IN THE MEADOW?

I always admired the Lisney building on Stephen's Green, which gave a suave sophistication to Dublin's most genteel square at a time when the city was far from suave, little more than a redneck provincial backwater. So when Anja the anarchist suggests that we meet in front of Lisney's I'm dazzled by her good taste which is just fine by me.

"I'll see you two thirty in front of Lisney's, the property people," she states on the phone with no touch of irony. I can hear Iggy Pop singing The Passenger in her background. She works for TVME, an independent production company specialising in cheapo no-presenter chart shows for Irish and European stations. Dublin is all agog, at the moment, with Iggy, Jagger, Puff Daddy, five thousand boy bands, and Mariah Carey, all in town for the MTV Awards tonight. I'm due to attend so I can be interviewed about the ritual by CNN afterwards.

Two thirty I'm standing obediently across the road from Lisney's staring at their fancy building, wondering what goes on in the upper floors behind the naff curtains that contrast brutally with the austere and rigid lines of a superficially modernist five-story complex.

I can't say I'm entirely comfortable about meeting this Anja,

155

though she looks good on paper. My rusty connection on her is an old revolutionary confidante, but how can I trust anyone from the old days now? Nevertheless there she is at two thirty-five walking through the doors of Lisney's the property people. A good looking blonde in her early forties, shortish, wearing common-as-shit Versace sunglasses and a baggy tweed suit that looks like she picked it up in a charity shop, albeit a somewhat superior charity shop. She clasps three property files in her left hand and clamps a Nike shoulder bag under her right arm. Her head rotates left to right and back again like a security camera while she rams her files into her bag. She spots me negotiating my way through the traffic, and waves enthusiastically like we're old lovers. My connection gave me a Polaroid of her and vice versa. My connection is anxious that me and Anja should meet. My connection, handing Anja's Polaroid to me, said: "Liam, this bitch is what you used to call a heavy trip on the brain but you know fuck all about what's happening in your own country and you owe it to yourself to meet the likes of Frau Anja."

There's some truth in this.

Soon I'm dodging cars with this sexy German woman determined to smash this sorry scheme of things entire and then remould it closer to her heart's desire.

Her Sam & Libby shoes, ingenue hairdo and sunglasses betray her comparative affluence. The dodgy suit may be some class of zany disguise, designed to throw somebody (me? Lisneys? the Guards?) off her trail.

There are pleasantries as we walk towards a taxi rank on the west side of the Green.

"We go to my place to talk," she says. "When I came here first I could cycle all over town but you can't do that now."

"When'd you come to Dublin?"

"1976. I was just a girl…involved with the Red Brigades back home. I'd done some minor terrorism—they didn't trust me with anything too serious—but I was mistress to a senior member of the gang when I was sixteen and he was forty-one…I was sent here to liaise with left leaning comrades within the Provos."

Her accent an interesting mixture of singsong Berlin and rough-as-sandpaper Dublin.

"This mission proved more difficult than you might imagine…at first at least. I got a job doing the cloakroom at McGonagles when it was a punk venue and this guy who sometimes played folk music with Phil Lynott came in one night and chatted me up, so I fell into those circles, playing soccer with Lynott and the boys out in Howth, a little low level dealing, going on the road with Thin Lizzy selling t-shirts and posters. After two years I sort of got my act together and managed to contact INLA guys, who were easier to locate…"

"Right. I know what you mean." I grin.

"Yeah. And I took it from there."

She grins back at me. I reckon we're going to fuck later.

"I think I know your face from way back then," she says.

"Probably. I think I could have met you at a party in the Libyan Centre or on a protest or something like that, " I suggest.

"Were you involved in Gays Against Imperialism?" she asks.

Her way of asking if I'm a fag. San Francisco and all that…

"No. No." I laugh. "But I remember that recherché little organisation. They used to meet in Trinity, right? My onetime wife was involved in setting it up. It was really like a Trot front and she was a pretty senior Trot."

My way of saying I'm straight.

"Yeah. I was involved too, through the women's movement."

In case I was in any doubt: 'I'm no dyke'.

Later we will fuck.

So it's all Commie rock'n'roll nostalgia all the way to the taxi rank, all the way to Memphis. Talk of a house off Leeson Street in the Seventies inhabited by Angry Brigade refugees from England and Luke Kelly from The Dubliners and a few agreeable drug dealers…that radical Catholic mansion in Rathmines run by the Jesuits where Daniel Berrigan hung out and the anti-nuclear movement did its photocopying…the night the Hirschfeld Centre got burned down…how when they opened Phil Lynott up in the hospital to see what was wrong with him they found his intestines already rotting so they just sowed him up again and waited for him to die. I never heard that one before!

She clams up once we get into the taxi and orders the driver to take us to Monkstown.

"What were you doing in Lisney's the property people?" I enquire gingerly.

"Looking for properties, of course," she snaps.

"Oh, right, I get it…we've had neo-liberalism so now we've got neo-anarchism."

This causes her to frown at my indiscretion, checking out our driver to see if he's heard me. But he's too caught up in listening to his tape of The Irish Tenors. I take the opportunity to mend my fences and change the subject.

"One of those guys," I say pointing at the tapedeck, "went to school with me."

"Oh yeah?" she is mildly interested. "I've just been editing this godawful in-concert video of them. Which one d'you go to school with?"

"The fat one with no legs."

"They're all fat and they all have legs."

Now the driver is not only listening to us, but eager to join in on the conversation.

"Yeah, well," I tell her, "the fattest of them went to school with me. His legs were totally gammy when he was a kid due to some birth defect so he had them cut off from the knees down when he reached adulthood and now he has prophylactics or whatever you call them."

"Prostheses," chimes in the driver, seeing his opening at last. "Me own wife has a prosthesis. An arm."

Anja lives on the top floor of a Georgian terraced house which looks out over Dublin Bay from the Southside, about five doors down from a place I used to go twenty years ago to score dope. Monkstown was a toney part of town then and even nicer now. Media people like Anja, a Def Leppard soundman who lives directly under her, a dude from a boy band who lives with his boyfriend next door to where I used to score.

Her two thousand CDs are the most cluttered thing about her bright white smart immaculate home. The pad involves a tiny bathroom and two huge adjoining rooms; a bedroom and a living room with kitchen utilities systematically organised against one wall. The living room furniture (two armchairs, a deal table, two Sixties kitchen chairs, student-style bookshelves constructed from concrete blocks and random planks) is mainly handmade by her boyfriend who, she tells me, will be joining us later.

The bedroom is different; an early Habitat chest of drawers with most of the drawers ajar, items of men's and women's clothing tumbling out, an ancient whorehouse-style brass bed complete with feather pillows and feather duvet, a Victorian piss pot (which sees active service) and four or five cyberpunk paperbacks strewn around the floor.

A Jack Yeats watercolour hangs on the living room wall, along with a massive poster for a recent Joseph Beuys show at the Museum of Modern Art in Kilmainham. She presses Play on her CD player and a Royal Trux CD already in the machine snaps into life. Evil but good music.

"The Yeats must have set you back a bit," I say, squinting to admire the thing.

"Oh, yeah," she involuntarily apes my wince, staring at the painting herself. "Stolen. Stolen about eight years ago during a raid on the home of one of the Guinness heirs. Coffee?"

"Yeah, please. You like Beuys?"

"Yes. I do. You like girls?"

"Yes."

"I used to meet Beuys when he'd come over here. The irony of his show being on in Kilmainham is that he was very involved in a little scheme to turn that building into a European cultural centre…" Her talk tapers off like she has fond memories of the artist, is thinking about the fact that he is now dead.

She busies herself for five minutes setting up the coffee while I go inspect the bookshelves. A lot of non-fiction and political stuff in German. More crap women's fiction than you might have expected…Maeve Binchey…Danielle Steel…Patricia Cornwell. The regulation selection of intelligent detective writing; Ellroy, Chandler, Highsmith. More cyberpunk.

I pull out an anthology of new Irish poetry and go sit in one of the boyfriend's armchairs. I get absorbed in the poetry and don't notice that she has disappeared into the bedroom. By the time I look up to see her she is pulling a computer case from under the bed. It's kind of mid-range flashy with a silver surface.

"Oh, shit," I sigh, "now you're going to show me all your poems and ask me how you can get them published."

"Ha. Ha," she says dryly. She has a sense of humour but it exists within well protected borders. "You like the case?"

"It's a nice case." Her question is just about as stupid as a similar question I've been asked by at least three different women: 'You like my tits?'

"A Zero Halliburton. Made from aerospace quality aluminium. I picked it up last month from Minimum on Stephen's Green. You should go there."

For a moment I think she has confused me with somebody else but I'm gradually getting the picture. Anarchist or whatever she is, this bitch is into her consumer durables.

She places the case on the table and summons me to come join her. She does the combination fast and flips the lid open. Inside are half a dozen of the nicest combat handguns I've ever seen in one place at one time.

"I got some Australian Lithgows too. Plus half a dozen Mitchell High Standards," she brags like a buff dude showing off his pecs.

I stare at her equivocally and nod calmly before examining the contents of the case: a Colt 45, a SIG-Sauer, a Fifties Browning Hi Power, a Glock 19, a Glock 20. I lift out a beautiful Smith & Wesson Sigma polymer-frame handgun. She nods approvingly like I've just chosen a fine wine.

"That one burps a bit," she says lovingly, pointing at the Sigma.

Royal Trux are howling about juicy juicy juice as the front door opens and in walks her boyfriend, a nineteen year old Irish kid called Ryan Lacken.

Ryan is a funny little guy that I like straight away; he has a winning way about him. He wears a silver silk suit which also looks second hand. Maybe they have a fetish about hand-me-downs or maybe this is their concession to anarchism. He glances at the guns and begins small talking to me. The MTV Awards comes up in conversation, the whole fucking town is talking about little else. I mention that I have a spare ticket and does he want to come with me. Anja is taken aback by this, which is my intention.

"I've always wanted to see Iggy," Ryan says laconically, walking into the bedroom where he gets undressed, revealing, first, white Calvin Klein jocks and, then, an Iggy-like cock that slaps against his thighs as he makes his way back through the living room and into the bathroom where he proceeds to shower himself with the door open.

Anja is watching me watching him. I form the distinct impression that she has heard from somebody that I'm queer. In my mind and my trousers I've already formulated a plan for putting her right on that score.

Which is what happens next. Royal Trux comes to an end and she murmurs to me: "Your turn to choose the music now."

I walk over to the disorganised piles of CDs and rummage. Picking music proves to be a big task but in the end I choose One Foot In The Grave, early Beck recordings I've not heard. They own lots of music, but not a whole lot that I want to listen to. I'm not into recent English rock bands like Stereophonics and Radiohead, but these two are into little else. Or maybe it's just that she is media people and this shit is her work. I don't know. I'm not getting any sense of direction from these people. Why am I here? This is supposed to be a meeting towards the writing of an article on the Irish paramilitary/subterranean underground for *Spin* magazine, and it's looking more and more like the makings of a colour spread for *Vogue* or, alternatively, something for *Guns & Ammo*. But anyway.

Ryan Lacken returns to us, drying himself with a big hotel towel. Also, presumably, stolen. Anja goes over to the bookshelves and picks up a designer condom box that she describes as an Alessi Cohndom Box designed by Susan Cohn.

"This one is made of a thermoplastic resin but you can also pick them up in stainless steel."

"Is this from Minimum on Stephen's Green too?" I say.

"Yeah. Exactly. Let's fuck."

All three of us hop onto the big brass bed which squeaks and grinds while we hump away merrily until I say it's time for me to catch a taxi to the Point. Ryan snaps out of a frenzy of sexual bliss and says there's no need for a taxi, he has a car out front. Us guys shower together, get dressed, and head downstairs. Anja is taking her shower as we leave. I don't make any plans for further meetings. Outside it is dark and cold but an Opel Omega, the sort of executive car that makes me totally uncomfortable, awaits us. Crossing the Liffey by Butt bridge, we're at the Point in twenty minutes. Most of the conversation along the way concerns Anja's tits, which I really enjoyed burying my face in.

"Hmm," Ryan laughs, "tits come and tits go but Anja is a remarkable lady."

"Tits may come and go but Anja goes on forever. Right?"

"Right," he chuckles knowingly. We both chuckle knowingly.

"How'd you meet her?"

"Well, as you know, we're both members of Cognitive Dissidents," he begins.

I didn't know this. I knew they were both in an anarchist terrorist group, but I'd been naive enough to imagine that that aspect of them, at least, was serious.

"We were in the same cell. My old man is a really rich architect—he owns our pad—and all the women in my family, going back three generations, are sculptors. My old man is on the far right, we had a dog called Himmler when I was growing up."

"So Dad is on one lunatic fringe and you're on the other."

"Exactly." Ryan laughs good naturedly. "And don't bother telling me about too far left being right and shit like that. Anja laid that on me when we first met. Her folks are screwed up and busted. Her old man is a dealer and her mother is this Jewish actress. A real old woman now, but still beautiful. Nice tits just like Anja."

We have trouble getting the laminates which let us into the Awards but it works out in the end. Some prick from a boy band introduces Iggy, saying "I hope *I* look this good when I'm seventy." Jagger introduces Bono, laying down some bullshit about how the fat boy still walks the streets of Dublin.

"Only the ones that he owns," chortles Ryan.

Afterwards there are five hundred different parties to go to. Choose one. I choose the one where Iggy is playing, at least I'll know the songs, and I get talking to Iggy's manager who is this smooth customer in a blazer, wary and deferential since he knows I'm on CNN later. But he tells me he used to work for the Stones, so we arrange to meet the following day to talk about Mannish Boy. The fat boy is up in the balcony with Jagger.

At midnight Ryan Lacken drives me to RTE to do my CNN thing, offers to blow me in the RTE car park, and goes home with me afterwards to drink lots of coffee and talk politics. It makes me really uptight when guys want to have sex with me but Ryan is both pleasant and sharp. Rare qualities in the new Dublin.

"That money you're spending on your lifestyle," I say to him with coke-derived Dutch courage, "should be distributed to the poor. If you guys were real anarchists you'd be a little bit more concerned about the lot of the poor and the disenfranchised, a little less proud of your fucking digital rubbers, or whatever they are. I can't write anything about you people...I've dialled a wrong number here. Did you really meet in a revolutionary cell or through a dating agency on the Net?"

Ryan is a good person. I see his type a lot in California. Anja is downright nasty and I suspect she's a CIA spy or something. She never once discussed politics with me. At least Ryan talked about that stuff until five thirty, when he headed for home, and he took it on the chin when I criticised his behaviour.

THE RESERVATION INDIAN

The world was getting nasty and modern. The thing I remember most clearly from 1982 is an article I wrote on a new phenomenon—the video nasty. My first video nasty was Nightmare In A Damaged Brain.

I don't recall the exact sequence of events with the clarity that informs my other recollections of Rory. What did I hear first? Was I happy or was I sad? How long after I stopped providing a safe house did the bad times begin? What are good times? I can't imagine that I was happy about it all because it was a crock of shit. Married women in towerblocks are a life experience I've kept far away from my own front door. Maybe that's why I never became a real writer.

I don't know how he came into contact with such a creature. Maybe it was via that damp murky world where Dublin criminals mix with Dublin Provos. Maybe it was through his day job, perhaps she cleaned the floors in his office. Maybe it was through drinking. I suspect it may have been through drinking.

The covert life of the dedicated revolutionary was grinding him down. I was the only one that he could talk to about what he was actually doing in his life. He only met the other Volunteers immediately before jobs, either at my flat or at other safe houses. He explained that he'd get to Donnybrook first and let himself in. The other guys, a pleasant enough crew who had nothing in common with Rory other than the obvious, would arrive separately over the next hour. They'd drive to the out-of-town bank or post office they were ordered to rob, do the robbery, and drive right back to the safe house. Rory would pick up takeaways and beers from the Chinese restaurant around the corner from my flat. Conversation would centre on post mortems of their robbery, what they'd read in the papers that day. Then they'd all go their separate ways. One of them would bring the money to a quartermaster later the same day. The comradeship of his rookie period, heroic male-bonding training sessions up the mountains, was a thing of the past.

He got pissed off with his work at the oil company. Being the surface regular guy lost its surface charm. He couldn't yap on about brave warriors like Cochise (who said: 'I was going around the world with the clouds and air, when God spoke to my thoughts and told me to come in here and be at peace with all') or Sitting Bull ('God made me an Indian, but not a reservation

166

Indian') favoured topics of one-sided but entertaining rants directed at me back in the old days, for fear of convincing his fellow employees that he was completely bonkers.

Rory'd enjoyed work at first; it was a sort of Zen joke with him and, also, he was taking home good money. He even got to fuck a few of the secretaries after office parties. A strong well built young man in his prime, he must have been desirable enough except for that coiled-serpent aspect of his personality. He sat there in the middle of the mediocrity of them all, his muscle-bound body hidden in a cardigan and slacks while, out in the world, his contemporaries were wearing bondage gear, Sex Pistols teeshirts, and putting theoretical anarchy into practice.

Maybe Una's husband drove one of the oil trucks. Rory's job involved assigning all the trucks delivering fuel to the four corners of Ireland. Wherever she came from, the craziness was never her fault, although almost everything else was. Craziness runs in families, in this case it came through a poisoned stream running from his mother into him and there wasn't a whole lot that anybody could do about it. Rory didn't grow old, he was always a boy at heart, but he grew weary of endurance as a lifestyle.

I don't think I was properly focused on the fact that the shit was going to hit the fan until the shit had already hit the fan.

Out there in cold rainy Dublin amid the ballad singers and the awful blues bands, Rory met a woman called Una. He was twenty-one and she was a bit older. She lived in one of the seven Ballymun high rises, famous for the fungus growing on the walls of the flats, the dripping wallpaper, and the fact that the inhabitants were forever throwing themselves from the top floor, searching for relief through instant death. Ergo the U2 song about seeing seven towers, but only one way out. Una was married with a four year old boy. Rory told me about his good fortune on the phone one day, his voice full of fevered joy.

"She has this kid, Larry, who is a really smart kid," he gushed with cringe-inducing sentimentality like an old school RTE presenter. "When I went to see them last Thursday I bought him a toy gun and he was just full of little smiles all evening. He thinks I'm his uncle so he really likes me. The father hasn't a clue. He's never there and she says he's a real cunt. A stupid cunt."

It was not a big deal that they were fucking. People all over the world are fucking right now in all manner of inappropriate circumstances.

Una and Rory used to get together in her towerblock home when the husband, called Noel, was out of town. When Noel was around, Una would make the trip across to Rory's flat in Rathmines. As the friendship grew and grew, he bought lavish gifts for her home: a bedside lamp, a washing machine, a coffee table, Waterford cut glass. On elegant, South Dublin shopping sprees together, he'd buy her shoes or jeans from Grafton Street boutiques. The class warrior of impeccable class background and his trashy representative of the great unwashed.

I was just being an asshole about it. I'd made up my mind about what sort of man he was and I didn't want him to break ranks with my preconception. Maybe it was his own business if he wanted to hang out with what seemed, from the internal evidence of his narratives, to be a very common individual whose main terms of reference were booze, TV quiz shows and soap operas. What Ma would call a tramp.

I really didn't buy the alleged attitude of her husband either. According to Rory, he never asked where the new (second hand) washing machine came from. It never surprised him that she had a new coat or new shoes or that their child had so many new toys that the kid must have thought it was Christmas every third day. Noel was forever away working, yet they were supposed to be perpetually broke. Rory slipped her about forty quid a week, and a great deal more when the bills came in.

There was nothing that I could do or say. What could I say? Unless I was willing to wade headlong into his whole scenario, which I had no business doing, I had to maintain a strict and neutral silence. Criticising a friend's lovers is a sure way of getting yourself into big trouble. Plus the better part of me knew I was just being snobby, stand-offish, and contradictory. Reading between the lines of his conversations, I surmised that all was not well with his IRA membership. History tells us that there is less and less time for fighting the good fight when there is good fucking to be done.

Like many a good revolutionary before him, Rory's attention drifted when sex became available on a regular basis.

Sex is an enemy of promise, just like booze, kids, and journalism.

THE FIGHTING RACE

When I wrote *Tyrant's Might* I failed to include Dan Breen's date of birth. I forgot, also, to mention the names of the policemen he gunned down in 1919.

The Tipperary Volunteers decided they could capture a consignment of gelignite being taken to Solohead Quarry by workers, protected by local Royal Irish Constabulary men. Eleven IRA men were mobilised and put in position to capture the explosives. Three days later when the explosives finally showed up there were eight Volunteers awaiting the well-guarded cart.

"Hands up," shouted Breen three times.

In response the RIC men raised their rifles and held them ready to fire. Seán Treacy opened fire first, Dan came in after him, and two RIC men were killed. The War of Independence was on. The freedom train had left the station.

The very same day, in Dublin, the independent Sinn Féin Dáil met for the first time. Both the parliamentary and guerilla aspects of the fight for freedom were under way, hand in hand. Solohead, an insignificant road crossing, became famous all over Ireland. People in Ireland were proud that on a lonely Tipperary road the Irish finally got around to saying "Enough!" to the English.

When I did my original research some old codger of an *Irish Times* reader wrote to me pleading:

Can you be persuaded to drop this biographical notion of Dan Breen which you appear to have? Take any of the godfathers of the Provos today and you have the Dan Breen pattern, commencing with the heroic action of, from a safe position, blasting to death the decent policemen engaged in their daily chores. How long will we have to endure these apocryphal tales that glorify trigger-happy thugs? If you must write a biography, find somebody who was good at making drains, thinning turnips or the like, for amongst these will be discovered the people who did more for their country than those who have undeserved fame. It is books like yours which motivate the immature ones of today with your depraved 'children-of-a-fighting-race' rubbish.

But I could not be persuaded. I included the letter in an appendix to *Tyrant's Might,* and slashed the old codger and his West Brit attitude to ribbons, Liston egging me on.

The so-called 'decent policemen' come back to haunt me today. Walking into Simon's coffee shop on George's Street I bump into Ben, who used to have a clothes stall in the Dandelion Market years ago, was later in a dub reggae band I wrote about in *Anna Livia,* now has a small clothes manufacturing company and seems well heeled. He has two children with him, a troublesome girl around five and a boy just out of nappies. The girl is testy and demands attention. Ben explains that he doesn't normally bring the kids into town but that he has to do some work at the offices and...whatever. I'm not too interested. Work and kids and getting around the city is life. Fuck it. We all have to deal with this stuff in our own peculiar way. In our own particular war.

So in between Ben keeping the girl's mouth full of chocolate fudge cake, while Beck and Ben Harper come through the speakers, we get to talking.

"I never knew you wrote a book on Dan Breen," he says to me merrily but out of the blue.

"That was a long time ago, Ben, I think before I met you." I laugh. I'm taken aback, a little wary to find he has the slightest interest in ancient history. Ben always struck me as being mainly interested in the sex, drugs and rock'n'roll aspects of life.

"Because I have a sort of personal interest in Breen," he says, as good humoured as myself.

Now Simon is playing a compilation tape of Diamanda Galas and John Cale. Collegiate coffee shop, I used to come here after the Trinity Ball.

"Oh, really?" I chirp, assuming that some distinguished relative of his was active in the movement.

"Yes," he says, pausing for effect. "My grandfather was one of the RIC men that Breen shot dead at Solohead."

"So your ancestor inadvertently changed the course of Irish history," I quip. I've had years to think about my attitude to the killing of those particular cops.

"Yes!" says Ben, taking my attitude well, for the slain cop is many generations away from him, and he'd not be a rag trade Celtic Tiger fat cat if Ireland was still under English rule.

"All his kids were ostracised after the killings. Nobody'd talk to them at school and they were shunned. The family was split up, the kids sent to relatives in the four corners of Ireland, their names changed so nobody'd know who they were, such was the hatred with which they were regarded once the war got into full swing."

A major row erupts between the children over chocolate cake so Ben shrugs his shoulders wryly and says he'd better go. I never ask him his great great grandfather's name. I have opened a can of worms. All the worms are dead. They stink.

The train is full of mobile phone freaks so I retreat to the dining car where I go over my lecture notes while chomping on an old-style mixed grill.

We reach Limerick Junction—minutes from where Dan started the Tan War—and I'm greeted by the chairman of the History Society, a pleasant, dapper school teacher and Irish language enthusiast in his mid sixties. He is all excited.

"We're expecting our biggest crowd this year and the local

Presbyterian Minister is coming, so for God's sake will you be careful about what you say?"

I feel like telling him to fuck off but decide to grin and bear it. I'm doing the lecture because I find it good to give my writing an airing in public, and because I always get a good trawl of new contacts at these gatherings.

The History Society chairman drives me to the Galtee Hotel in whose wood-effect ballroom I am due to speak at 8.30. He guides me into Reception, fixes up my room with the wench behind the counter, and departs. The wench asks if I'll be wanting a meal so I order tea, sandwiches and a few bottles of Ballygowan to be sent to my room.

About 8.15 I get a summons to join the Committee in the bar for some very brief socialising prior to my talk. Mainly schoolteachers and the more cerebral Fianna Fáil types. All attest that they've read *Against Tyrant's Might*, and I don't doubt them for a second.

As we make our way into the ballroom I see that this will indeed be a busy night. A long queue has gathered outside the admissions kiosk and for just one moment I think it's 1972 and that I'm Horslips. A dancehall sweetheart at last!

Eventually there is such a crowd that the hotel manager opens uncontemplated balconies and, half an hour late, I speak for seventy minutes to a hot smoky hall. I know they're here because of Breen and his pals, very local heroes from just a couple of miles up the road, and not because of me. But still this is gratifying, not least because they keep perfectly silent while I speak and the fierceness of their engagement is obvious.

I'm not long into my talk when I notice, as I always do, the four wolverines halfway down the hall. Black leather jackets, ruddy complexions, fierce fearless eyes, muscles like steel.

I'm talking about what Ernie O'Malley said about the mountain people, their wildness and their ability to change. I'm going house-by-house through the community where Breen came of age. I'm recalling Tipperary IRA Volunteers who went on to die in the Spanish Civil War. I'm drawing on my new researches, painting a picture, through their own words, of the indignities suffered by the IRA men who lost the Civil War:

> I was arrested on 8th March 1923, as were also about ten others from my area. After spending five months in Tipperary Jail a number of us were transferred to Kilkenny where orders were given to shoot whenever a head was seen at a window. This order was carried out in about five cases during the next twelve months. About the end of October a hunger strike was started as a protest against being kept in jail without the right to look out the window.

I get carried away by the size and concentration of the crowd, I'd only intended speaking for forty minutes. When I finish I'm hoarse but agree to take three or four questions. One of which is the usual moronic "What do you think Dan Breen and the lads would make of the Good Friday Agreement?"

My inquisitor, one of the Fianna Fáil intellectuals from the Committee, is waiting anxiously for me to say that Dan would be gung-ho behind the way things are going but I sidestep him by saying it's impossible to predict what a man who died thirty years ago would make of anything that's happening today.

"I mean, what do you think he'd make of the Internet?" I quip. This stumps him and amuses my audience, most of whom probably don't know what to make of the Net themselves.

The Chairman announces that there'll be refreshments afterwards after thanking all and sundry. If this was a book signing I'd have sold over a hundred books but alas it isn't so I end up signing about fifteen tattered copies of *Against Tyrant's Might*, two *Punk Rock Girls*, and a copy of *Anna Livia* which some smelly weirdo who looks like a refugee from the Van Morrison Fan Club clutches feverishly.

When most of these folks have faded away like polite ghosts I notice the wolverines make their way towards me. They're local men, they give me their names but don't really need to introduce themselves.

We talk for twenty minutes about the theory of mountain ambush as it relates to the Tan War in Tipperary. They're wary about the peace deal and it seems obvious to me—if not to them, for they are men with good hearts—that they're about to jump ship. They're in their late thirties, don't have many years of active service left in them, but little sentences they let slip (deliberately) tell me that, for them, the fighting isn't over yet.

"When Ireland is united…" one of them begins a sentence, his simple preface betraying the teenage boy trapped inside the guerilla's body.

The Committee members grow anxious, flutter close to our conversation. The Volunteers make their farewells, the tallest of them leaning over to whisper into my ear: "Tiochfaidh ár Lá."

Our day will come.

THE DESERT SHORE

Life moved on within me and without me. The Stones began 1982 with Waiting For A Friend and ended it with Going To A Go Go. I saw a photograph in *Time* magazine of a sexy model with sixty four kilobytes of computer memory, whatever that was, on a little plastic thing about the size of a beauty spot, just under her left eye. We were buying liquid crystal display stuff like plastic watches and plastic alarm clocks.

I was approached to write the life of an infamous recently-dead poet. I agreed, took crate loads of papers into my flat, and abandoned the project five weeks later, unopened crates returning to a disapproving widow. I started working on *Fog, Amphetamine, and Pearls*, a study of songwriters and bands who took up the challenge laid down by Dylan. Like most other Dublin literary projects, I never quite got that book finished. Later, when I moved to America, I rejigged the concept and *Fog, Amphetamine and Pearls—Inside The Paisley Underground* became my first book since *Tyrant's Might*. A minor book but one that sold a fair few copies and got me going internationally. It still changes hands for good money in second hand shops in Dublin.

Working real hard on hack work, harder than I'd ever done before, I wasn't doing a lot of looking after the ones that I loved. I was spreading my wings. Travelling abroad from time to time: to London every four or five weeks for interviews, to America for the first time to check out bands, to the usual boltholes for the usual drugged out holidays—Greece, Turkey, Morocco. Ma complained caustically that I never rang and didn't get down to Kilkenny to see her anymore. I wasn't watching out for the people who'd watched out for me in other days. Fat fees from foreign magazines arrived from time to time and I was thinking to myself that I should rent a house. I was looking at trendy clothes in shop windows, buying new shoes twice monthly. It didn't cross my mind that poor old Rory was wallowing in a very different fantasy world involving wife and family, loved ones and neighbours. He had nothing to compare his situation with because his own family were so weird, indifferent, and fucked up.

I quit my Donnybrook quarters with six months rent due, moved to a comfortable smaller place where Rathmines drifts into Rathgar. One very cold and wet Saturday towards the end of 1981 Rory came to call on me with big news. He'd phoned first to say he had something important he needed to talk about. Having long abandoned the hope that important conversations between us might be to do with revolutionary politics, or even good movies we'd seen on the TV, I was resigned to hearing the latest instalment of the irritating sexual soap opera which now occupied all his non-working hours. I was being shitty again, stand-offish about sex, determined to be a grown-up. A grown up with a Mohawk haircut and shocking pink mirrored shades.

I should have been glad for him because he'd never been content in all his days, always downcast and pessimistic; now he felt totally free while I was none too happy about his weird exhilaration. My own relationship with Dee had plateaued out into an actual adult thing. We had sex when nobody was looking, we went to events together. I don't think we ever imagined we'd end up married to one another. We did think we had a short-term good thing going that'd fizzle out in the fullness of time. Marriage came later and was a reflex action. Ours was a cold and warm arrangement; the high drama of Rory's dalliance was not the kind of thing that us cynical ex-UCD phony punk types— who'd successfully worked out alternative middle class lifestyles to suit our pockets and our genitals—were likely to get involved with.

He told me his plan when he arrived at my new home, where most of my stuff was still in boxes about the place. He would sell everything including his car, give up his work, and move to London with an instant family—Una and her son Larry. It would happen in a matter of days rather than weeks or months. He was going to quit his job the following Friday.

He was finished with the Provos. They were too cautious, too moderate, their agenda unachievable because they were using revolutionary means for non-revolutionary ends; they just wanted to do for the whole of Ireland what Fianna Fáil had done for the South. He had a big bee in his bonnet about Sinn Féin. He said such a public front was very bad for a secret army. It allowed access to infiltrators. It gave succour to the cautious windbags who'd always been the backbone and the bane of Irish freedom movements throughout the centuries; the singers of rebel songs so despised by Ernie O'Malley for wanting the songs but not what went with them.

"These days I have more respect for the INLA," he said conversationally. "At least they have balls. I know they're psychos. I know they're always killing one another rather than the Brits."

"Oh, yeah?" I said. "I told you all about my little dalliances with the INLA? They're fanatical puritans, assholes. They have a thing about dope dealers…they have hang-ups about dope smokers…they have hang-ups about queers…I think they even have hang-ups about sex itself! The only thing they don't have a hang-up about is alcohol. And slaughtering one another with meat cleavers."

"Yeah, I know all about that shit," he laughed, irritated. "This alleged genocide is not necessarily a bad thing. But, seriously, the only way anything real will ever be achieved here will be if we fight on and on unto the last economic consequences of our actions. We must be willing to fight to the last drop of our rebel blood. And then rise up and fight again."

"But Rory...you hated London the last time you were there," I pointed out when I'd digested this. He'd never been so windbaggy about his politics before.

"Yeah," he said, lighting a Benson & Hedges, "but I'm not going there to be with the English. I'm going there to be with Una and Larry."

"Will you go back to squatting?" I asked as the coffee percolator bubbled and Nico moaned through Desert Shore on the stereo.

"No, of course not," he said all humpy, already acting the part of the responsible pater familias. "I'll go working on the sites again and rent a place in Brixton or Clapham or somewhere."

"Yes," I said, rolling a big fat doobie, "you'll have several mouths to feed."

UNTIL MY DARKNESS GOES

On the last Friday in September 1999 I deliver *On The Run* to the publishers—Sub Urb—and I pick up the second half of my advance. To celebrate this exchange my publisher takes me to Café En Seine, one of the smart new places where all his slick provincial Dublin pals gather after work to congratulate themselves on having come so far so fast.

Do they hate me because I escaped?

Sub Urb is a prosperous outfit, probably funded by drug money like much else in Ireland. Much of what they publish is well turned out trivial stuff. The main man—my patron—is James Coady, a shaved-head fashion victim in his late thirties. His family used to own a chain of newsagents all over Dublin so I guess he comes—peripherally—from a publishing-related background. We're drinking for an hour when we're joined by James's boyfriend, a hideous megalomaniacal old queen who works as an interior designer.

"I've just had a completely disastrous meeting," he whines. "For three months now I've been working on this new office building for an accountant friend of James's. Yesterday I finally submitted the plans to him and now I've just come from the meeting. I'd designed him a building entirely based on the pyramid principle, which I think is magically harmonious. So we had our meeting today and it lasted five minutes! He puts my plans down on his desk and says to me 'We can't build this! You should know that the feng shui of this design is totally wrong.' So I said to him that in Egyptian magic the pyramid was regarded as the symbol of harmony and he says 'You above all people should know that the pyramid has no place in feng shui.'"

Was it for this that we sent out certain men the English shot?

The nicer people I used to know have either accommodated themselves to the new consensus—gotten with the programme—or they've been brutally sidelined. Dublin has joined the international community of cities where intellectual life is a scary fringe activity and only money matters. Ireland? Me, I fled. I walked before they made me run. I could take no more of their rancid mediocre thinking. Now I'm fleeing again. But, before I run, I have to go see for myself.

I quit Café En Seine in time to catch the last train from Connolly Station to Belfast; the same Dublin to Belfast line on which Davit nearly got blown to bits.

In Belfast I book myself into a small private hotel in the redbrick university part of town. Saturday morning I walk the whole shattered city full of fiercely battered people whose lives seem utterly hopeless. God, ironically enough, died in Belfast a long time ago. I walk from the town centre to the Falls Road where disenfranchised Nationalist youth loiter outside miserable shops and stunted parks.

Directly across from a Sinn Féin Information Centre I notice a street corner building, an impressive Victorian redbrick. The windows on the bottom two floors are sealed up. Seven security cameras are focused on a steel front door. Endless other cameras jut out of the walls, observing specific parts of the building and spots on the streets around it.

Suddenly the steel door flies open and four guys in their mid-twenties slide onto the street, cool panthers in black jeans and black leather jackets. Each of them an essay in physical co-ordination and muscle tone. Every one of them looking somewhat like Rory. The four stalwart Volunteer lads eye me warily, no two of them scrutinising me at the same time, a carefully co-ordinated and lethal hydra.

I smell an old familiar presence of masculine danger. The glamour, the glory, and the danger. My nostrils actually expand to breathe in the same air as them. But those days are gone. For them, and certainly for me.

I WANNA BE SEDATED

A real slick withdrawal from Dublin the next weekend was planned and executed with military efficiency. I got Rory's book collection and some records that he knew I wanted, mainly collectors-item soul albums that he'd paid too much money for when he first started working. Una's husband Noel was conveniently away in Galway that weekend. A taxi to the airport, a plane to Heathrow, and the first week spent in cheap hotels around Earl's Court was the drill.

Then there was a one-bedroom flat in Shepherd's Bush and, when he'd been working on the sites for a couple of months, a semi in Croydon. This time around I didn't get any letters at all. I did get two pornographic postcards and a birthday card with a £50 record voucher. Nobody loved me much that year—with good reason—and the only other present I got was a good overcoat from my mother. I was in London from time to time but I didn't have Rory's address. I'm not sure I wanted to see him anyway.

Growing old is a remorseless process of covering yourself up and watering yourself down. You're supposed to settle your scores with society and, like an old gunfighter, settle down. In your mid-twenties this is happening to you but you're still too young to spot it. That day when you feel tired, that cheeky teenager who irritates you, that beautiful girl who thinks you're an old fool. Only with decrepit retrospect do you understand what was happening to you in your twenties.

It'd been a long long time since Rory and me were two boys walking around that schoolyard in Fursey's shouting at each other about Frank Sinatra. I was too old to be a real jerk anymore. Time is on nobody's side. We had both become men and he was swimming out into the dangerous strong currents of life while I was taking stock on the shore. Punk rock, particularly the restless spirit of New York punk rock, had rescued me from a certain complacency. Punk rock eventually made me take music so seriously that I devoted my life—a very superficial thing—to writing about it.

"Come on," I said to Dee in bed the night Rory moved to London with Una. "Let's rock and roll to the Ramones."

I Wanna Be Sedated on the stereo filled the darkness.

When we came I whispered: "This is rock and roll radio. Stay tuned for more rock and roll."

I was writing Ireland's first big article on a thing called AIDS. In July a San Diego security guard who'd lost his job killed twenty people and said by way of explanation, 'I don't like Mondays'.

I didn't want to think too much about what Rory was doing. I thought he stayed intelligent, I still trusted his wise judgement in certain ways, I thought he was a good man, a man with ideals and a vision of improvement. Somebody (that somebody should have been me) should have told Rory that people are not guns. You don't just pull a trigger when you want them to go off. Sometimes people will explode in your hands.

For a while things proved idyllic enough over there in London for the two wandering Irish. They became the consummate family unit with English money and English friends. The youth who fought the English grew up to be the man who went drinking with them on the weekends. I don't really understand, although I still think about it, exactly what trip that family were on. Una was not the woman she seemed to be and her Noel was not the dimwitted idiot that Rory had assessed him as being.

My friend forgot his military training, forgot what Che had to say about gathering intelligence. Poor folks behave badly towards us middle class folks because they think we've got it all, that we're enfranchised and they're disenfranchised. From their perspective they've got a point, and that's why—if you come from where the money comes from—you can't trust poor people.

One hot day in June of 1982 Rory got home from work in the evening, sweaty, itchy, in need of a shower, to find a young Irish couple, Una's older sister and the sister's husband, sitting in his kitchen. When last heard of, this crowd were living in Dublin on welfare. He'd never met them before, and they looked him up and down like he was a leper. They were friendly and chatty to her, hostile to him. They explained, while Rory served up drinks, that they were just on a shopping spree in London and decided to drop out to Croydon to see Una.

"You could almost reach out and touch the tension. As if fucking gobshites like them would even be able to find Croydon! He looked like Popeye The Sailor Man and she looked like a fucking fat sow. When they left," Rory told me months later when everything had turned so very sour, "I asked her what the fuck they were doing there. I said where the fuck did they get the money to come over to London, and what the fuck kind of shopping were they doing? Were they buying crisps, or lucky bags, or what? She convinced me that it was cool by giving me a blow job and I was such a stupid dopey cunt that I went to sleep that night, my knob all happy and the rest of me all worried!"

That was the last he heard about the sister's visit; the subject was never raised again. He just worked on and on, a big Irish mutt making money, breaking sweat for the English, doing overtime, drinking, playing the father. The English were pretty much rebuilding London in the early Eighties. Working as a builder's labourer did great things for Rory's muscle tone. He drifted away from boyish ideals but began to look more like the Red Indians of his intelligent boyhood fantasies. Liberated from the repression of playing the regular guy for the Provos, he grew his hair back to the shoulder-length vogue of the mid-Seventies. This made him look out of place in the squeaky-clean Eighties but you look out of place as you grow older anyway. And Rory didn't live long enough to witness the Eighties full on.

He bought a remote control colour TV, a three-piece suite, a big double bed, a span new Audi, a microwave, fitted carpets, a dishwasher, a thing for making fresh pasta, an automatic washing machine; what he later called "Every kind of shit known to man. Italian shit. Japanese shit. Plastic shit."

Another strange evening came around in Croydon. I still feel so very sorry for him when I think about that evening—it was the end of everything for him. He came home from work to find another big surprise awaiting him. As he put it to me:

"It was like a scene from a fucking Burt Reynolds movie only the joke was on me."

His home had been stripped bare by real professionals. Each piece of technology, every appliance, the pasta-maker, the plastic shit, even the carpets were gone. Even the rubbish gas cooker that came with the house was missing. A note taped to the kitchen door explained that Una was going back to her husband. He kept the note of course and, when he eventually returned to Dublin, showed it to me. A folded, unfolded, stained, worn sheet of copy-book paper.

Don't bother trying to look for me. I'm not going back to the old place. I'm doing this for Larry—it's woeful to be rearing a kid away from his Daddy. Noel has kicked the drink and he has a great job now. Things are really looking up for him. I had the time of my life with you, it was just fantastic, but now I want to put it all behind me and go back to a normal life.

Una's world was a foreign land to me. Her idea of normal life was a freakshow in my world. I didn't understand it or want to understand it. I couldn't make out the signposts, and I declined to buy a map.

Una misjudged Rory very seriously and didn't know him well enough to understand how much at home he was with revolvers, violence, sawn off shotguns and killing. A man who has brandished a gun in the face of some scared provincial bank manager wouldn't be discouraged by a note telling him not to follow his onetime lover to the ends of the earth (or, as turned out to be the case, to suburban south Dublin).

Rory flew back to Dublin two days later.

REAL IRA

The Provos have called it a day, deciding that they, having reached a certain respectability and stasis, can finally draw a line under Irish history. They're middle aged but ideals don't age.

There is a quote from Parnell which adorns his statue in Parnell Square:

"No man has a right to fix the boundary of the march of a nation. No man has a right to say to his country: Thus far shalt thou go and no further. We have never fixed the *ne plus ultra* of the progress of Ireland's nationhood and we never shall."

The Provos have decided to go no further, that Ireland need go no further than them, and right now they're enforcing this decision on their brother-rebels in the INLA and the Real IRA. I think of Rory's dashed life, the dashed lives of people he and I perceived as our enemies, people blown up on their way to work or play, and it almost makes me cry to think that this is what it was all about: so that Gerry Adams could get mobile phone calls from Willie Nelson, so that Belfast would have a few road signs in Irish.

I'm lying alone on the double bed in a Belfast hotel room, checking out MTV, which is full of propaganda for the awards I attended two days ago. The Corrs and Boyzone and a blast from the past called the Rolling Stones and news that Gary Glitter has been given four months for keeping kiddie porn on his computer and Bob Marley being tortured by Lauren Hill. My hotel is in the only part of Belfast that hasn't been maimed by thirty years of war. The phone rings, so I pick it up. This is it. It's the real thing. Just do it.

"Mr Crowe? Your car is here for you."

"Oh? They're early!" Half an hour early. "Tell the driver I'll be down in ten minutes."

I'm dressed and standing in the lobby waiting when my driver, a good looking teenager with dreadlocked skate kid hair, strides laconically through the hotel's revolving door. An athletic looking boy in torn combat trousers, Rancid teeshirt, and Vans trainers.

"Sorry to be early." He smiles casually. "I had to drop my girlfriend off at the airport and this was on my route back."

Which is complete bullshit.

Outside the hotel we walk in friendly silence to a pricey new Jeep Wrangler whose driver—another skate kid—gives me a high five. Punk haircut, moonwalker trainers, an ancient Iggy teeshirt that must have belonged to his older brother.

Dreadlocks tells me in a prosperous Southern accent that his name is Kevin and that he's from Kilkenny; he seems to know I'm from there too. Moonwalker is called Cathal, has a harsh Belfast gurrier accent, and doesn't have much to say. Both boys have dark intense eyes which speak of a great seriousness.

As soon as we pull away from the curb we travel at speed until we reach a motorway which takes us south and away from the city. Kevin reaches for the stereo and inserts a mix tape of Aaron Copeland, Miles Davis and Tortoise.

"Liam," he says to me, "we're delighted that you want to do this interview with us. Things are getting very dangerous for us. We've been visited in our homes by our former Provo comrades and told individually that if we don't lay down our arms we'll be shot. In the last six months two of our most important men have died in car crashes. Each and every one of us fears execution at the hands of British intelligence or the Provos."

Our journey takes fifty minutes and eventually we're in the pitch black bandit country of South Armagh. There is no need to blindfold me because I'd never find my way back here. We pull into a laneway leading to a one storey farmhouse with a large concrete farmyard out front. Parked in the farmyard, I note, are seven cars and three motorbikes. Our jeep grinds to a halt at the front door, where me and Kevin alight. I can hear dogs barking in the distance but I can see no dogs. Cathal doesn't join us but drives away in the jeep; I assume there are lookouts lurking somewhere in the darkness of the fields and that Cathal is going to join them. But this is not really a high security operation.

"Please follow me now, Liam," Kevin says very gently. He walks through an ajar front door. I follow into an old fashioned country kitchen. A cold chicken rests in a Pyrex dish on a work surface. Three loaves of white soda bread, some onions, a saucepan full of washed and quartered potatoes. On the wallpapered wall a modern framed print of The Shepherdess by Millet, a young girl saying her Angelus. Beyond the kitchen an open door leads into a sitting room where Johnny Cash is playing on a stereo. The subdued murmur of conversation can be heard along with the music as Kevin turns to me, smiles, and beckons me to follow him into this gathering of the Real IRA.

A woman in her mid-twenties, her back to me, is walking towards the stereo to lower the volume. She turns her head around to look at me, smiles gently, turns back to the stereo. There are two other young women in the room, sitting on a battered old couch talking to one another, and six men sitting around on stools, kitchen chairs, and armchairs. They're all dressed like any cross-section of trendy young society except for two older men who wear old fashioned denim trousers, store-bought jumpers, and strong sensible shoes. This room is not used to large gatherings and, I guess, is not the living room of anyone in this assembly.

There is general talk about this and that, I accept a beer, Johnny Cash gives way to Gram Parsons, people are smoking Marlboro Lights and Benson & Hedges. The generational nature of the music makes me wonder if, maybe, this is actually the home of one of the older guys, Frank and Michael.

Out of the stew of chat and music and drink and smoke, it emerges that Michael is the boss man with Frank as his lieutenant. As befits a boss, Michael doesn't go in for a whole lot of chit chat and, when I settle down to do my interview, it is Frank who makes most of the running, Kevin interjecting more often than Michael. The woman who turned down the stereo—Nuala—also has a few things to say.

Frank says their organisation is not as structured as the Provos, that their current strength is about sixty volunteers, that they're in touch with disaffected INLA and Provo activists all over Ireland.

I ask if this is the entirety of the Real IRA?

"No," Frank replies with a vehemence which makes me think he is lying. "We're organised into cells and, at the moment, things are very much in a state of flux. People are humming and hawing, hedging their bets. There are lads in the Provos who are tired of the war—many of them ex-prisoners—but who're sympathetic to where we're at. Those lads are more inclined to help us lay our hands on armaments than to get actively involved themselves. They've done their bit, done enough."

A lot of water has gone under the bridge since Frank or Michael were street fighters but the serpent, while under control, is merely coiled. The same cannot be said of their younger comrades all of whom are taut and lean, desperately loyal to one another like old school friends.

When I ask the inevitable question about the Omagh massacre it's Nuala, a good-looking petite woman with long curly jet-black hair, who provides the response. I wonder if this is a deliberately worked-out strategy for dealing with the thorniest of questions.

The nasty comes over as being less nasty when delivered by a beautiful female.

"All I can say about Omagh," she says in an annoyed tone like she was the very one who argued against that bomb being planted, "is that it was stupid, egotistical, and immoral. It was also a mistake, but that is a different matter. The IRA has occasionally made mistakes that result in atrocities or carnage but the British forces have committed vile, obscene offences all over the world and virtually none of those were accidents…"

This is not really a comprehensive response, more your typical neo-theological Irish obfuscation. We talk an hour more. I explain that, while I don't approve of the consequences of Omagh, I have no problem with their politics. When we've talked enough I suggest we quit while we're ahead. This brings a murmur of polite laughter from the uneasy, twitchy volunteers. I turn off my tape machine and make my farewells, explaining that I'll place my feature in a prominent American publication. Kevin says he'll go find Cathal and, oddly enough, it is Michael who walks me to the door.

"I enjoyed your book on Dan Breen," he says like a man who finds it difficult to make small talk. This is a very hard guy trying to be friendly.

"Oh, God!" I laugh. "The worst cover in the world!"

"Aye," he smiles. "But you did a good job there. Most of your other books are on music, aren't they?'

"Yeah. I used to write about music in Dublin before I moved away to America."

"Oh, I know that," Michael says gently, like a sensitive farmer. "I was studying Engineering at Belfield the same time as yourself. I used to see you with all those beautiful women in the corridor of the Arts Block. I used to envy you. You were on the inside and I was just a big thick down from the North on a British grant."

I stare at him in the half-light of the farmyard. The look on his face tells me that he knows I can't recollect him.

"Fuck, I don't ever remember seeing you at Belfield," I say, but I'm grinning at him because us university types are always delighted to bump into one another, even in the middle of the night in Armagh under the aegis of the Real IRA.

"No, of course not," he laughs. "As I say, I was nobody. Sure I'm nobody still. But we did almost meet one time. You don't remember that either. We both attended a meeting at Pearse House in…God…it must have been around 1978. The whole lot of us got arrested and you escaped on the bus."

"Oh, Christ, I remember it all too well. I didn't really escape," I admit. "Which one were you? Which one were you?"

"Ah, I looked different then. I was the one with the Graham Greene book striking the pretentious pose."

"But you didn't stay pretentious for long. Obviously."

"I suppose I didn't."

The jeep creeps up on us. I give Michael a collegiate bear hug before climbing in with Kevin and Cathal. An hour later they leave me off at my hotel. I return to my room where I turn MTV back on and fall asleep thinking that I liked those people a lot. There is no real guile or double-talk about them. How long will they live? What will become of their cause?

EXECUTIONER'S SONG

Paramilitary training kicked in like a cocaine rush. If you want to kill somebody you've got to be patient—to be a watcher.

Séamus, by 1983 a top man in his department, chairing five important committees, managed to get Rory his old job back, and Rory began to recall a few of the things that Che had to say about intelligence gathering.

He rented a spartan four-room unfurnished flat close to Rathmines Church. It was the top floor of a four storey terraced redbrick. The house was divided that way—a flat a floor. I never went there much because he made no effort to make it homely and was rarely in homely mood. He had tons of space but he did nothing with it. There were no floor coverings in any of the rooms, just rough bare floorboards except for the bedroom where somebody, back in the romantic mists of time, had painted the floor black. He had a big double mattress on the floor in the bedroom, a fake Deco bedside lamp alongside it. Clean clothes were organised neatly in different piles on the floor; shirts, jeans, jocks, socks. Little piles of paperback books systematically stacked against the walls. A kitchen that never saw any cooking; beer in the fridge, Chinese takeaways brought in for eating. Two bizarre ancient armchairs Séamus brought in from Pádraic's old room at either side of an open fireplace in the living room. A bookshelf full of magazines and paperbacks: detective novels, revolutionary memoirs, science fiction, blockbusters. A new portable TV balanced on a two foot high pile of old newspapers. That was it. An old Hoover in the bathroom—left behind by a previous tenant—with a Doors sticker on its handle. Throw-away razors and coal-tar soap on the glass shelf over the sink.

He was remarkably calm, if crushed. Like he'd flushed a

bucket of poison out of his brain, only nothing had replaced the poison. He laughed at his own stupidity and to some extent was his old self, ranting and raving about Norman Mailer, about fake revolutionaries, anarchism, Conor Cruise O'Brien, and about his favourite worst enemies, the Dublin-based leadership of the Provos. He was putting out new feelers in the direction of the INLA. He had a meeting with some comrades in a Northside pub and then there were some other meetings, but I never heard exactly what happened or where it led.

"I know the INLA have this hang-up about drugs," he said one night, "but sometimes I wonder if the whole fucking lot of them are on drugs. For sure they're off in a world of their own. Not to mention totally preoccupied with one another. They're like a religious cult or something."

He'd been back at work three months when he bought a fresh well cared for secondhand Ford. This car caused us to have some final great times together. Five times we drove to the West of Ireland for the weekend, staying in cheap bed & breakfasts, doing magic mushrooms. We listened to compilation tapes I'd made while Rory put the boot down and transported us two men through the surreal mountains of Connemara. Those were good days for laughs and fresh air. Those trips to the last bastion of Irish Ireland—where some of the people actually spoke Irish from time to time—were an epilogue to our friendship.

The Ford was the first weapon that he needed. Empowered by wheels, he devoted his Dublin Sundays to hanging around outside a respectable well maintained Crumlin council house where Una's mother and father lived. On his fifth surveillance Sunday she showed up with her boy Larry. Cool as a cucumber, he didn't fly off the handle or intervene but waited until they left,

Una holding the little boy's hand and talking incessantly to him. They caught a bus to central Dublin, he followed the bus in his car. They walked from the bus stop to the Tara Street DART station where they went up the steep stairs leading to the south platform.

Rory parked the Ford, bought a one day travel pass at the Tara Street kiosk, waited at the bottom of the stairs until he heard the DART approaching. Then he bounded up the steps in seconds and, just before the train doors closed, leaped on board. Mother and child didn't get off until they reached Killiney, on the far south side of Dublin Bay, staring across at Howth on the north side. Making sure Una didn't spot him, he held himself in superb check and, fifteen minutes later, his patience paid off completely: "I couldn't believe my luck, it was like fucking for the first time, I was just saying Yes! Yes! Yes! to myself. This is really happening. I saw her walk right up to the front door of her new home, a shitty council house on a crap estate, the fucking place had this kind of damp green slime dripping down one side of the building. She takes out her key, and she goes inside. The poor little kid dragged along behind her. I wrote down the details— the street name and house number—and I left it at that. Now! Now I know what I'm doing, where I'm going, and there will be no real problem."

Two weeks later she took a bus from her hovel to the nearby Killiney Shopping Centre, a dour cramped Sixties vision of consumer durable optimism. Rory followed her—in the Ford— and parked in the shopping centre's forecourt. While she was inside shopping he sat in the car with one eye on the exit, one eye on the *Irish Press*. He saw her walking in his direction, got out of the car, pretended to be as amazed as she was by their chance meeting. She was smart enough, feral enough, to get real nervous at the very sight of him but Rory insisted he was just totally delighted, thrilled to bump into her. He took her for coffee in the shopping centre's musak-fuelled cafeteria, an invisible orchestra playing Hey Jude and I Just Called To Say I Love You. As they talked she grew shit scared as the reality of his having found her sank in.

Rory was always a great actor—after all he'd led most of his adult life in a state of permanent sublimation. So he insisted that there were no hard feelings. Indeed, he explained, he was delighted that things had worked out between herself and Noel for the sake of the child. He asked her how Larry was, coming on all concerned.

"I never told you, Rory," she told him in a tone of soap-opera regret, "but poor auld Noel has had a real bad heroin problem. Do you know what I mean? He has been like a fucking saint, that man! So when me sister came to see us in London she brought a letter from him, explaining that he was off the stuff, that all he wanted was to be a good father and husband. So I rang him and we arranged to give it another try. But that fucking didn't work out either. He went back on the gear and I'm down here now. I live near here with me boyfriend."

Rory was a real gentleman about it, told her he was really pissed off about the stolen household goods, said that it was a shitty thing for her to do to him: "You knew me well enough Una. You knew I'd've given you the fucking washing machine and all that shit if you'd wanted it. You should have just said you wanted to come back to Ireland."

And on and on. According to himself he put on a great performance. No doubt he did. So convincing, as it emerged, that they were fucking again within the week. She would come to his new flat in Rathmines and this time it was purely mattress work. No day trips to the seaside with the kid. No presents, no furniture, no talk about a future. Just her sneaking into town on shopping escapades—her boyfriend didn't work and sulked around the house all day—and Rory picking her up in the Ford.

He said he was sure she didn't trust him yet. "The fucking bitch is an animal, you know, she can sniff and sense trouble in me. Just like a filthy dog. Even though she can't see it or smell it. Even though I hide my disgust completely, some little third eye inside her is still watching me with caution. Telling her to look out. Look out! Look out! And that voice is right. Perfectly correct!"

He just kept on fucking her like a dog until she needed the sex more than she cared about the risks:

"Now I've gotten her where I want her. All she wants now is cock and more cock. She wants it up the back hole. She knows I'll never give her more money. Now we have a very simple arrangement which suits this stupid cunt so well! It suits me fine too. Now I've got her. Now she is unawares."

Una was unaware, hurtling ninety miles an hour down a dead end street.

I never met this woman. I never once saw a photograph of Una. All I ever heard was cardboard cut-out descriptions. First she was 'really fucking beautiful'. Now she was 'a fucking whore'. I had a vision of her in my mind that I never checked out with him. I imagined that she was about five foot ten, pudgy, inclined to trouser suits and perms, old before her time, with desperate stupid eyes. She was obviously a stupid woman—she should never have gone near him that second time.

One hot Saturday morning in the summer of '83 I was feeling pretty sorry for myself. The night before I'd been to a gig to review Princess Tinymeat for *Anna Livia*. My throat was dry as dust, tight, swollen and sore. I got out of bed at eleven and dashed to the shower. I dried myself off afterwards, listening to Kraftwerk naked. I'd just started a liquid breakfast of coffee and restoring orange juice when my doorbell rang. I pulled on a pair of jeans and went down to see who was there.

Rory stood on my doorstep beaming, happy and alert, the very picture of robust good health. I offered to make some breakfast for the two of us and he was on for coffee and toast but didn't want anything more elaborate. He wanted to go for a drive up the mountains, and this seemed like a good idea to me. I said he should come back in an hour, that I was totally fucked up, that I'd be in better shape to greet the day in an hour.

"What'll I do until then?" Rory asked, all boyish and confused.

"Go to the supermarket and buy some fruit juices and some spring water and some booze, why don't ya?" I threw him my keys and he slouched away. Obedient and passive.

I got back into my shower again, stood still with hot water flowing all over me. I stepped naked out of the shower and drank more coffee. The phone rang and I let the answering machine take it. It was Dee wanting to see me that night.

When Rory returned—exactly an hour later—my mood was much improved. I'd gotten so maudlin and strung out under the influence of my fresh smelly Moroccan dope that eventually—contradictorily—I cheered up. As Rory walked into my sitting room I had Peter Tosh reggae on the stereo and I was tucking my cock into my jeans. He danced around the room—he was a good vulgar dancer—singing the lyrics, shouting: "You know that

198

American radical one, Emma Whatshername, the one who said You can dance at my revolution...Emma Goldman, that's her!" Still pretending that he was vague with his quotes, the Emma Goldman line a favourite of his since 1976.

"I don't know what I am anymore," Rory shouted over a duet by Tosh and Mick Jagger, "but I think I'm an anarchist or a Trotskyist. I guess I must be an anarchist. I can't get along with anybody except you."

"I don't think the dictionary defines anarchism as being able to get along with me," I said, getting up to dance opposite, but not with, Rory. "But I do regard myself as an anarchist. A punk anarchist. I still fucking just go crazy for the New York punk rock jingle jangle."

Due to my dope smoking we didn't get going until three o'clock—by which time the roads leading out towards Bray and the Dublin Mountains were jammed with Saturday afternoon suburban traffic. Eventually we left the city behind us and climbed into the forests in the hills around Dublin, the landscape dotted with occasional golf clubs, bankrupted white elephant health spas, and Old Guy nightclubs advertising forthcoming appearances by Hank Locklin, Charlie Pride, and Dickie Rock. The Dublin Mountains a beautiful escape from the life of the city, the air so vividly crisp and clean up there. That Saturday there were few cars on the narrow back roads we traversed.

The car radio was turned on to RTE Radio One, the current affairs and arts station. A once-popular Irish TV presenter was being interviewed about his conversion to Buddhism. The presenter asked the TV star how he'd like to be remembered.

"As a human being," murmured the star, "I would prefer not to be remembered."

"God!" exclaimed Rory, "those Buddhists are such egomaniacs!"

In between the chat the presenter played records by Dean Martin and Neil Sedaka. Rory sang along to Little Old Wine Drinker Me and The Queen Of 1964.

"That fucking Neil Sedaka is a sick disease," he laughed. "So nobody wants an over aged groupie now!"

It was getting on for dusk when we drove down an unpaved mountain path leading right into the depths of the forest where we stopped for a piss and a beer. He rambled off alone into the woods and I leaned against his car, daydreaming, rolling a joint. He didn't come back for twenty minutes—I have no idea where he went or what he was doing—by which time it was virtually dark and I was stoned and tranquil.

"I got something to show you," he said, opening the back door of the Ford and leaning inside to get out a large powerful flash lamp. Then he walked around to the back of his car, instructing me to join him.

He pulled open the boot, shone the flashlight into the boot, and said "Look!"

Lying there on a dirty tartan rug was a big hatchet, a butcher's knife, and a roll of Agent Orange-coloured synthetic rope.

"I'm going to get her to the flat and fuck her. Then when she's all emotional and sleepy, smoking her fag and recovering, I'll stun her with a punch or two and tie her up. Then I'll kill the fucking bitch with this," he said, brandishing the hatchet in his hand, and shining the flashlight onto its thick metal blade, so shiny and new that the light reflected from it, mirror-style.

"But you'll get caught!" I almost shouted, not particularly worried by the moral aspects of his proposal.

"I don't give a fuck," he said quietly, gently placing the hatchet back into the boot and slamming it shut. "I just don't give a fuck. I have nothing to live for, I never have had, and that fucking whore screwed me up so that I don't give a fuck about her or what happens to her or me. I hope you never fuck up your life the way I've fucked up mine, Liam. You're the only person I could ever trust. I know that now."

We got back into his car and drove around those dark hills for a while. Rory turned on the radio again, turning it up loud. The Buddhist celebrity interview was over and now RTE were presenting a dramatic adaptation of Jane Eyre. Rory flicked around angrily looking for music while I stayed silent, caught up in my own perturbed stoned thoughts. From time to time cars coming in the opposite direction, their headlights blinding us, passed us by. He found lots of music on his radio—heavy metal, country & western, American rock—but nothing suited the mood he was in right then so he turned the radio off. We climbed higher into the hills, parking eventually at a lay-by from which we could see the orange streetlights of Dublin stretch off into the far distance where the sea and its darkness replaced the land.

AN END TO TERRORISM

December 2nd, 1999. Direct British rule of Northern Ireland is over, the British claim. Ireland drops its territorial claims over Northern Ireland, about this there is no doubt. Provo grey eminences get good fat jobs in the new government. The gravy train is full to overflow.

In the last days of the Dan Breen project I found myself

thinking about Rory all the time. In all the years I've lived in America I've rarely thought about him. His recurrent memory one of the reasons why I quit Ireland in the first place.

The night I finished *On The Run* I had a white-fear nightmare about Rory: a journey through dark heat. In my dream I was standing on a North Dublin beach in the middle of the night. A huge gale was blowing up and the wind howling like a banshee. The air carried both rain and sea spray. I was wearing sports gear and wild looking trainers and I stood erect with my hands in my pockets staring out to sea, my lips pursed against the cold, my cheeks numbed into indifference. In the dream I could see myself, and it looked just like the real me, right down to the clothes and the shoes.

Suddenly the presence of the cold wind was replaced by the emphatic presence of Rory; I could not see him but he was all around me, much as the wind had been all around me just a moment earlier. He was there, he was older, he was angry with me, angry that I had lived on.

"But I've grown old, Rory," I didn't move my lips but I said this to him. "My memory is failing, I can't even remember properly what you looked like, I don't understand the world any more…just be thankful for the times we shared together. All the things I wanted have turned to shit and the world I wanted is turning to shit around me. At least you escaped all this. All I ever wanted was to be free and I'm totally fucking trapped."

Rory wanted me to come with him, and like a succubus he tried to suck the life force out of me, to take me away to some place where the dead roam naturally, as if to the manner born.

I woke abruptly in a strange place. Got out of bed and stumbled to the mirror, stared at a strange face. I was standing in my room in Summerhill Parade in an icy cold sweat. I could hear a police siren on the street outside. I went downstairs to the den, put on a CD, turned on CNN.

A plug for the Sheraton Hotel in Cambodia...Holidays in Cambodia!

Cut to Tina on a publicity tour of America, calling for Irish-American funding for terrorism to be halted, calling for an end to terrorism...She irritates the shit out of me.

I saw her extraordinary interview twice that night.

THE PRONTO GRILL

The Stones disco remix of Undercover Of The Night was my soundtrack in '83. A supergrass, a failed assassin and a bully, was responsible for twenty-two IRA men getting sentences totalling four thousand years.

Towards the end of his life, his last six months on earth, Rory smoked a lot of dope, drank a lot, became congenial in a middling kind of way. When he was too drunk or too stoned he tended to ramble on and on, but he'd always been a bit of an orator—even when he was a kid—and I was usually happy to hear what he had to say until it descended into irreversible gibberish. At the end he was on heavy tranquillisers, and they didn't go well with the drink. I saw the end coming, only I mistook it for something else entirely.

In the days that followed our drive into the Dublin Mountains I devoted a lot of time to thinking about what Rory told me and showed me. I decided to play Devil's Advocate and ask him a little more about his plan. We arranged to go see some arty Japanese movies together, so he dropped by to pick me up at six.

I didn't go in for a lot of home cooking, usually it was just cheese and crackers in my kitchen, so we shuffled around the corner to an old greasy spoon called The Pronto Grill, where they did infinite different things to hamburgers, cans of tomatoes, and chicken legs. Suave Ranelagh, nestling between the elite ruling class splendour of Donnybrook and the up-from-the-country flatland squalor of Rathmines, was an incompatible mixture of influences. Still elegant like a village green, still boasting its own cinema, full of studenty flats. I always liked Ranelagh but I never lived there, dividing my time between what I satirically called my Donnybrook bohemian love pad and various cozy sanctuaries in Rathmines. But the Pronto Grill was just about the only decent cheapish eating place in all three suburbs.

We had a fine crisp evening, with a clear sky and a full moon, for our chat. All kinds of residents from the district gathered inside The Pronto, hunkering over red check tablecloths and modest victuals. Ike and Tina's bizarrely futuristic Nutbush City Limits blasted out of an ancient tannoy system, the weary old speakers delivering Ike's wild wolf howling-at-the-moon guitar with precision and clarity.

Rory didn't mind discussing the gory details of the planned execution, not even in a dive full of respectable local residents. He'd had a few drinks before picking me up, but not so much drink that he was morose or bitter. With just one or two drinks in him he could be flashy, debonair, funny. Now, of course, he was not exactly funny but he was certainly in control. I ordered Chicken Kiev with chips and a side salad. He got steak, mushrooms, and chips. The Pronto didn't have a license so we drank coffee relentlessly. Ike and Tina Turner gave way to Blondie, Rory extolling the great virtues of Debbie Harry's beauty, me bullshitting about where punk rock went before it disappeared, like I was reciting one of my own articles.

"When exactly do you intend to do her in?" I asked, stabbing my fork into half a cold tomato and pushing the whole lot inside my mouth.

"Friday week," he said calmly. "She's away down the country now visiting some gobshite country cousins. She comes back on the Thursday so Friday week I've taken the afternoon off work. The cunt's coming around at two. I'll fuck her until five and she'll be dead by half past."

"Do you think you'll really be able to go for it?"

"Of course I can fucking go for it. I'm a trained killer," he said, not proud or boasting, but brainy enough to know exactly what sort of dark night lurked up ahead. He smiled over at me, searching my face for the uncomplicated friendship that existed between us when we were boys. I smiled back in the same spirit although complications go hand in hand with adulthood. I liked him still but it distressed me way too much to see that his life had come to such a pathetic pass.

"You won't get away with it, you know?" I said as we left The Pronto after he paid our bill.

"I can get away. I know how to move real fast. They trained me in escape too," he said nonchalantly, taking the car keys from his pocket.

He did know how to escape; I'd seen this for myself.

We got together for dinner in The Pronto again on the eve of the planned killing. I'd grown a little restless about the whole proposition and so, of course, had Rory.

"So you going to stick to the plan?" I asked, half hoping he'd changed his mind but knowing that this was unlikely.

"Yeah, I'll stick to the big plan," he said, emphatic but none too happy, sort of Robert Mitchum-like, a man standing alone against society, in front of a kaleidoscopic landscape of hills and valleys. "By this time tomorrow they'll be putting bits of her into plastic bags."

"And you? You'll be...."

"Me? I'll feel a whole lot better than I do right now," he said confidently, looking me straight in the eyes, no tremble in his voice. Only the slight twitch of his lower lip revealing what he was going through.

THE RETURN TO NORMAL

A week before I finish *On The Run* I go to see Father Joe at St Paul's, the Jesuit retirement home in the Wicklow hills south of Dublin. I drive through miserable rain in my hired car, listening to Nina Simone singing. A live album from 1986. Then a Jimmy Cliff tape. I've not seen Joe since 1982 when I revisited St Fursey's to do a Back To School feature for a series of that name in *The Irish Times*. Back then Spunk was still cock of the walk, gliding along on a superb wave of ego, quickness, zeal and neurosis.

I pull into the grounds of St Paul's. The rain stops and there is a break in the clouds. A short tree-lined drive gives way to a pebbled courtyard. A big old gentry house. Most of the Anglo-Irish quit Ireland in the decades after the Tan War and many of their houses fell into the hands of Irish religious orders, who found these colossal buildings convenient for convents, boarding schools, abbeys. St Paul's is spruce and well-maintained. Double-glazed windows take from the line of the building, but no doubt add to the comfort of the old men living on inside.

A young fresh-faced novice comes to the door to greet me, very friendly, his Munster accent seeming all the more rough and ready to me now that I no longer live in Ireland.

The boy leads me into a lounge full of comfortable old armchairs, central heating turned up full blast. A TV in the corner is on with the sound down, showing an old black and white cowboy movie.

"Sit down Mr Crowe," he almost whispers: "Father Joseph will be with you shortly."

He's hardly left the room when Spunk shuffles in, his schedule no longer so very full.

Old and frail, vain and arrogant, Father Joe has forgotten nothing, has never changed. Every stitch is immaculate, smells of dry cleaning. His firm head of grey hair, bouncy and freshly washed, reeking of medicated shampoo. Once Joe was a man of action. Now *The Irish Times* has better tame Catholics willing to crawthump in public for the delight of the crowd. Joe is on the back burner, he has been used up just like Rory got used up by the Provos. The next thing I will read about Joe in the papers will be an obituary in *The Irish Times* which my mother will cut out and post to me, which will attest that Joe was a good holy moderniser, not the reactionary megalomaniac I remember him as being.

Time has mellowed the two of us. He says to me that I'd always been a great fellow and a bit of a character.

"You were before your time, Liam! Before your time."

It is like he can see everything clearly now. Way back—during the Golden Age of Rock'n'Roll—he thought I was the Devil incarnate and he told me so.

He guides me into a large book-lined study where a roaring fire keeps death away, reminding the old men of the sexy bounce of real life. He presses a buzzer on the wall beside a black marble fireplace.

"Please, Liam, sit down. Sit down and tell me how things have been for you since we last met."

Making smalltalk, I don't talk about my divorce or *Mannish Boy*. I do tell him about *On The Run*—the religious always love to hear about history, even unpleasant history. I tell him about reassuring things; how well my mother is, that my daughter is very bright and cheeky. Ten minutes later a stout housekeeper brings in a tray carrying a silver pot full of steaming tea, milk in a silver jug, sugar in a china bowl, two china cups with saucers, ham sandwiches, chocolate biscuits, silver spoons, napkins. When the housekeeper enters the room Joe clams up—an unreconstructed snob and misanthrope to the last—and I follow suit. We both just stare nonchalantly into the strong unhinged flames of the wood fire, the deep homely smell of burning wood fashioning the atmosphere. I listen to the crackle and hiss of the wood, the clink of cups being laid and the gurgle of tea being poured, wait for the old woman to leave. When she quits the talk inevitably moves along to Rory.

I say I'd not seen Rory for years before his death, but that I'd been deeply shocked to hear about it. Joe seems to think Rory killed himself because his fiancee broke off their engagement. I don't clarify things for him—stories like that are how the middle classes translate the unacceptable into their own language.

"You know his younger brother Tony committed suicide also?" he says confidingly, glancing at me, sipping his tea, his voice descending to a whisper.

I'm confused but not necessarily surprised. Rory was so proud of Tony, had such conventional brotherly aspirations for him. That he'd do well in life, excel with women, become the normal man that Rory himself never actually wanted to be.

"Ah yes, the father sent him to St Fursey's too. Young Tony was very similar to Rory. Very serious, very dedicated. But, well now, how would you put it…not…political…that class of thing…those days are dead and gone anyway. Thank God. Things are much better now, there will be permanent peace now and everything will return to normal." For reassurance Spunk clasps his two bony knees with thin veiny hands.

Old men always expect things to return to an island called normal.

"Yes, Tony drowned himself during his final year at UCD. The parents were devastated. He was studying Engineering at Belfield, a most brilliant boy. He got worried about his exams. I think it all got the better of him."

As if you'd kill yourself over exams you could repeat in the autumn.

Father Joe stares off into the distance, away in the lost world of his own normality. His left hand trembles slightly. Maybe he feels he'd failed those two boys. Then he changes the subject.

"Whatever became of Badger McCarthy?" he asks chirpily, a wry smile crossing his face.

I've only seen Badger once or twice since Dark Space. "Badger McCarthy? Oh, Badger became an anarchist," I say with relish.

"An anarchist!" Spunk gasps in disbelief, his old right-wing self coming back to haunt me. "You mean Badger is totally alienated from society?"

"Yes…I suppose you could say that," I reply because Badger has certainly grown alienated. Last time I saw Badger, 1990, I was a homeowner in San Francisco and he was a free spirit living in a squat in Amsterdam, listening to trash metal, wearing a Sepultura teeshirt a bit too tight on him, sporting a silver stud through his left eyebrow.

"But Badger was on the football team!" shouts Joe Spunk in confused dismay.

Maybe the world is not going back to normal after all.

Badger on the football team. Me into the Rolling Stones. Rory into Che Guevara. Joe Spunk on the BBC.

GIMME SHELTER

I didn't get up until lunchtime that day. I had a disturbed sleepless night, all tossing and turning, wondering what the day would bring and where my life would take me. Once during the night I woke up with a dry bitter taste in my mouth like I'd been drinking rot gut for a week. Looking out my window in a half-sleep, imagining I saw blood dripping from the full moon, I considered ringing the Guards to inform on Rory, but that thought passed in the night like a waking dream. When I finally got up I knew I'd be a shithead, allow the drama to pan out however it panned out, be true to my pal in my bittersweet way. Una was due to arrive at his place at exactly the time I was due to do a live radio show on RTE.

The first thing I did was ring my taxi firm and book a car for 2pm. Then I put on a pot of coffee, some clothes, and a Ramones album, all in that order. I tried to call Rory but there was no reply.

While my coffee was percolating I put on tight new shoes and ran across the street to get a paper plus some milk from the allnight shop. When I got back to the flat I tried Rory again. Still no reply. I thought about calling the cops again but the years and what I called my politics meant that I was in no position to turn informer on him. An alternative was to go around to his flat and try to interfere but that messy proposition filled me with conventional dread. I did nothing, I had a radio show to appear on—and that's showbiz!

When my taxi arrived to take me to the radio station, I just walked out my front door and into the car on autopilot. In that mode I was driven to the studio front door. The driver tried to talk with me but I think he thought I was preoccupied with the broadcast I was about to do.

"What'll ye be talking about today, Mr Crowe?" he asked while Dolly Parton sang Coat of Many Colours on the radio.

"What?" I'd barely heard him.

"Will ye be talking about music today on the radio?"

"Oh that, yes. Yeah. I'll be talking about the new bands around town."

"Me nephew, now, is a drummer. He wants to go professional. The whole lot. Do ye know what I mean? Brian Downey from Thin Lizzy is me cousin and I was asking Brian for advice on behalf of the boy's mother, me sister. What do you think yourself?"

"Huh?"

In an underground studio I spoke to a million listeners about local controversy, said bad bands were very good bands, thought about what was happening, at that moment, in a bad room in Rathmines. Perhaps, in keeping with his plan, they were already slow fucking.

The second I got off the air I made for a phone in the production room and tried Rory. No luck. I decided not to call his number again. I killed time talking to the show producer and some of my fellow guests. Then I went to a pub in Donnybrook with this girl who reviewed movies for the *Irish Press*. She wanted to ask me odd personal questions (Did I ever want to be a priest when I was a boy? Did I think I took after my mother or my father?) but she saw I was preoccupied. After drinks I caught a taxi with her into the city centre where I went to a movie on my own. I don't know what movie or who was in it; I didn't absorb a single thing though I sat in the front row.

I got home in the late evening and went to bed early for me, my phone unusually silent. In the morning I rose about eleven, went out to check the dailies, but found no reports of blood-murder or psycho mayhem in Rathmines. I made my coffee, played Gimme Shelter over and over again, rang people to pass the time, picked up gossip and dished out a little of my own. Hash and chat relaxed me so much that when the doorbell finally rang in the early afternoon I leapt to attention, all tense, so unexpected had his arrival become, so successfully had I persuaded myself that this was not really happening.

Rory was green with shock and weariness when I let him in and poured him a coffee, rolled him a joint. All that day he was morose and silent. He rarely intimidated me any more, but I was intimidated then.

"The whole fucking thing was a complete fiasco. A mess!" he rasped one time, staring at the ragged Persian carpet on my floor.

In the middle of the night, when he'd calmed down just a little, I got the specific details out of him. He assumed that she was dead, but she'd been very much alive when he last saw her.

"We had fucking brutal…bestial sex…first a blow job and then up the ghastly gully," he chortled drily. "While I was washing the shit off my cock in the bathroom afterwards, she was lying back on the bed smoking a joint. I watched her in the bathroom mirror, delighted with herself after her stuffing. She was about to nod off when I marched out of the bathroom swinging my axe, the one you saw up the Mountains. She didn't see me coming for her until I was right on top of her again and then I made a mistake all my training should've taught me not to make—I waited seconds too long before striking the first blow. She'd moved out of my way like a tiger by the time I got in with a first good whack. The axe took a tiny skelp of skin off her left thigh but she was on her feet right away, screaming out these pig-like sounds, heading for the door. She was in such a terror that she could feel nothing, she was just howling and howling. Oink, Oink, Oink. I got my calmness back and with my next lunge—she had her back to me—I planted the fucking axe right between her shoulder blades. She fell forward onto the floor, pounding the ground with her knees and fists…a dervish kind of thing. I pulled the axe right out of her back in order to aim it at her head…it made a sucking sound coming out of her…but she got out of the way just in time, grabbed a poker from the fireplace and smacked me in the balls with it. I fell onto the ground myself and she clawed her way to my front door and out into the corridor beyond."

The small dark bedroom was enveloped in fresh smelly blood and, by the time he got to his feet, she had left a trail of the same hot blood all over the stairwell, all the way down to the ground floor and out the front door. He gave chase with his axe in one hand and the poker in the other, caught up with her just as she ran through the front door, screaming, crying, bleeding, onto the front steps of the house. There Rory whacked her across the back of the head with the poker. By then the other tenants were coming to their doors or looking out their windows in horror.

"The whole fucking house was covered in her fucking blood!" he said to me like a proud serious kid. "She was making sounds I never heard a human make before. She was vomiting, bleeding, screaming, kicking at me. Green snot out of her nose, pissing, crying. People were gathering on the footpath and I knew I'd better quit if I wanted to escape. We were both bollock naked and psychotic. I could see she was kind of failing, that soon she'd lose so much blood that she'd give out. So I got in three more good whacks with the hatchet, once in the tit. I should have buried the fucking thing in her face but I was freaked and, anyway, I wanted to get away. I'd a getaway plan worked out so I put that into action."

His plan was very clever, very military. Abandoning Una alive on the front steps, he walked back inside, closing and locking the front door behind him. He strode up the stairs, dropping the axe as he went, marched into his flat, and double locked his door, which sported a paranoid's lock—a good Chubb. He had a set of dry-cleaned clothes and new sneakers waiting in his wardrobe. He went directly to the shower and scrubbed the blood off his body and out of his hair. He didn't mess around, reckoned that he was out of the shower in two minutes, all the time aware of

214

the commotion gathering on the street, outside his door, and inside his head. Then he towelled himself fast, dressed in the clean clothes, climbed out a window and down an old drainpipe into the back garden where all was calm suburbia. He could hear sirens in the distance which he assumed were coming for him. He walked to the back wall of the garden where a little used wooden door led out onto a narrow laneway where his Ford was parked. He had a knapsack packed with money, clothes and food in the boot of the Ford.

He drove away, never speeding, heading east towards Ballsbridge and out into the rush hour traffic making towards the seaside resort of Bray. When he got to Bray he parked on a backstreet close to the seafront and, with his knapsack, walked out along Bray Head, a Victorian clifftop walk running parallel to the train tracks. He climbed down the side of the cliff onto a concealed grassy plateau where he smoked some dope, considered the events of the day, and went to sleep peacefully for the first time in months. At dawn he walked off Bray Head, back to a totally deserted Bray beach. He stripped naked, folded his clothes under his knapsack and swam in the ice-cold sea for twenty minutes. He ran up and down the beach to dry himself off, dressed again and, knapsack on his back, took the DART into the city centre where he got a flat-top haircut, had something to eat in a workingman's cafe, and caught a taxi to my flat, where he stayed for six days, only venturing out under cover of darkness.

After that first night, we didn't talk all that much, and when we did talk it was about the Stones or Blondie. Never about Una and only very occasionally about the IRA. We watched RTE's one TV channel until it drove us demented, listened to a lot of the black music he wanted to hear, very little of the white music I liked, and sniped at one another a lot. During the daytimes I went about my normal business as a journalist.

THE SEVENTIES

A taxi picks me up and takes me to the airport. The taxi driver, a blond woman about my own age, was a big fan of Horslips and Thin Lizzy when she was a girl. She says her nephew is in the next Boyzone. "Did yez ever think of moving home to Ireland?" she asks me in her rough kind voice after I've paid her.

"I don't think so," I say to her smiling politely, my fake accent tinged with an American twang.

"Things is very good here now. It's not like the old days," she says.

"I preferred the old days." I heave my shoulder bag onto my shoulder. "I've been gone a long time. I only remember the old days. I'm gone too long."

I move away from her car. She leans over to wave goodbye.

"Keep rocking!" I shout to her.

She gives me a clenched fist and a Seventies grin.

I am forty, and restless ghosts already encircle me.

Inside the airport building I check in my shoulder bag before heading for a coin box. I spend my last Irish coins calling Ma before heading for Departures.

We are invited to board according to wealth and social status. I travel economy, and we're the last to get on. Just before I step into the plane I notice these free postcards Aer Lingus are giving away: Irish Nobel Laureates for literature. I pick up twenty cards featuring Yeats and Beckett. My final action of the *On The Run* project. I step into the plane and escape to *Mannish Boy*.

Rory never escaped.

Rory lived on until the Eighties.

BITCH

Una didn't die, funnily enough, for she was a tough survivor whereas Rory was not. She did spend months in hospital and more months going back for physio, corrective surgery, and treatments. I heard she was disfigured for life with a gammy jaw, but made a good all-round recovery in the long run. She was able to give the cops a full and spiteful account of Rory, his life, his family. IRA membership and all. The many Rathmines witnesses confirmed her story, the naked blood-covered couple screaming like mad dogs at each other on the flatland weekday afternoon.

When he rang his folks from a coinbox in Ballsbridge three nights after the attack his mother screamed at him for five minutes before ordering him to give himself up to the Guards, who were calling to the house day and night, staking it out from across the road, and probably tapping the phone.

"Rory, you have to resolve this somehow. You're up to your neck in trouble. Go see a solicitor. Get him to go to the Guards with you," Maeve whined.

"If that's the only advice you can give me, you can fuck off!" he responded before slamming the phone down.

For once Maeve was a voice of sanity, or at least she gave him a big fat reality sandwich to chew on. After telling her to fuck off he stormed back to me in a taxi, despondent and racked by confusion, spoke soberly about his position, about the trouble he was in and the trouble he'd caused. The next three days he drank a lot of vodka, talked bullshit, indulged his obsession with the minutiae of terrorism.

He wouldn't shave or wash, began to complain about the food I cooked, odds and ends concocted from indifferent tins and packets. By the time he left I was saying things like:

"It's not my fucking fault we can't go around to the fucking Pronto Grill for steak and chips."

"I know this is a stupid situation for you, you can't have anyone around, I'm fucking up…messing…I'll go away," he murmured apologetically the day he left.

"Rory, why don't you go back to England?" I suggested like a traitor. "You'd get away on the ferry no problem."

"Nah. I don't want to go there. I wasted myself there already. Twice." He spoke with a strange staccato confidence, authority in his voice, in the spirit of the schoolboy Rory.

"Well then you should go somewhere where you can get lost a while." I was thinking of continental Europe.

"Oh man," he said to me and it was the only time in his life I saw him close to tears, "I've been lost a long time."

He disappeared out into the dark wet city of Dublin and I didn't hear from him until six weeks later when it was all over bar the shouting. He rang his father at work and Séamus persuaded him to go see the family lawyer, "just to talk the whole thing over."

The lawyer, a pinstriped suburban jerk, arranged to meet him in a backstreet pub behind The Four Courts. That Rory agreed to such an assignation, in a part of Dublin always rancid with Guards, was indicative of his mental decline. The lawyer, a wills and probate merchant freaked out by this salacious attempted murder, set him up. He never showed, but Rathmines detectives did appear with a warrant for Rory's arrest.

Rory got charged with attempted murder, assault with a deadly weapon, and numerous of the other usual tagged-on things. A new lawyer—a liberal criminal law specialist—got him out on bail, warning him that he could expect to do ten years. It was one of the conditions of his bail that he go live with his folks. He no longer had a place of his own, in any case. His landlord dumped his stuff in a charity shop after the cops had finished with their forensics on the flat. I saw him intermittently after that, usually when he needed to escape for a few nights from Howth. He was fiercely subdued and depressed, surviving on strong tranquillisers prescribed by a shrink who, when the court case came up, was going to appear as a witness in his defense.

"They're going to argue that I was mad!" he laughed ruefully. "And I feel like telling them that I was totally sane, that it's the most rational thing I've ever done."

I went along with him to his first court appearance, a preliminary hearing at which there was no question of him being locked up. I met the father and mother for the first time since schooldays. Séamus was all sort of creased in on himself, wrecked by his life and the sheer unavoidable physical wasting process. But he looked like a senior civil service mandarin. Maeve looked the selfsame, highly strung, sedated suburban housewife she had always been. Resentful. Still looking for somebody to blame. For everything. They were both in shock, terrified as hares confronted by hounds. They'd probably never been in a courtroom before and here they were, confronted by their profound failure as parents, by everything else, by me too.

Maeve certainly blamed me for leading Rory astray; she made that clear: "You and your IRA! God damn you! Couldn't you leave him alone?" while Séamus murmured: "Ah, Maeve, Maeve! For God's sake." They didn't know how to deal with me nor I with them. Rory's little brother Tony'd grown up to be a tall handsome adolescent sporting long hair, combat trousers, and a tasteless brown leather jacket of the sort then in fashion. The boy was thin as a whippet and didn't yet have his brother's brooding stockiness. I didn't get to say much to Tony—adolescent boys are professionally sulky.

After the hearing Rory got rid of the family and we went to a pub across the Liffey from the Four Courts.

"Jesus Christ, Liam, I'm totally freaked by the thought of going to prison. I don't know if I can handle it. I've met a lot of the lads who've been in Portlaoise and it sounds like fucking hell. In the political prisons, at least, they have one another for company. I'll be in Mountjoy with all the fucking robbers and murderers and junkies," he said, staring at me with a weird intensity, sucking on a Major, his feet tapping the ground in an unbearable staccato rhythm.

"Stop tapping your fucking feet," I said to him.

"Sorry," he said all hangdog.

"Maybe you really should escape while you still can."

"Nah."

He picked up his pint from the table, drank about a fifth of it, placed the glass back.

"I'm going to top myself, Liam, I'm going to end the whole fucking thing for everybody. I'm going to put the whole fucking lot of yez out of your misery. But most of all, myself."

Then I didn't see him for weeks until we bumped into one another outside The Abbey Theatre one sunny June 1983 lunchtime. I was on my way to eat with a friend in The Abbey's basement vegetarian restaurant—The Silver Tassie by Seán O'Casey was playing upstairs. "A triumph" according to *The Irish Times*, and they should know.

Rory looked like shit, his face puffy from drink and sedatives, his clothes shabby and wrong-fitting. He told me he was just out of hospital, that he'd swallowed every pill in the bathroom back home (quite a number given his mother's dementia and his own problems) the previous week. Maeve hauled him off to hospital to have his stomach pumped. He looked old for his age—he looked like a dead man.

"I see Seán O'Casey is having another triumph at The Abbey," I quipped helplessly, pointing to a poster on the wall.

"What?" he said, bleary eyed and confused. "What?"

The last, last time I saw him was five days later when he showed up drunk and maudlin at my flat. It was the middle of the night but I was up, busy preparing for an important interview I had to do the following morning with our notorious Prime Minister, Charlie Haughey.

That last night I talked to Rory for hours during which he mumbled vague sentences about very little, just the shell of a man with nothing left inside.

"I had so many things going for me." He paused for the longest time. "Didn't I? I had everything going for me."

"Yes, you had it worked out perfectly," I smiled sadly.

"But I fucked it up?"

"We all get around to fucking it up one time or another," I answered wearily, pessimistically.

Eventually I persuaded him to go sleep on the couch in the sitting room, which he did after swallowing four hexagonal sleeping tablets. Some time before morning he woke me up, poking my shoulder vigorously, asking if I'd help him kill himself.

"No. I won't," I said. "Just go back to sleep. I could never do that for you. I think you should never do that to yourself."

He stood alongside my bed staring at me through the darkness with the never before seen, never foreseen, look of a whipped dog on his tired face. He apologised for being such a mess, and said he'd be gone in the morning when I got up.

He was gone in the morning when I got up, true to his word. I shaved, showered, checked my batteries for the Haughey interview, went into town.

True to his word he was dead within days.

I was at *Anna Livia* writing up Haughey ('His eyes are two slits, make any snake proud. His face is the kind of face that any painter would want to paint. What a pity he favours such mediocre portraitists.') when Ma rang. She'd seen Rory's death notice in the *Irish Press*. Deeply regretted by his grieving parents, brothers. Suddenly. At home.

I lied like a good son and told her he'd died after a traffic accident.

I didn't go to the funeral. I wrote a letter of sympathy to his parents but they never replied. *Anna Livia*—with Charlie Haughey on the cover and my byline in lime green directly under his name—hit the streets the week after the funeral. I was the talk of the town.

A year later a girl I was seeing, who came from Howth, told me how he died.

He hung himself from the banister at the top of the stairs.

It was Maeve who discovered him. She was in and out of mental homes for the next year.

CLASS REUNION

I'm blocking the sun. I work for a system I don't understand or trust. I hope I'm more like the boy that I was than the man that I became. I'm waiting in the station for a train that departed much earlier in my life.

Ma calls me all excited. A Father Timothy from St Fursey's has been on the phone to her wanting to know if she's my mother. She proudly tells him that indeed she is—that I've just gone back to America. He says to her that they're organising a 25th anniversary reunion of my class at St Fursey's. They've looked all over the place for me and not a trace could be found, not even in Borders or Spin. Somebody found her number in a Kilkenny telephone directory and Timothy was calling on the off-chance. Did she know where I was?

So she gives him my address in a foreign country and then she rings me in that country to tell me all about it.

Today some photocopied pages sort of designed up on Photoshop arrive at my distant front door. The event to be organised by three of my old schoolmates, one of whom I recall. Now he calls himself William, then he was just Billy, a frightened blond kid obsessed with soccer. Another of these worthy gentlemen is one of the three John Murphys who were in my year. Perhaps it's the one who almost choked me to death when I told him he was a fucking moron. Rory restrained him and, but for Rory, that John Murphy would probably have killed me.

They've arranged, William and these Johns, a dinner dance at the Tower Hotel in the city, with overnight accommodation available at a privileged rate, based on two people sharing a room. What kind of music will they play for us to dance to? Will it be some nostalgic Seventies covers band, or will a DJ play records from the Golden Age of Rock'n'Roll or will it be just a jumble of anonymous everything from each and every awful era that we middle-aged men have witnessed thus far in life? Will I go?

The morning after the dance, one of the photocopies informs me, there will be a golf outing to Waterford Golf Club.

Will I end up out there on the ninth green, stoned, cold, and lonely, an eccentric vision surrounded by comfortable family men who were once my friends and enemies? While Rory's young bones lie in a grave in Howth Cemetery, not far from my Uncle Alan or Phil Lynott from Thin Lizzy whose tombstone I noticed when Ma and me buried Alan in Howth one wet and freezing January Tuesday in 1995.

What would Rory say?

"Fuck those idiots and their fucking golf," he'd say.

God made him an Indian, but not a reservation Indian.

Sometimes I think he died for Ireland.

IRISH HISTORY—MOVING **TARGET**, SCREAMING **TARGET**

BY JOE AMBROSE

Irish anti-imperialism divides into two intertwined strands: the physical force tradition and the constitutional movement.

Constitutional thinking has its roots in Daniel O'Connell (1775-1847), an equivocal character whose great achievement was Catholic Emancipation. Up until the time of O'Connell the native Irish Catholic population were generally disenfranchised, enjoyed limited property rights, and were victim to all manner of legislative repression. But Daniel O'Connell's great work for his people was achieved in the foreign London Parliament. O'Connell was aware of this, yet his second great campaign, to repeal the Act of Union which in 1801 made Ireland an English colony, was a failure.

The next major constitutional figure was Charles Stewart Parnell (1846-91), a liberal Protestant landlord of much integrity who also operated out of London, albeit to great effect. Parnell, like O'Connell before him, never got Ireland its freedom but he did mould a community, a climate of opinion within the Catholic nationalist element which made eventual separation from England virtually inevitable. Parnell, the most prominent parliamentarian of his epoch, so dominated Westminster that occasional commentators suggested that, in the event of his winning Home Rule for Ireland, he would have remained on at Westminster to become the British Prime Minister.

The most charismatic politician in London fell foul to one of those fabulous sex scandals which dominated the final years of the Nineteenth Century. Parnell's infamous relationship with the scarlet married woman, Mrs. Kitty O'Shea, brought about his undoing—he was brutally smashed. James Joyce said that Parnell held out the hand of friendship to the Irish people and that the Irish snapped it off. The Catholic bourgeois consensus he'd moulded turned nasty.

Cast out into the political wilderness, Parnell courted physical force extremists and became an icon of dashed recklessness for young Irish intellectuals like Yeats, Joyce, and the embryonic leadership of the IRA. Parnell had always coaxed the physical force element—'the men of the hills'—in from the cold. They've been invited into the parlour several times since then.

The roots of Irish terrorism, guerrilla fighting, and revolutionary politics can be traced back to relatively minor and screwed up movements like the United Irishmen (1791-98), the Young Irelanders (1842-48), and the Fenians (1858-1916).

For all its legendary status, Fenianism was a somewhat damp squib. But it did give rise to a lively tradition of paranoid subterraneanism which thrives within Irish paramilitarism up to the present day. Ex-Fenian Michael Davitt created, with Parnell, the Land League (1879) that forced the transfer of agricultural land from the pro-British landed gentry to the resident tenant farmers.

The 1916 Rising, the wild experimentation of Joyce and Yeats, and the Irish language revival movement were just three of the phenomena which exploded out of the cultural fermentation taking place in Dublin after the destruction of Parnell. The 1916 leaders included an old Fenian, Thomas Clarke (1857-1916), the important socialist theoretician and agitator James Connolly (1868-1916) and the notable educationalist and minor poet Patrick Pearse (1879-1916).

On the surface 1916 bore all the trademarks of previous bungled armed struggles. It is hard to see how a sensible and serious man like Connolly allowed himself to get involved with such a foolish scheme. What is certain is that Pearse, with his slightly daft poet's sensibility, felt he had to destroy himself, to be killed in a Mishima-like blood sacrifice. He wrote that his own death would rekindle the then-dormant demand for a free Ireland which was totally disconnected from England. Perhaps Connolly agreed with this somewhat cracked notion.

The funny thing about it is that history has proven Pearse totally correct. The British summarily executed the best and the brightest in Dublin in a frenzy of bloodletting; teachers, writers, agitators, and other provincial intellectuals. Connolly faced his firing squad strapped into a chair (unable to stand because of an injury sustained in the Rising). Fifty nine year old Thomas Clarke was marched naked to his death.

These men were familiar faces on the streets of Dublin, well known in political and cultural circles all over Ireland. Their deaths caused a spirit of revolt and anger to spread throughout the country. Teenage rebels like Ernie O'Malley and Dan Breen decided that enough was enough. In 1919, via Breen, the IRA took shape in the popular imagination. On the day that Breen and the IRA (new name, new people, mainly teenagers) swung into action, a rebel Irish parliament elected by popular mandate, met in Dublin. Armed struggle and democratic forces in unison.

The War of Independence/Anglo-Irish War/Tan War (1919-21) brought about the deaths of 405 policemen, 150 military, and 750 IRA members and civilians. It ended with the 1921 Truce and the Treaty with England which Michael Collins signed. This deal offered limited freedom to 26 counties and ceded control of six northern counties—the North—to the English.

The Civil War (1922-23) was fought between two factions of republicans: those who accepted the Anglo-Irish Treaty, and those who rejected it as being well short of the republican ideal. Pro-Treaty elements tended to be the Sinn Féin politicals, although their real leader was the gunman Michael Collins. Anti-Treaty people tended to be in the IRA, although their leader, conversely, was the political de Valera. The IRA lost the Civil War, and it was some years before Dev formed his ex-IRA constitutional party, Fianna Fáil. Via the ballot box Fianna Fáil wrested control of Ireland from the hands of Dev's enemies.

The fact that the sedate liberal democracy now administered from Dublin has its roots in the slightly demented and covert blood sacrifice of Pearse, strikes terror into the prosperous Irish political elite. If that mad unlikely 1916 dash for freedom—which enjoyed no popular support at the time—gave rise to the sensible mandated administrations of today, then what sophisticated response can Irish democracy make to out-on-a-limb fringe movements opposed to the Provo cease-fire?

They say that whenever the English solve the Irish question, the Irish have a habit of changing the question.

The most intriguing general history of modern Ireland is **Ireland Since The Famine** by FSL Lyons (Fontana, London). Dan Breen's autobiography is **My Fight for Irish Freedom** (Anvil Books, Ireland). Ernie O'Malley's books—all published by Anvil Books— are **The Singing Flame, On Another Man's Wound**, and **Raids and Rallies**. **The Boss** by Joe Joyce and Peter Murtagh (Poolbeg Press, Ireland) chronicles the decline of Fianna Fáil into scandal and outrage under the control of Charles Haughey (1925-) whose lurid Seventies lifestyle is the stuff of mythology, a worthy contribution to the disco era. **The Parnell Split 1890-91** by my friend Frank Callanan (Cork University Press, Ireland) is the best study of the enigma that was Parnell. **The Oxford Companion to Irish History** (Oxford University Press), edited by Professor SJ Connell of the Queen's University Belfast, will clarify the nooks and crannies of Irish history, albeit with a strong revisionist bias; they don't call it the Queen's university for nothing.

JOE AMBROSE has worked as a journalist, historian, art curator and publisher, as well as a DJ and musician. His biography of Dan Breen, instigator of the Irish War of Independence, was published in Ireland when Ambrose was in his twenties. Ambrose has also co-written a biography of William Burroughs, and interviewed the likes of Paul Bowles, Frank Zappa, James Ellroy, Nick Cave and the notorious former Irish Prime Minister Charles Haughey. His first novel 'Serious Time' was published to wide acclaim in 1998 (Pulp Books) and his short fiction has appeared in numerous literary magazines and anthologies including 'Allnighter' and 'Shenanigans'. A frequent visitor to Berlin and Morocco, these days Ambrose mainly lives and works in London and in Ireland, where he contributes to Lyric FM, the Irish national classical music station. Joe Ambrose knows next to nothing about classical music, but a great deal about many other things.